IN THE MOMENT

AARON L. ASHFORD

Where Literary Stars are born.

Dedication

This book is dedicated to my mother, Ola Mae Ashford. Thank you for always being my number one fan and my biggest cheerleader. I could never pay you back for all that you have done, so I simply say thank you and I love you.

Moments are what define us as individuals, a collective people, and have defined generations both past and present. There are consequences for living in the moment once it has come and gone.

Chapter One

My life had become a sick joke. I had contemplated at least a dozen ways to end my suffering, but I just couldn't bring myself to acting on any of them. It wouldn't be fair to my family, especially my son. For once in my life I simply did not have all the answers. I only had questions. I didn't own a gun, hated swallowing pills, was afraid of heights, and I definitely wasn't going to hang myself. How could I have allowed myself to end up on the verge of suicide, in a state of depression no less? In this moment I couldn't magnify my blessings and make them bigger than my problems.

Normally I would just take a long run and forget about everything and everyone. That was how I escaped my problems. Not even I could outrun this pain; this hurt. I was searching for a reason to go on. That's when my phone rang. I looked at the caller ID in disappointment, because it wasn't her. It was Marcus, my best friend and now he was vying to be my agent. I really didn't want to be bothered with either version.

"Hello."

"Kennedy…you sound like crap. That doesn't sound like happiness to hear from your agent. I have some good news man!"

"Good news," I replied sarcastically.

"Clean the wax out of your ears and listen up. I sent those sample chapters to a couple of publishers and industry big shots to gauge their interest and we appear to have some major interest!"

I paused for several moments. This had been the opportunity that I have been waiting on all my life. I should be bursting at the seams with excitement and doing a serious Holy Ghost dance all while speaking in tongues. I was excited deep down, just not like I thought I would be. Not like I should be. Not even news this good could wake me from this state of depression that has consumed my being for the last few weeks. I couldn't stop thinking of Jacqueline Tate. Breaking up with her has been the hardest thing that I have ever had to do. Falling in love had to be the invention of a fool, not a sane or rational person. My life made no sense whatsoever.

"Say something man. I am gonna take your silence as you being speechless."

"I am here…excited man that's all, just excited. You are the man Marcus."

"This I know", he said with all of the arrogance and bravado that I have come to expect from him. "On another note…you ain't still trippin' over that Jackie broad are you?"

"Her name is Jacqueline and I would appreciate if you didn't refer to her or any other woman as a broad. To answer your question I just have a lot on my mind, none of which you would understand."

"Yeah, yeah, whatever! I do know one thing."

"What's that?"

"I know that a new woman is the quickest way for you to get over Jacqueline or anybody else. Besides she is a married woman for goodness sake."

That big dose of reality hit me like a ton of bricks falling from the Empire State building. It reminded me of why I did what I did. I had to pull away, because in spite of what we felt, the fact was that she was a married woman with a husband and two children. As much as I hated to admit it, Marcus was absolutely correct. At least about the fact that I needed to move on and get pass Jacqueline. I needed to focus on my career and getting my affairs in order, literally and figuratively. I had been separated from my wife Marley for the last year and a half after being married for 14 years. For some reason we have not made our divorce official despite the reality that happily ever after had long ended for us. We both wanted what was best for our son Miles.

"So…..who took the bait on the incomplete manuscript?"

"At least two editors at major publishing houses said they wanted it. Another felt as though it had big screen potential. They wanna know how fast you can finish it."

"Are you kidding?"

"Kennedy King, would I pull your leg about business? You know I don't play about my paper, so I wouldn't joke about yours, especially since in this case they are co---mingled. Anyway, they said that you need to finish ASAP!"

"Wow", was all I could get out of my mouth. I couldn't believe that this was happening. Since I could remember I have always loved writing and to think that someone else was finally seeing my potential was so surreal. My mood began to improve with those thoughts in mind. I could finally put Jacqueline out of my mind and focus on my happiness for a moment.

I knew that Marcus was serious because it was the first time in nearly 15 years he called me by my entire name. He had been calling me K2 since I can remember. I had one of those weird double last names. My mother said she wanted to name me Martin after Dr. Martin Luther King, Jr. but decided against Martin since my last name was already King. She said that she didn't want to make me to have to walk around hearing all the MLK jokes from the other kids. She named me Kennedy instead. My mom thought that JFK, and MLK were two of the most selfless and influential people of her time and she thought the name would be perfect. When you are named after two men that were both assassinated in their prime it made you a little suspicious and you hope it's not in the name.

"Just set it up, you know I am on board. Good job," I said with much more enthusiasm.

Okay, I will hit you with all the particulars.

One more thing!

"What's that?"

"Who da man?"

We both laughed at his humorous side. "You da man Marcus! You da man."

We hung up the phone still laughing. That was what I needed; it actually helped me to feel better. Marcus was a workaholic and even though it wasn't quite 9:00 AM, he was making things happen.

I opened the blinds to allow some sunlight into my dark and cluttered condo. The sunlight revealed both a gorgeous day on the outside and a person's life in disarray inside. From my view I could oversee Centennial Park, The Atlanta Aquarium and the Coca Cola Factory. There was so much life going on, children playing and people going about their normal day in the pursuit of their respective happiness. Meanwhile doom and gloom consumed my world, nothing resembled life in here. I hadn't cleaned my place in about two weeks, and there was clutter everywhere. There was a stack of Atlanta Journal Constitution papers that I hadn't even read, my voicemail was full, the sink was full of dishes, and I had trash that needed to be taken out. My postal mail, email, and hygiene had all been neglected at this point. As I began to think of Jacqueline I decided to do the one thing I enjoyed the most other than writing or being with her and that was running.

I figured that I was already in need of a shower, and that it could wait until I really worked up a sweat. I threw on my tights, a tank top, reached for my iPod, and grabbed my best running shoes. Since my life was already an uphill battle, I figured that I needed a challenge. I would conquer Stone Mountain.

Going into the bright sun that Atlanta had offered on this day was almost blinding. I felt like a vampire at daybreak. I ran back in for my shades and I was set to go. It had been at least a couple of days since I have left my home, so it felt good to get out. I had risen from the dead. My GPS device told me that Stone Mountain was a little over 15 miles from downtown Atlanta, which would take about 27 minutes. What would I do without this Garmin? Even though it was nearly fall, this down south heat and humidity was for the birds. I didn't think that I could get used to it. I had only been in Atlanta for a year and a half since leaving my hometown of Lorton, Virginia.

Marcus urged me to come to Atlanta as a way of getting a fresh start and refocusing. He was like many other young aspiring professionals that migrated to Atlanta in search of something bigger and better.

We had both gone to Hampton University for undergrad. Marcus and I were not only good friends; we were fraternity brothers as well. We pledged together, thus we have experienced nearly a lifetime worth of memories. Some of which I would just as soon forget. I shielded thoughts of Jacqueline as I pulled up to Stone Mountain. This paid parking pass came in handy since I frequently ran either around the mountain or up the mountain. I didn't have to pay a daily rate.

In a moment of weakness I decided to send her a text to let her know I was thinking about her and wondered if she was thinking of me. Naw...I thought to myself as I tossed my smart phone on the floor of my car along with the keys and began stretching in preparation for my run. I've had my Honda Accord since I graduated college. It hasn't let me down yet as I approached nearly 300,000 miles. Didn't figure anyone would be looking to steal it now.

I drowned out all thoughts of Jacqueline and our two-year affair by turning up my iPod full blast. Track after track was a reminder of her since she loaded nearly all of the songs. Our playlists mirrored one another. The truth was that although I was closer to 40 than I was to 30 reminded me of the importance of keeping my body in shape. People thought that I was lying when they found out my age. I stretched my hamstrings, calves, and groin muscles; didn't want to risk pulling one. I admired a few women either walking or jogging that were worthy of another look, but all that did was remind me of what I was trying to forget. Every woman that I met I found myself comparing her to Jacqueline, and the truth is they don't even compare. I was pathetic. I was in love with another man's wife. What a disgrace I thought to myself; embarrassing. I knew that I was better than this.

CHAPTER TWO

I took off on my quest to scale the 1,686 feet of elevation that made up Stone Mountain. In spite of a nice mix of my favorite tunes across nearly every genre of music, my mind settled on Jacqueline. I could not get her image out of my mind. I was married to a woman for 14 years of my life, gave her my last name and a child and I have never felt for her what I feel for Jacqueline. That was crazy. The sad thing was that it wasn't a knock on Marley. She was no slouch at all. Marley and I met back in college at a Mid-eastern Athletic conference track meet. She went to Norfolk State University by way of Jamaica. We were both runners; in fact we both ran the same events. We were sprinters. We ran the 100 and 200 meters and we anchored the 4 by 100 meter relay teams. Speed was our greatest asset and probably our biggest detriment. We definitely hurried things in the relationship department as well.

We had everything in common at the time. That was a time when running was all I really cared about, and it was how my education was paid for. Marley and I would train during summers and spend alternating weekends either in Hampton or Norfolk, Virginia. Most of my undergrad experience aside from pledging pretty much centered around her. It didn't take long for our romance to blossom. Marcus was always trying to get me to be with other women. He said that it wasn't natural for a man to be with one woman. Those are words that he still lives by today. Guess I was a bit more traditional. If that were the case, how could I have shared a man's wife for 2 years? I felt like a huge "S" was branded on my forehead which stood for Stupid or maybe Sucker. Either one could apply to me right now. I pondered those thoughts as I climbed in altitude along my run.

I was getting some stares which could have had many interpretations. Not many guys wore tights uncovered, which made me suspect that maybe some of the guys were enjoying the view a bit too much. This was Atlanta after all. Not that I had anything personally against gay guys, just as long as they missed me completely with it. On the other hand I was appreciative of the not so subtle stares I garnered from the beautiful women that I passed along the way. I began to pick up my pace as the mountain steepened. I was beginning to perspire, which let me know that I had neglected both my passion for running and my personal hygiene a little too long. Nonetheless, I kept on climbing;

kept on going. I envisioned that I was climbing higher than all the problems this life had offered me. The more I thought of Jacqueline the more I ran; the harder I pressed. I ignored the burning in my legs and within my lungs. I struggled to maintain my perfect running form. It was funny, but I could even smell Jacqueline. If 100 women wore her trademark fragrance I could pick her out blindfolded. Nobody wore Juicy Couture quite the way that she did. Just the thought of her drove me crazy. It made blood flow to places that it didn't need to right now; especially wearing these tights.

Before I knew it I was mentally back in the place in time that we first met. Marcus and I were hanging out in Charlotte, North Carolina for the CIAA weekend. Once again he was trying to mix a little business with pleasure. We were celebrating another of his clients who he had recently signed. At the time Marley and I were still together under the same roof, but far from the illusion of being each other's soul mate. Marcus was getting on me to finish writing my book which at the time was very incomplete. Writer's block definitely had the best of me. It was beating me down like Kimbo Slice. I was facing some difficult realities in my life and writing was the furthest thing from my mind. Reluctantly I hung out with Marcus and we frequented most of the events throughout the weekend affiliated with the tournament, all VIP treatment nonetheless.

Even though I wasn't the flashy type like Marcus, I had to admit that it beat standing in those long lines just to get into all the venues. The CIAA was a big deal in this region of the country judging by the huge crowds of people, probably most of which didn't even go to CIAA schools but just liked having a good time. I was a MEAC type of guy myself, but I had to admit that there was a lot to be desired as far as our tournament went. We were hanging out at a spot called Club 935 that had a line wrapped around the corner just waiting to get in. Rolling with Marcus had its perks as we bypassed the long line to an entirely different entrance from general admission to VIP. Over the years I had lost my attraction for what clubs used to provide in terms of excitement. It was mostly the same tired looking guys saying played out lines, while women just wanted free drinks and gave out fake names. I mulled over that thought as we found our way inside. It was pretty nice I thought to myself as I looked around. We passed a bar with a smaller dance floor off- set by a huge projection screen showing the video to the song that the DJ was spinning, or should I say programming on his fruit themed laptop. Nobody spins records anymore; I guess technology has even advanced DJs. I will always be a fan of the needle to vinyl sound from back in the day. I stopped at the bar and ordered a drink. I wasn't a heavy drinker so I ordered a beer. Marcus got a dirty martini. That was one drink that looked like it was appropriately named. It looked very unsanitary.

"I see you're still a Heineken fan," he said referring to my beer selection.

"Yeah, I like to stay consistent."

"I hear ya. You need to be looking for some new talent. From where I stand there is a lot to choose from. "I may even hold an audition for a spot or two on my roster," he said while nearly breaking his neck looking around.

"Man there is nothing for me in here...not trying to replace one problem with the next one," I said as I thought about the realistic possibility of officially splitting up with Marley and divorcing. Marcus just looked at me as he rested on my words. He didn't even comment. He was focused on scouting new talent.

Marcus was a guy who worked hard, but played even harder. He enjoyed the life that he was living. I was a guy who prided himself on stability and being consistent and it was hard to have that interrupted. We walked to the coat check area and surrendered our jackets as we embraced the warmth that this many people under one roof had suddenly provided. I was wearing a nice buttoned down shirt with some dark Guess jeans; not flashy at all. Marcus on the other hand stayed decked out. He was wearing a nice designer suit, expensive shoes, and monogrammed shirt with his initials on the sleeves, and no tie. He definitely dressed the part of an entertainment agent. We made it to the VIP area that was really only slightly elevated and separated by a velvet rope with some plush lounge chairs to sit down. It didn't seem that exclusive to me.

I became mesmerized by the women dancing onstage separate from everybody else to pass time. Marcus entertained more than a few women and wooed them with free drinks for the majority of the night. I didn't see the sense of it all. Men buy drinks and telling lies, while women accept the drinks and tell their own lies. It seemed like nobody told the truth anymore. A big waste of time I thought. Women put themselves in awkward predicaments time after time without even knowing it. A man would buy drinks all night if he felt like it would get him closer to the inside of a woman's panties. Why couldn't people just meet and say "let's screw a few times and see where this goes?" It seems like it would save everyone time and money. I sipped more than a few beers and eye danced with the stage dancers, song after song, and move for move. Although it frightened me to fathom being in the 21st Century dating game, I knew deep down that it would be my reality. I cringed at the prospect of dating in an era where Facebook, camera phones, and Skype existed. Marley and I were on borrowed time, and time was coming to collect itself any day now with penalty and interest.

After more beers than I could recall I decided to go to the restroom and get our jackets. Once I had relieved myself and collected our jackets I scanned the crowd for Marcus. He was a party animal and it was obvious that he was having a good time. The crowd was beginning to dissipate and people were moving towards the exit. That was when it happened. I turned in search of Marcus, but what I found was the discovery of a lifetime. Never had a mistake been more perfect. I accidentally stepped on the toes of a young lady. Although I apologized profusely at the time, I would later find out that it was the perfect alignment of the planet and the stars. With the audacity of Columbus I proceeded to explore this new venture.

"I am so sorry," I exclaimed out of sheer embarrassment.

She paused as she looked down to examine her shoes and toes that peeped through her pumps. "I'm okay."

For a moment I feared a nasty response that would have been uncalled for, but she was very different. Her eyes were the brightest most beautiful eyes that I had ever had the pleasure of gazing into. There was so much life. They were both innocent and sensual all at once. We stared into each other's eyes for minutes that seemed like hours before we even exchanged names. In that moment the crowd didn't matter. In fact everyone else was moving slow like those scenes from the Matrix trilogy. I only saw her. There was immediate attraction, but not the typical physical attraction that I have experienced since I could remember where beautiful women were involved. This was on a deeper level. It was almost spiritual.

"I'm Kennedy. What's your name?"

"Nice to meet you Kennedy. My name is Jacqueline."

"I didn't mean to step on your foot. In fact I didn't even see you. Guess I was not paying attention."

"You sure that's not how you pick up women?" She smiled. "Just step on their feet and play like you didn't see 'em…. Is that it?"

"I can assure you that that's not how I do it." We both laughed.

Jacqueline told me that she was out with her friends for a girl's night out. I told her that I was out with Marcus, pretty much doing the same thing I guess. We both looked at each other with the "married people don't do this stare" and probably dismissed it just as easy. Every relationship was different, that's for sure.

Jacqueline told me about her job, her twin boys, and her 7 year marriage. She told me that she used to be a social worker until she realized that her student loan payments exceeded her salary. She figured that since she loved helping people that she might want to start with her first. She told me that she was into marketing but didn't really elaborate. I told her about Miles, Marley, and my never ending job as a pharmaceutical sales rep. That was just a government sanctioned version of a drug dealer. I guess if the FDA could regulate a drug and Uncle Sam could tax it, it was legal. Told her about my on again off again novel that was far from complete. I was no more than an aspiring author. Anytime you aspired to do something it just meant that you hadn't done it yet. It was just something about her that made me comfortable sharing that.

We became engaged in conversation totally oblivious of elapsing time. It may have been the beer that I consumed or whatever she was drinking, but I don't even remember whose idea it was to exchange numbers but we did. In retrospect I guess we both blamed it on the alcohol and kept moving. I noticed Marcus from my peripheral waiting on me. Jacqueline and I parted ways reluctantly. I was not looking forward to the interrogation that Marcus had waiting, but I was looking forward to hearing from Jacqueline Tate very soon.

CHAPTER THREE

As the crowd dissipated Marcus and I went in the direction of once eager party goers, who were now just intoxicated people in search of the nearest Waffle House or hotel room toward the exit. All the while I wanted to look back to steal a glimpse of Jacqueline. Wondered what she looked like from afar; wondered if she was looking at me. That was silly I thought to myself as I fought that urge with everything inside of me. I just couldn't help but feel a moment of awkwardness and intrigue. I know that didn't make sense, but I was trying to wrap my mind around what just happened inside a night club of all places. This woman I didn't know from Eve or her sister had piqued my curiosity in the worse way.

"I'm starved man let's get some grub," Marcus demanded as he yawned a tired man's yawn.

"That's cool" I asserted and kept it moving.

The temperature outside seemed like it dropped at least twenty degrees and the rain from earlier had returned in the form of sleet. A cold front moved through the area bringing in temperatures that made me see my breath when I spoke. I clutched my jacket and pulled it tighter to keep my warmth from being consumed by the hawk that was out tonight. I was used to cold growing up in Northern Virginia, but I did not expect it to be this cold in Charlotte. Right now I was one cold dude ready to get to inside of something that provided me with warmth. I blew into my hands and rubbed them together as Marcus and I waited on the valet to bring his car around. We boarded his Lexus GS 460. There were more horses under this hood, than on an average sized farm. The heated seats were just what I needed as my body melted and seemed to come back to life in no time. Times like this made me wish I had bought a new car because my dated Accord would have both of us freezing damn near to death. I chuckled inside and decided to keep that thought concealed where it belonged. Marcus used his voice activated GPS system that guided us to the nearest IHOP.

Her fragrance lingered on my hands. It was not one that I wasn't familiar with, but was suddenly growing on me with every passing moment. I inhaled and exhaled her with every breath. Marcus and I made small talk over veggie omelets and cheese grits at 3 AM. IHOP was packed like a club. I tried to imagine the money that Charlotte was making as a result of all the people who attended the CIAA. Marcus was busy yapping about how many women he had met and what his plans were for them. He never stopped. He was so busy talking about himself that he never bought Jacqueline up, which was great for me. The times that he was interrupted by calls or texts on his iPhone gave me opportunities to think of her.

I was at the top of Stone Mountain overlooking the best view in which to see Atlanta. With my hands on my hips I began stretching again to control my breathing and to ensure that I didn't pull anything. Not even running could totally clear my mind of Jacqueline, but my mood overall was greatly improved. My brain was suddenly overtaken by endorphins and for the first time in weeks I felt like I had a purpose. I trotted back down in the same manner in which I had climbed. Only this time it was easier to reverse what I had done in the first place. At least this applied to running, not as much in relationships. Before I knew it I was back in my dated but reliable Accord heading back to my condo.

With my sunroof open I enjoyed the breeze that 85 miles per hour granted me as I crossed multiple stretches of highways to get back downtown. Once inside I decided to give my place a much needed cleaning. I plucked my iPod in its stationary dock so that my tunes could blare and fill every square foot with noise. It felt as though I had been in silence for too long. I listened to random tunes from Alicia, Ledisi, Laura Izibor, Maxwell, Jill Scott, John Legend, Musiq Soulchild, Michael Jackson, Marvin Gaye, Miles Davis, Lenny Kravitz, and Mary J. I even had some New Edition pumping. Although the music helped me to restore my place to a sense of cleanliness, it also kept me in a place where I was once again filled with thoughts of Jacqueline. I took my phone out and decided to call my son. The most difficult part of being separated was not being able to see Miles every day. Now that I was in a different state all together made that even more painful. He was a great kid and to Marley's credit she helped with the transition. I had tons of frequent flier miles going back and forth to Virginia to see him. Miles was 14 years old now and I knew that he needed me more than ever at this point in his development. He was extremely resilient in handling the separation so far. At his age most kids are so consumed with a rush of hormones and bad information that they screw things up literally and figuratively. I was much younger than Miles when my parents split and it was not a smooth transition whatsoever.

My folks argued like any other couple, but I had to admit that I didn't see that coming. I just remember one day my dad did not come home. That day turned to weeks, which turned to months and eventually he was remarried with a family of his own. Talk about one to grow on. I hated his ass for years. To this day I have never gotten over how a man could just walk away from his family like it was nothing. To add insult to injury he left my mom for a white woman; not a glamorous white woman like Pam Anderson or pretty like Jennifer Anniston. He picked a Meredith Baxter reject. I wasn't racist in the least bit, but he obviously had issues with color. That's the straw that breaks the camel back when it comes to black women. My mom could pass for white in some circles and compared to my dad she was. My mom is beautiful like a doll baby. She is the type of woman that wakes up flawless. She looks like an older version of the singer Tamia. My dad is dark as the keys on a piano. He made Richard Roundtree look light skinned. At the end of the day he felt as though he needed the real thing and despite my mom's complexion she was what she was. A light skinned black woman. It was sad that people still saw color and that prejudices even existed within races.

Daddy grew up in a small town in Mississippi called Natchez. He told me that he got called nigger in every way possible for a person to be called nigger. So much that he thought nigger was his first name. The weight of those jokes and taunts destroyed any self -esteem that he may have had.

He hated the word and anyone who used it. He even hated himself deep down. It offended me like hell when he told me that he married my mother because he thought that she was light enough that his kids wouldn't have to go through what he went through. They wouldn't have to be called spooks, darkies, jiggaboos, and porch monkeys like he was; even by other blacks. He fed me that lame excuse as if it would help me somehow feel better that he just walked out on his family. I hated him then, now I just feel sorry for his ass. His theory proved wrong because I ended up being only a shade or two lighter than him, but dark nonetheless. The difference is that I love the skin I'm in. It is what it is. Thanks to him I have a white stepmom named Jane and three half siblings Richard, Charles, and Catherine.

Despite his flawed ways I never rejected them no matter their makeup. Kids didn't ask to come here in the first place. I already knew what that was like. I already knew that having him for a father was enough of a burden to bear. There were many nights that I had cried myself to sleep wishing I was never born. The pain of his absence was too much initially. Maybe not having him in my life was a blessing in disguise because I seemed to be the only one of his children that's never been on drugs, arrested, or having children out of wedlock. That thought gave me some solace when it came to that situation. I dialed the number to the residence that used to be where I laid my head. The phone rang a few times before someone answered. It was Marley.

"Miles is not here Ken." She said that with some attitude.

"Well hello to you Marley. How do you know I am not calling to talk to you?"

She hissed at my question. I could tell that she had one of her major "tudes" in full effect.

"Look," she paused. "If you were truly concerned about me...then you would be here and not in Atlanta or wherever the hell you are so save it. Miles is out with his friends so call him on his cell phone arie." Her Jamaican accent increased its presence which let me know that she was in rare form. I decided that I didn't want to take part in the latest episode of back and forth all the while getting nowhere really fast. Especially not over stuff that was not going to change. I took the out that she had provided and decided to cut this conversation short. I ended that call and called Miles on his cell. I laughed to myself thinking about how technology has spoiled everyone. At 14 my mom knew where I was gonna be from dusk till dawn. There were no cell phones. You went to school and came home. You played until the street lights came on and you went home to do it all again the next day. Now you have to text your own kids and hope that they respond on the phone that you pay for. Something just didn't make sense about that, but here I was texting my son who didn't pick up my previous call.

CHAPTER FOUR

After my chores had been completed and I was showered I found myself dozing off with thoughts of Jacqueline front and center. She dominated my left and right brain and every neurological pathway in between. I was a prisoner to the melodic nostalgia and the lifetime of memories created in a two-year span. This was a mere fraction of my life, but maybe one of the most significant periods nonetheless. After we met, there was infrequent dialogue exchanged back and forth, but nothing major. I was still in Virginia and she was in Charlotte so distance was an issue. That's until my job started going through some major restructuring in light of the state of America's declining economy.

I couldn't understand why pharmaceutical companies were having problems surviving when my CEO pocketed a cool 20 million in bonuses during these harsh times. One thing was for sure; Americans loved drugs both legal and illegal. We were a nation of people that loved instant gratification. We'd try anything to alter our minds and distract us from the ills of society. I was just waiting for the instant orgasm in tablet or liquid form. People wouldn't even have sex anymore; they would just pop a pill or two and call it a day. It was just how things were. I thought that I was in a pretty secure line of work. Recession proof if you will. I was given the option to relocate or get downsized, so I chose to take the Atlanta market. This move would prove useful in a few ways. It created some much needed space between me and Marley; put me in a place to finish writing my first novel; and it put me closer to Jacqueline. This seemed like three plusses and no minuses so far.

Jacqueline and I decided that dinner would be appropriate. No strings attached. The truth was that we had both been drinking when we met and only had sketchy images at best of one another. We met in a part of South Carolina called Greenville that was off of Interstate 85, kind of midway between Atlanta and Charlotte, but much closer to her than me. I had some medical offices that I supplied antidepressants or erectile dysfunction drugs that were nearby as I was learning my new territory. She was fine because it was far enough away from Charlotte without being too far in case she had to get back quickly. I didn't know much about the area, but one of the doctors named Felicia told me about a good restaurant called Smoke on the

Water. It sounded good, so that's where we met. I was really nervous about meeting her again. I feared that she might not be as hot as I remembered. Maybe I had drank one too many. I also feared that she was very pretty and what that would mean as well. Then I told myself that no matter what, this was just dinner. Nothing more and nothing less, we were both married after all.

I arrived first and went inside. I must say that I was impressed with this tiny rural metropolitan like town so far. Not impressed enough to live there, but impressed enough to get a decent meal. I was feeling overdressed. I had on a suit and tie because I had just finished my work day. She walked in and looked around. Jacqueline was dressed very casual in jeans, a graphic t-shirt, and some high heeled sandals. Her hair was curly like I remembered. Her eyes were beautiful just like I remembered. They were dreamy and mesmerizing, but at the same time there was an undeniable innocence. When I waved her over her reaction said that she wasn't disappointed in me either, but maybe she was disappointed that she was under dressed compared to me. We exchanged pleasantries and she sat down. There was an awkward moment where we didn't know whether to embrace or shake hands. It was comforting to know that neither of us seemed too comfortable in this situation. She immediately confirmed what I was thinking. She apologized for being so casual. I brushed it off and told her that I only wore a suit because I was just finishing up my workday. I told her that I wished I had brought some jeans and a t-shirt as well. The truth was she was wearing the hell out of those jeans so I didn't mind one bit. Her heels made her legs bow just a bit and displayed her curvature.

We made small talk while we ordered our dinner. She and I both ordered glazed salmon atop collard greens. The waitress assured me that the greens didn't have the slightest bit of pork influence so I was cool. Jacqueline talked about her children. Said she was glad that she had twins so she would never have to go through childbirth again. I could tell that she was an excellent mother; very maternal. She reminded me of Marley in that regard. I told her about Miles and how much he has changed since going through puberty. I thought of myself at his age and how similar we both were. I had to admit that he was an even better version. Neither of us really wanted to regard the elephant in the room that was our respective spouses. We danced around that one all night like two highly skilled prized fighters. Pacquiao and Mayweather would be proud. Things got a little more awkward when our food arrived. I offered to bless the meal much like I always did prior to eating by extending my hand to hers. She seemed as though this was out of sorts; foreign even. I decided not to delve into her religious ideations at this point, and dismissed the whole thing. The conversation flowed perfectly as we enjoyed food, fellowship, and two glasses of Pinot Noir.

Jacqueline seemed pretty familiar with the Greenville area and she suggested that we take a walk at a nearby park. Since I wasn't in a hurry I went with the flow. I followed her lead. When the check arrived I took one of the hundred dollar bills from my jacket pocket and settled the $60 dollar debt without thinking. It seemed as though she expected it, but I didn't say anything. I wondered why women only wanted to be traditional when things suited them most. A man would pay for dinner, wine and dine until the cows come home if he knew he could gain access to a woman's inner thigh. No questions asked. I guess my treat was getting to watch her switch her hips as we walked out of the restaurant. I couldn't ignore that if I tried.

The weather was nice. It was just past 7:30 p.m. on an August evening, which meant the temperature had broken considerably. I took my jacket and tie off and left them inside of my car. It was about as comfortable as I could get. Jacqueline's toes were freshly pedicured which told me that she was into taking care of herself. The park was beautiful. People were jogging, kids playing, and others just doing what the hell they were doing. She talked about her interests in photography but indicated that it was nothing serious. She appeared to be scanning the park using only her imaginary camera capturing life as it happened, meanwhile regretting that she hadn't carried her equipment with her. It seemed like she would get some good shots from here judging from the view. She sensed my hesitation when we were about halfway in the middle of a bridge suspended high above the park. At least it was higher than I cared to be, because everyone else seemed fine. I could feel the vibrations as others jogged by which made me feel very uneasy. She didn't put up a fuss as we turned around and opted for an alternative route.

"So…we're afraid of heights I see." She teased.

"Ohh.. Is it that obvious?" I laughed and kept it moving; didn't even deny it.

Once we made it down to some benches that sat in the middle of the park I really got to see the bridge from the bottom up which was a safer point of view for me. Jacqueline seemed preoccupied by her cell phone. I saw her text at least three times during dinner and ignore at least as many calls. I told her that she might want to take that to help ease whatever was uneasy with her. She continued to talk and text; talk and text again and talk and text more. If this was a real date, I would have split so long ago, but I stayed. In light of that, I didn't really know how to gauge this encounter whatsoever. What in the hell was I even doing? In hindsight I guess that it was a real date. I doubt seriously if either of our spouses would approve. Despite our misses that evening, there were far more hits where she and I were concerned. Our date proved to be the confirmation that there was mutual interest by both parties involved. How was this going to play itself out?

What followed would be a series of next dates between Jacqueline and me. Our dates would include more dinners, lunches, and even breakfasts. Over those dates she would prove that she was a more than competent dresser. She had a very versatile style that ranged from business to casual and she wore them very well. Jacqueline made an impression on me every time that we met. She was never the same. Our intimacy level deepened as we could talk about any and everything. It was scary how transparent we both were with one another without even being physical. It prompted me to ask her if she knew what she was doing, because I sure as hell didn't.

"Are you sure you know what you're getting into?" I asked. She replied, "I'm just going with the flow...just enjoying getting to know you. I don't have any crazy expectations or nothing like that. You know?"

I nodded to let her know that I felt the same. We were both creating something that couldn't quite be qualified, but at the same time had huge potential. Over that time of our romantic infancy she asked me out of nowhere if I thought it was possible to love two people at one time. In my past this question would have made me bolt like the former track star that I was. Somehow I didn't because I knew exactly what she meant. We had both began to catch feelings for one another. The thing about feelings is that they come easy but die-hard. Two people that were both married would be unwise to catch feelings for someone else. That would be the advice of any rational person. I had to admit that I hadn't been completely faithful to Marley throughout our marriage. I probably was a little too young and immature when I got hitched, but there was never anyone that I felt this close to and that was the scary part about Jacqueline. Before her I had only had a few one-night stands while on business trips. There was no connection beyond that. I just knew that I could get lost in her and I didn't even put my guard up. I didn't try to prevent this train wreck from happening. I simply went with the flow and threw caution to the wind.

CHAPTER FIVE

I never thought that I'd see Kennedy again after that night we met. There was a part of me that desperately wanted to see him again and there was a part that knew better. The truth is I had been waiting on someone just like him. Sure I was married and all, but a part of me felt like every day I was dying a thousand deaths being with Dwayne. Despite the fact that he was a good father and provider didn't excuse him from sucking as a husband. I felt like I had been married to a man that I had given my virginity to, had his babies, and he just couldn't see me with 20/20 vision and a set of binoculars. He was blind to who I was as a woman; couldn't see my needs. I felt like I was flat lining and all of a sudden Kennedy gave me the jolt I needed to breathe again. He was pure electricity. The way we met was so strange I kept telling myself it had to be fate. It was the perfect alignment of the moon and stars. I would never give a guy in a club the time of day, especially not after he stepped on my brand new Jimmy Choos.

I had never put much stock into love at first sight, but he made me think and rethink that theory. It just felt like something I couldn't even explain. Felt as though I'd known Kennedy my whole life. Maybe even a lifetime or two before this one.

That familiarity was a major reason I held off contacting him for the first few months. I was really searching Dwayne and trying to see the smallest glimmer of hope that things would somehow change. That he would make me feel like I was the only thing that mattered aside from the boys. Every girl wants to know what that's like. In typical Dwayne fashion he never ceased in disappointing my expectations. Sometimes in life people showed you very early on who they were, and they rarely if ever changed. I was just one of those people that wanted to see the best in people despite them showing their worse. My girlfriend Gabby would just say, "So what. Go screw someone else already!" It made me laugh just thinking about her quick wit and potty mouth. I just wasn't the type to give myself to a man without feeling connected to him. I know this to be fact because I have turned down lots of men who have offered "no strings attached" sex. It just wasn't my thing. Maybe I was just old fashioned. Maybe I was just plain old stupid. Either way Dwayne knew that the likelihood of me stepping out on him was as slim as Rush Limbaugh supporting President Obama.

I'd be lying if I said that a small part of me didn't wonder how it felt to lay with a man and walk away afterwards without any emotional attachment or baggage. I could almost hear my mother now, "Remember Jacqueline no man will want a woman that's made her rounds. The greatest way to honor your husband is to give him something no other man has had. It's worked for me and your father and we've been married over 36 years." If I had a dollar for every time she sang that lecture I'd be in Oprah's neighborhood. I became brainwashed by my mother's teachings and held onto my virtues. Let's just say that decision didn't make me very popular with the boys in high school or college. Sure they tried to take a crack, but when they found out that no meant "no", I didn't get many second dates. All of my girlfriends had lost their virginity by at least 11th grade which was added pressure. Since the extent of my mom's sex talk was "save it," I felt so slutty when I discovered that touching myself was an awesome thing. Very awesome! Sometimes I would touch myself so much that I would climax and feel like I was about to go into convulsions. Even though I wasn't having intercourse, I knew exactly how I liked and needed to be stimulated when the time came. No pun.

Dwayne dropped off Evan and Michael at school on his way to work. He was a high school principal so his school started later than the boys did. I had a couple of meetings scheduled for later in the day so I found myself with a little free time before I had to be up. Normally this would be the time that I would call Kennedy and lure him into a little naughty time over the phone that would drive us both insane and usually end up with some sultry phone sex. We were so in tune with one another that it was scary. I guess that I was speaking in past tense because lately we haven't even spoken. Sure we've had hits and misses in the past, but never have we gone this long without talking or seeing each other. I felt like I was a heroin addict experiencing withdrawals in a major way. I missed his touch; his caress. I missed the way he gazed deeply into my eyes as if he saw who I really was. I missed his breath against my body; missed the way he felt when he entered me. Each time felt like the first time. He was never hurried, always took his time to make love to me as if I was his. Kennedy never made me feel like I was his mistress or his side piece. Just thinking those thoughts had me turned on in a major way. My clitoris was pulsating like a pressure cooker. I needed a release like Halle Berry needed to feel good in Monster's Ball. I wished Kennedy was here to put out this fire like only he could. I had no choice but to help myself. I pulled out my vibrating dildo and turned it on. I let it massage my clit, which only made me hotter and wetter. I needed penetration. I needed Kennedy but he wasn't here. I did my best to imagine that it was him penetrating me; soft and gentle. He was filling me up with every inch that he had to offer. At this point I was so loud and on the brink of climax that I feared the cops would be knocking any minute. It was a bittersweet orgasm. I had the release I needed, but the reality was that Kennedy wasn't here. There was no one holding me like they'd found their true purpose in life. No one was telling me how beautiful I was or that they had never felt this way about anyone before. All of a sudden none of those things existed.

As I lay in my empty king bed I was consumed with thoughts of the man that I was desperately in love with, all the while resenting the man that I was stuck with and married to. It almost felt like a prison sentence. My mother would say that life had a wonderful sense of humor. I wasn't sure how she viewed what was humorous, but this was definitely a joke done in poor taste. I checked my phone, but he hadn't called or texted me. No emails since his last one over two weeks ago. He said that he couldn't take it anymore. He said that he loved me and that he had never loved someone the way that he loved me, which was why he had to leave me alone. We had both pulled away for some reason or another in the past, but something felt different about this time. As hard as it was I had to begin to accept the fact that our relationship was no more. I had grown in ways with this man over the last two years unlike anything I could categorize. Other than my boys and fond memories of the past, I didn't feel much towards my own husband. Dwayne couldn't hold a candle to what Kennedy and I have developed within obvious limitations. The tears began to flow as the finality of it all was crystallizing. I was grieving a loss of catastrophic proportion. Part of me wondered how you could love someone the way he claimed to love me and walk away like I was nothing. Then there was part of me that knew exactly where he was coming from. That part of me bared more rational thinking. It wanted to give my marriage a fair chance regardless of what Kennedy and I have shared. It was the reason why I was here and Kennedy was there. It was why we weren't together. It was why he gave up on the fantasy that we'd created of happily ever after.

I'd contemplated many times about leaving Dwayne and being with Kennedy. I wondered how our love could blossom without restraints and secrecy. I wondered how great it would be to profess my love for him to any and every one instead of keeping the greatest thing next to the birth of my boys a secret. I was feeling so much pain. There was so much confusion. I had to get this man out of my system if I was going to be any good to anybody. I had imagined being atop mountains hand and hand with Kennedy and professing our love for one another to the heavens above; let the angels bear witness to our union.

After I had showered and dressed I hissed as I discovered that I was running late. I had tons of things to do and I was seriously off schedule. This man had me way off my game. My phone vibrated indicating that I had a text message. Please be Kennedy I thought to myself. With disappointment and regret it wasn't. It was Gabby which reminded me that I was late to my hair appointment with her. The fact that we were really good friends did not allow me to take Gabby for granted. Gabby took her business very serious. I didn't wanna hear her mouth; at least not today. I texted her to let her know I'd be there in five minutes, which was a lie. It sounded better than saying that I haven't left my house which was the truth. Figured she could stomach that one better. I knew I had to hurry up if I was gonna get things done. This was Bronner Brothers Show week, which in my profession was like the Super Bowl to the NFL. It didn't get much bigger than this when it came to hair shows. This was the pinnacle in my profession. I had been a marketing consultant with Genesis Hair and Beauty for the last three years. Genesis was one of the few companies that made beauty and hair care products for black women that were black owned. I would have never figured that Koreans had such an interest in black women's hair. I guess they were more interested in the billion dollar industry that black hair had become. I was wheeling my oversized SUV en route to Gabby's salon or the G-spot as she called it. Gabby had quite the imagination, and the girl could do some hair. I jumped out and entered the salon in anticipation of her verbal assault on the importance of timeliness and professionalism that I have heard before.

CHAPTER SIX

We were halfway through with my hair before Gabby decided to break her silence and communicate with me. I guess it was her way of punishing me. You would swear that she was bipolar or something the way she could go from hot to cold like a Porsche goes from zero to sixty. She medicated herself in one of two ways, either booze or weed. Maybe the two glasses of Riesling helped put her in a better mood. The G-spot was her version of an upscale beauty salon. It had a lounge feel to it; very posh. You almost didn't mind being there for the hours it sometime took to get your hair done. Gabby was the owner and had the biggest clientele, but she surrounded herself with some talented stylists. Tonya had been here since I began coming, which was about four years ago. Raymond has only been here about a year. He is not the first guy that Gabby has had styling; but he has been the only one that seemed immune to her vicious mood swings and lack of sensitivity at times. K 'Neisha operated the station in the back where pedicures and manicures were done. Gabby had nearly thought of everything when it came to beauty, which is why her shop has been considered tops, not just in Charlotte but the entire country according to Essence magazine.

"Did you figure out how many models we are going to go with? I wanna know how many people I gotta style and do make up for."

"Yeah," I replied knowing that she wanted me to be specific, "16 girls and 11 guys." I braced for her reply. "Damn, Jacqueline that's a lot of prep time and work for that many models. We didn't have that many at the last show." "I know Gabby, but I want our display to be bigger and better than it was the last time. I want people to leave impressed with Genesis, even our competitors. This is Bronner Brothers for heaven's sake!" I paused. "Don't worry you're gonna get paid well for your wonderful talent." She smiled. For some people you just had to speak their language. Gabby's language was dollars and cents. If it didn't make money, to her it didn't make sense. She seemed calm at the thought of making some extra dinero.

Moments later my weave was done, my eyebrows threaded and nails and toes were flawless. In my line of work I had to be on top of my game at all times. Beauty was the name of the game and I was in it to win it. Dwayne hated me wearing weave and I wasn't a big fan of it myself, but it made styling my hair quicker. Besides, I really wasn't that high on what he thought anyway. Kennedy didn't seem to mind, or at least he never said anything to me. When I thought about it 1500.00 dollars was a bit excessive for a hair do that consisted of some Indian woman's locks, but I had to represent for the industry that I was into. Besides, you had to pay for quality these days. There was nothing worse than looking like you were wearing a weave, other than looking like you were wearing a tacky weave. At the end of the day it was another expense afforded to me on Genesis's dime.

Raymond was talking about some married man that he has been seeing on the so called "down low." It disgusted me to think that you couldn't look at a man without wondering if he was suspect. It's one thing that they cheat with women, but men cheating with men that are married to women is a concept that I will never get used to. If you're gay then be gay all the way. Although I didn't particularly subscribe to Raymond's chosen way I respected him a whole lot more than guys who pretend to be something they are not. Gabby must have sensed my disgust and chimed in with gossip of her own.

"Have you talked to your boyfriend lately?" She teased. I looked around in embarrassment not wanting Raymond or another stylist to hear her. They were all busy listening to his latest anal exploits. I smiled knowing deep inside I wanted to cry because I hadn't spoken with Kennedy. Gabby pretty much knew everything about us. She was the only confidant I had regarding these matters. "I haven't heard from him for over two weeks. This is the longest period we have had with no contact." A troubling look consumed me that was obvious enough for Gabby to pick up on. "Don't worry about it. Look we will be in Atlanta this weekend and I am sure you guys will more than catch up if you know what I mean." I smiled hoping she would prove prophetic in this instance.

When I left the G-spot, I left gossip of down low trysts and the smell of numerous chemicals all in the name of women's beauty with a renewed optimism of my own affair. As I made it to my car and monitored my time for all remaining errands before the boys were out of school I wrestled with thoughts of "what if." What if I left Dwayne to be with Kennedy? How would all of that look? There was so much to consider. He lives in Atlanta for now and I am in Charlotte. He has his own issues with his wife to consider albeit they are separated. The boys think the world of their father and he is a good one. Would Kennedy even want to blend our respective families? How would his son Miles react to me? Would he want to have more children? What if our love wouldn't stand the test of time? Even though we love each other, these were serious factors to consider. If it weren't for my boys I probably would have left Dwayne's ass a long time ago without batting an eye.

It felt like torture as I listened to Maxwell's Bad Habits song for the fourth time. I just kept on starting it over and over. I kept on torturing myself. Call me a glutton for punishment. This song made me think of Kennedy. He was my bad habit. He was a habit that I didn't wanna break. I was caught up in the moment. I could feel him breathing down my neck and caressing my body without missing one single curve or crevice. The mind was a very powerful thing. I am embarrassed to say that I was totally aroused in that moment. Finally I switched tracks to something a little less scintillating. I wondered how he could all of a sudden become so cold and distant to me. It felt like anger towards me after he made it clear that he had never loved anyone the way he loved me. He certainly had a funny way of showing his brand of love all of a sudden. Who the hell breaks off a relationship via email? Hate had to be better than this. He didn't even have the decency to do it face to face.

When I pulled up to my next destination I looked around to make sure nobody was looking and removed my suddenly moist panties and put them inside of my purse.

After I checked with the manufacturer about the product we needed for the show and the specifics on shipping I met with my team about the details of the layout for our display. I covered everything from A to Z twice over to ensure things were just the way I wanted it. My level of thoroughness was not to everyone's liking, but I really didn't give a damn. I had a job to do and getting it done was all I really cared about. They didn't hire me at Genesis to make friends. They hired me to take their sales to another level and that is what I have been doing. When I left the meeting I called the Westin Hotel in Atlanta to confirm the reservations made months ago. Sometimes hotels developed amnesia whenever big events came to town. It was customary for the Bronner Brothers show to bring in about 80,000 people. My reservations were all accounted for and I let the lady know that we definitely still wanted the rooms. I made sure I had a private room just in case Kennedy wanted to tuck me in. A girl had to have her bases covered. I pulled into the carpool lane to pick up Evan and Michael like I customarily did. There wasn't anything or anyone I loved more than my boys. Sometimes I wondered how I was able to co-sign something as close to perfection as they were. I kissed my babies and buckled them into their child seats as we headed home.

CHAPTER SEVEN

Back down memory lane my mind traveled like a time machine as I slept. It was about six months after we had met. I was remembering the first time that Jacqueline and I made love. She was in Atlanta for some hair show away from her husband and her two kids. We met for dinner at Justin's restaurant on Peachtree. It was minutes from her hotel and not far from my condo either. I didn't wanna be presumptuous and invite her to my place so we went to a restaurant instead. Prior to that night we had managed to build some serious intimacy without being physical. In fact we had only made out and there was not a real clear road map as to where we were headed. I had to admit that this was foreign territory to me. I always measured intimacy with acts of physicality where relationships were concerned. I could tell that I was rubbing off on her because she seemed much more comfortable as I blessed the food. Jacqueline told me that her husband was not the most spiritual brother and that over time she has gotten used to a lot of silent prayers. That made a little more sense to me. For a minute I thought that she was an atheist. I wasn't exactly the Apostle Paul myself, but I was grounded in spirituality. While that didn't mean that I was perfect by a long shot, it just meant that I had sense enough to know that a higher power existed in my life.

She looked stunning adorned in a multicolor maxi dress with a sexy pair of silver t-strap heels with an open toe. As usual her toes were eye catching. She had a design on them that looked like small diamonds. Jacqueline really put effort into her look. She was radiant. We conversed over soul food as our respective souls became further intertwined. I remember thinking that this moment couldn't get any better. We later had a few drinks in Atlantic Station at a place called Strip. Jacqueline seemed more relaxed. She started moving very rhythmically as if she had a song going on internally. "Let's go somewhere and.....dance." She asserted. "Whatever you want." I called Marcus to get the lay of the mature and happening spots that evening. He put me on hold and told me to go to the Velvet Room. Marcus stayed one step ahead and forwarded me the directions from his iPhone. He told me to ask for the manager to get all the rights and privileges that they normally extend to him when he comes. Once again his connections served as beneficial to me.

Once we got inside true to form we were treated like celebs. Jacqueline ordered a martini and I had a Heineken. This time she sat closer. With the decrease of her inhibitions courtesy of the liquid spirits she didn't care about anyone seeing us together. Charlotte and Atlanta aren't exactly worlds apart. They are closer than you might imagine, especially within the circles that we both ran in. She pulled my hand and led me to the dance floor. It seemed as though all the guys had their eyes on Jacqueline as she moved her body with the rhythm and fluidity that goddesses were made of. She was responsible for creating mass hysteria inside my pants as we danced close and seductively. I took advantage of the moment and surveyed her body with my hands song after song. By the time Usher's "In this club" went off I knew every single curve of her body. Dancing could be an invasive form of interacting and this was clearly no exception.

"I want you." She whispered softly in my ear. I tried to maintain my composure. I tried to play like I didn't wanna grab her hand and run out of the Velvet Room like there was a fire drill. I just acknowledged her words with my eyes. I searched her to see if she had any regrets or hesitation. Wanted to make sure she knew what she was doing. I sure as hell wasn't gonna deny her or myself for that matter. I closed out the tab and we were inside of a cab headed back to the Westin. It's funny how the influence of a woman can make a man lose his mind and face his fear of heights in the same instance. I threw caution to the wind as the elevator rocked and zoom to the 46th floor. It felt like a rocket was taking off. When we got inside, things simmered down for a moment. It was as if she wanted everything to be perfectly scripted. There was no spontaneity in this moment. "Let me freshen up, I'll be right back." She seemed fresh enough for me; I was ready like Tevin Campbell. "I wanna play something for you." She turned her laptop on to her musical playlist and played a track. It was from Chrisette Michelle's first album. "I want you to listen the words and you will understand me" she insisted. It was the track entitled "If I Have My Way."

I wondered why she didn't play something like "Sex Me," "Your Body's Calling," Bump n Grind," or "Let's Get It On." Any of those would have delineated how I was feeling. I had to admit it was a beautiful song. Sometimes it was hard expressing yourself with your own words. I guess this was her way of telling me exactly what she wanted to say without uttering a single consonant or vowel. Before the song ended Jacqueline was out of the bathroom. She appeared like a vision of love. My mom had taught me that patience was a virtue and only now had that made sense. I was glad I waited. She was adorned in a white negligee that hung low on her breast line and climbed high around her bountiful hips and thighs. Her hair and makeup were touched up and the Juicy Couture was permeating my olfactory in the most perfect way. I was inhaling beauty. She held two glasses of champagne and extended one towards me. This was reason to celebrate. She sipped hers as I gulped mine.

Jacqueline sat beside me as her playlist continued to play random songs that sang of love and possibility. She stared into my eyes as if she was searching me. Whatever she saw seemed to put her at ease. You would have thought that it was her first time. I kissed her as she unbuttoned my shirt. We kissed very deeply and with great passion and intensity. My heartbeat increased as her breathing became heavier. Heat had risen between the both of us. For a moment I felt like I was a virgin. Felt like I hadn't known what it was like to be with a woman. That's how Jacqueline made me feel. She simply took my breath away. Jacqueline got up and sauntered over to the king bed and pulled the covers back. I followed her as I left a trail of my clothing all the way down to my boxers. I even removed my socks. My manhood was pushing against my boxers as if to say it wanted to be personally introduced to Jacqueline.

In all the excitement of passion and lust I was reminded that I didn't have any protection whatsoever.

Damn, I thought to myself. "Stop...for a minute!" She said. "I want you to know something."

These were the awkward moments that men wanted desperately to avoid. No good conversation has ever happened with a man and a woman that has preceded sex. There probably were very few after sex, it was just that an orgasm made almost anything more tolerable.

"I just want you to know that this is new for me Kennedy. I have only been with my husband and no other man has known me other than him. I just wanted you to know that." She seemed as if a major burden had been lifted. I didn't exactly know how to process that one. Maybe when the blood from my erection returned to my brain I could wrap my mind around it better. In that moment I wanted to wrap my hands around every inch of beauty that was her body and deal with the rest later.

She pulled her straps down and released her mountainous breasts. There was more than enough to go around. I licked them as she moaned and turned her head. I teased her nipples with my tongue, saturating her areolas. She really seemed stimulated evidenced by her increased moaning. Caught up in the moment I guess, or maybe it was shear curiosity but I wondered what she tasted like. Jacqueline's body was what guys affectionately refer to as thick. Her waist was small, but her hips and thighs were wide like canyons. Jacqueline was the Brick House that the Commodores were talking about. She wasn't wearing any bottoms beneath her top. If her body was a map of the east coast I was rapidly working my way down I-95 south in search of Virginia. Once I made it there, I exercised caution and slowed down to a nice speed. I tasted what was good. Jacqueline was pre-pubescent in her genital area, there was not a trace of hair. I was glad because I liked seeing what I was putting my mouth on. She reacted as though she was about to scream as she clutched the back of my head like a vice grip. I teased and pleased her clitoris to and through her orgasm. Her thighs felt like two pythons squeezing my head until after she came. Her legs fell away as she recovered and attempted to regain her strength. Jacqueline removed her negligee completely as she handed me a condom from the nightstand.

Once I rolled the condom on and entered her she exhaled and moaned the sweetest sounds I had ever heard. Jacqueline grabbed my face and kissed me so passionately that my erection grew stronger. We were face-to-face and genital-to-genital. It didn't get any closer than this. I took my time. I didn't wanna rush at all. I wanted this moment to last a lifetime. Jacqueline had gone to that place where satisfied lovers go. She had an orgasm once again. She was in the lead 2 to 0. I guess I didn't mind, maybe it was the Libra inside of me. I had an innate drive to please others. She must have been feeling a little more aroused and comfortable with me because she asked me to turn her on her side. I turned her on her left side and entered her pleasure walls. As I penetrated her deeper I could tell that the level of arousal was more intense. The curve of my manhood was hitting her sweet spot as her moans grew louder. I stroked her faster and harder as I was more stimulated. She was wetter which made me harder. The sounds of her moans filled the four corners of her hotel room and no doubt the neighbors knew my name. She beat me to the finish line again, only this time I wasn't far behind. I finally yielded to the force of the orgasm and came. The score was now 3 to 1.

When she spoke, she sounded out of breath "That was amazing Kennedy. You've got incredible stamina. You sure you're not taking Viagra or something?" I laughed. "Just because I distribute those sexual enhancement drugs doesn't mean I use them. I just try to take care of my body that's all. It's all about blood flow, so the running helps." "Blood flow huh? Whatever you're doing, don't stop." She slid closer to me and turned her back in that spooning position that all females love after sex. Normally this would be the part where I was wiping off and putting my clothes on, but I lingered instead. There was something that kept me there. Something kept me in the moment.

CHAPTER EIGHT

After I had gotten home and fed Michael and Evan, listened to them talk about their day, checked over their homework, and given them baths I could finally exhale and relax. It was amazing that two otherwise identical people physically could be so different in regards to their personalities. It was hard for me or Dwayne to tell them apart at first glance because they looked so much alike. I remember being pregnant and the doctor alarming me when he originally thought that there were serious birth defects with the one child I was led to believe that I was carrying. He even suggested that we terminate the pregnancy. That was a reality that I didn't wanna have to come to grips with. Then he discovered that there were two instead of one. While it was good news that they were both healthy and normal I became a nervous wreck at the thought of double duty as a prospective first time parent. Two breast feedings, diaper changes and burping. One thing was for sure, I knew that my life would never be the same. Dwayne was not the most hands on father initially which meant that everything was on me. Evan and Michael have brought me so much joy that I would do it over again in a heartbeat.

For kindergarteners, they had tons of schoolwork. It was encouraging to know that they both seemed very enthusiastic so far about school. They insisted that I read them each a story before bed as if they weren't in the same room. True to form I couldn't resist them. I loved them more than life itself. They were once again asleep before I finished reading about Curious George's museum fiasco. I kissed them both and turned out their lamps before I left their room. As I was heading down the hall I could hear the garage door opening, which meant either we were being robbed or Dwayne had gotten home. Somehow the first prospect didn't seem as frightening as my own husband coming home. I really had lost all my zest for his weekly tirades that usually accompanied one of his faculty meetings.

Being the wife of a principal meant that I was somehow grandfathered in as a part of the staff whether I wanted to be or not. I was forced to listen as he talked about teachers complaining about being underpaid and overworked all the while standardized test scores not being where they needed to be. With the present state of the economy Dwayne would be forced to cut at least 10 positions and implement furlough days across the board from top to bottom just to come close to satisfying the new budget cuts. Dwayne and his other administrators would have to take 10 days while the teachers would take 5. I couldn't imagine the strain that those cuts would impose on most families. We wouldn't feel it based on the fact that Dwayne's pay was in six figures and mine was vastly approaching it as well.

Who knows, this time next year I could very well be out earning him all together. I wondered how his fragile male ego would take not being the top money earner. He has thrown that in my face since I could remember. Dwayne said that I should just be a volunteer for the money that I made while being a social worker. He said that with all the arrogance that I have come to despise about him over the years. That was before I went into the beauty industry. By the time I made it up the hallway away from the boys I could follow his trail of clothing from the kitchen down to the basement. There were his shoes by the door, his brief case, shirt, jacket, cufflinks, and his bowtie, car keys and wallet on the island in the kitchen. The man had practically stripped before he made it to the basement on the way for a nightcap.

When we built our house Dwayne insisted that we have a basement complete with a bar so that he could have his personal space and play bartender whenever we had company. I could tell how his day went according to what he was drinking. The darker the liquid spirits the worse his day was. He was listening to Marvin Gaye's "Distant Lover", the live version; needle to vinyl. I wondered why he refused to throw away those dusty albums and synchronize all that crap to digital format like everyone else in the 21st century. "Get an iPod already", is what I wanted to say. I retrieved his items and put them in the appropriate place. His keys were on the key rack and his shirt and jacket were in the dry clean only basket in the laundry room. He must have thought that I was his maid instead of his wife. It was like picking up after 3 boys instead of the 2 that I should be picking up after. Lucky for him I could not stand a house filled with clutter and out of order. I guess that I got that honest from my mother, because her house was so clean that you could probably eat off the floor. My mom was a neat freak if I have ever seen one.

I heard him call my name. "Shit." I thought to myself. I hoped that he would just play his music and drink enough to fall asleep. When I made it downstairs he was halfway finished smoking one of his cigars that he dipped in expensive Cognac. I hated smoke, so he did agree to only smoke downstairs with the door open so that the smoke would escape the house; most of it at least. Why were smokers so inconsiderate? It was as if their lack of appreciation for good air quality superseded our appreciation for it. "How was your day?," he asked. "It was pretty good. I had a few errands to run to get some things done before the show this weekend." Dwayne never asked me about me day, so I knew that he was up to something. He was sitting on the sofa with his right foot propped up on the ottoman. His stomach protruded over his slacks and his left hand rested on his crotch. It was as if he was trying to be sexy or something. It took a lot for me not to laugh. He kept on with the small talk and asked me to sit beside him. I knew that he wanted to have sex, but I didn't...at least not with him.

Dwayne hadn't exactly kept up with himself over the years and he was really showing his age. He was only 40, but he could pass for older. I know that his job was stressful and all, but the drinking and the smoking didn't help either. He thought that a gym required a passport or something because he wasn't trying to go to one anytime soon. Men always complained about women letting themselves go, especially after having children and getting married. The truth was that he could stand to lose about 15 pounds. Some crunches and a few bicep curls wouldn't exactly kill him. It might even help him look better in that tank top he was wearing. I know that it was wrong, but I couldn't keep myself from comparing his body to Kennedy's. It was wrong because there was no comparison whatsoever. Kennedy treated his body as if it was a site to behold, and it was. He exercised religiously and watched what he put into it. Most importantly he didn't smoke. I thought that Dwayne would grow out of the whole cigar thing. Thought that it was just a phase he was going through. Guess that I was wrong, because now he smokes more and more frequently.

He wondered why I stopped kissing him. I could not stand the taste that it left on his tongue. With much regret and hesitation I had sex with my husband on the sofa in our basement as Marvin Gaye crooned in the background. The only thing was that my distant lover was in Atlanta while I was in Charlotte. I had put him off for several weeks, and I was growing tired of the accusations that something was wrong and that I was seeing someone. Knowing deep down that he was right on both accounts. There was something wrong, and it was there before Kennedy ever came into the picture. During the whole encounter I thought to myself how he didn't have a clue of how to make love to me. He didn't know how to hold me, touch me, or make me purr the way Kennedy did. Seven years of giving myself to someone that really didn't know my needs or who I was made me grow restless by the day. As I lay there in body with

Dwayne, I was mentally and spiritually with Kennedy; totally disconnected from the events that were taking place. I lay there about as disinterested in him as a republican at a democratic national convention. After he grunted and tensed up it was over, he was finished. I hurried to the shower to conceal my tears and wash away the encounter.

CHAPTER NINE

I decided that enough was enough. As much as I hated to admit that maybe Marcus was right in that I needed to move on in order to get Jacqueline out of my system for good. I had finally moved forward with my divorce and I would be a free man in 60 days. I had even taken the ring off my finger. Like Usher I was ready to sign the papers and so was she. It was what was best. For the last 14 years I was married to Marley and heavily involved with Jacqueline for most of the last two years, hanging on to the thought that she would one day be mine. Emotions could make you think and want the most impossible things despite the reality that they could or should never be. That was where I was with the whole thing. I was focused on what could be and not on what was. Jacqueline was married, she had two kids and home was where she wanted to be. It was where she was supposed to be, regardless of whatever scenarios we had concocted about being together. It was what it was. I had to close my mind to that chapter and begin a new one.

Marcus and I were hanging out in downtown Atlanta. He wanted me to meet his boss at a get together they were having at the W hotel. I figured that it would be a good opportunity to see fresh faces and to busy myself so that I wouldn't be reminded of what I was trying to forget. I even got GQ for the event and wore a suit. When we got there I quickly got into the groove because the music was nice and the women were plentiful and fine. Atlanta was heaven for a single man. There were so many gay guys and down low guys that women were always receptive towards a manly man. It was like taking candy from a baby when it came to getting a woman. The downside of that was the fact that you never knew what you were getting because some women had been with guys that slept with guys. That thought made me pause for a minute. It made me uneasy about the prospect of dating women in Atlanta or anywhere for that matter. It definitely made me thankful that condoms were invented.

Marcus waved me over to a table where he was talking to a guy. I walked over and he introduced me to his boss. "Kennedy King this is Kevin Wade." I shook Kevin's hand and told him it was nice to meet him. "So this is the guy you've been telling me about Marcus?" he added. Marcus nodded. "Yeah this has been my boy since college." We made small talk as we all took notice of the beautiful scenery that was the many women that walked by. They returned our stares with stares of their own; stares that said they were interested. Marcus couldn't help himself so he went over to the bar to no doubt show off his deep pockets and buy a round of drinks and see which one he could add to his roster. Kevin and I continued to talk to one another and get better acquainted. He told me that he read my book and that he liked it too. He said that it helped him get over a difficult time that he had gone through. Kevin told me that he moved back to Atlanta a few years ago to run his sports and entertainment firm.

While we knocked back a couple of drinks he told me all about his brief NFL career and his dream of helping others to succeed where he had failed. He hired Marcus when he realized his vision of expanding beyond athletes to entertainers as well. Kevin had practically cornered the whole southeast. He was building a very impressive roster of clientele so I was humbled and impressed at the same time to be a part of it. In five years he had gone from being fired as a mortgage broker to building an entertainment empire. Now he was playing golf with Tyler Perry, having lunch with Jay Z, and he was on everybody's VIP list that was somebody. This guy could have his way with any woman he wanted to. For a minute, I found myself somewhat envious of him. Then I snapped back into reality.

The truth was that envy really didn't look that good on me. I simply admired him in that moment.

Kevin explained that he liked it so much that he was arranging a meeting with some people to seriously negotiate making the book into a screenplay and putting it on the big screen. I was in a state of disbelief after he had confirmed what Marcus told me. Even though nothing was concrete just the thought of something that I had written becoming a featured film was exciting. I somehow contained my enthusiasm. After talking business Kevin started asking personal questions to get better acquainted. He said that he prided his firm on being just like a family. I told him all bout Miles and my soon to be status as a divorced man and starting over. He smiled, but not at my situation. He told me that he had gone through a divorce of his own and that he had custody of his two children. I asked him about the whole adjustment and how it was moving on. I was curious about his newfound status as a single man with increased social status. "It's like this. If you've been to Baskin Robbins and had all 31 flavors, you just don't get that excited to try them all anymore. You already know the one you like the most and you stick with it, but if you haven't tried them all then you will always wonder what you're missing out on." I absorbed his words like a dry sponge taking in water. He made perfect sense to me.

"Speaking of my favorite flavor here she comes right now." Must be butter pecan I thought as we were joined at the table by this fine specimen of a woman. Her complexion reminded me of honey and her body had enough curves to make a man dizzy just looking at her. "I'm sorry I'm late, traffic on 285 was murder." She kissed him on the lips. Kissed him like she was the owner of his lips and she wanted them back. His whole expression lit up when he saw her. It was like no other woman made him feel the way that she made him feel. I knew exactly what that was like, because it was the way I felt about Jacqueline. It was the way that she claimed that she felt about me. "Hey baby, I want you to meet Kennedy King. This man is a brilliant writer and I am proud to say that he is a part of our family." She extended her hand until it met mine and introduced herself as Lisa Ellis, but not Lisa Ellis-Wade. Neither of them had any rings on their finger but there was an undeniable connection. They had the stuff that folks dreamed of having, they exuded love. It was as if they ignored all of the societal pressures to force titles on one another. They were moving at their own pace and obviously it was working. I told them that it was nice meeting them both and I left the two lovebirds alone and busied myself by mingling with others.

As I sat at the bar I cringed inside thinking about the whole dating routine that I was unfortunately about to be getting into. The truth was that I had needs that only a woman could meet and I was not about to let those needs go unmet much longer. I had met a few women and had a few conversations and even did the whole cell phone number exchange, knowing deep down that I probably wouldn't be calling them. The games people played, I thought to myself.

After watching Kevin and Lisa's interaction and going back and forth with thoughts about Jacqueline in my mind I didn't realize that I had probably had more drinks than I intended to. I found myself under the influence of the moment and all that it had to offer. I was greeted by a young lady who was at the bar waiting on a drink. This was kind of rare because she was probably the only woman that was paying for her own drinks in this place. We made eye contact initially, which told me that she was interested in at least knowing who I was. "Can I get you a drink?" I asked her. "No thanks." She retorted. "But, I will buy you one." This was odd I thought. Most women would have taken the free spirits without hesitating. She was letting me know that she paid her own way. My ego could take it. In fact I thought it made her even sexier. I hated a woman all up in a man's pockets as if it were her birthright or something. She introduced herself. Told me her name was Kristin and that she was in town on business. Interesting, I thought to myself. I gave her my spill, name, occupation, and locale. I kept it light. Kept it moving. Sometimes less was more.

Kristin was beautiful. She was about 5 "5" without those 4 inch heels that she had on. She was wearing a navy skirt and white blouse and looked like she was just getting off. Her lack of southern twang when she spoke let me know that she was a long way from home. She had a nice rack on an otherwise petite frame. Her blonde hair was straight and hung shoulder length and her eyes were blue. She was of European-American persuasion. I motioned for her to pull up a chair as if I owned the bar. She accepted and we engaged in mutual small talk. Kristen told me that she worked as a data analyst for some company that I'd never heard of that housed their headquarters in Atlanta. I told her about my legal drug dealings as a pharmaceutical rep. I didn't mention the writing interests because I figured she didn't need to know. I guess I still wasn't comfortable identifying myself as a writer even though it was what I enjoyed doing.

I decided to pace myself with the drinks and increase my hydration with some water. Kristen had put back a few shots of Tequila and seemed in no hurry to halt her pace. Must have been one hell of a meeting I thought to myself. The more she drank the more talkative she became. At this point I knew all about her upbringing as a military brat and just about every state that she has ever lived in. I knew that she had no problems making friends and that she now lived in San Diego. She told me that she couldn't believe the racism that still existed in the south, even in the 21st Century, even after the election of America's first black president. Kristen said that she thought that I seemed different, unlike most that she'd encountered during her travels to the good ole south. I didn't quite know how to take that. Sometimes people could be offensive without trying to be offensive. Race was and will always be a touchy subject in America.

I reminded her that I was not from the south. I told her that I had been born and raised in Virginia. She laughed hysterically; as if I was Eddie Murphy doing standup; back when he actually did stand up. "What's so funny?" I insisted. She was laughing too hard to respond. At this point her face was turning red. "I'm sorry." She inserted. "Kennedy you do know that Virginia is a part of the south don't you?" "You ever heard of the Mason Dixon line? I do believe that Virginia sits to the south of it." She went back to laughing after she had given me her impromptu third grade geography lesson. After she stopped her hysterical laughter I attempted to further clarify myself. I explained that the attitudes and progression of people in general were better in Virginia versus the Deep South. It wasn't exactly the

Carolinas, Georgia, Mississippi, or Alabama.   The more we talked and laughed the more stares we garnered from on lookers who no doubt were mentally stuck in the stone ages. In some people's minds they could never fathom black and white relationships.   To every black woman present, I had become their public enemy number one. It was a thing that I had come to know too well being that my stepmother was white.

As I scanned the room I saw Kevin and Lisa making their way to the exit. Their romance was bittersweet for me. On the one hand it reminded me of what I couldn't have in Jacqueline, but inspired me that in due time it could happen with someone else. Marcus spoke before he left. He gave me the head nod and winked as if he was a proud father watching his son do something that he approved of. It gave him peace of mind that I was moving on. Kristen was really cool and down to earth. She was someone that was easy to talk to and seemed fun to just be around. I could tell that she felt the same about me because I wasn't exactly holding her hostage or keeping her from exploring other options. She motioned for the bartender to come over.   Kristen slapped her platinum American Express card on the bar and told the guy to clear our tab. She did that against my approval, which was obvious. She signed the slip and I left the tip. "You're not used to anyone doing anything for you, huh? I'm not one of these poor damsels in distress that needs a man to do everything for them." She chuckled and mumbled "Mason Dixon line." That remained amusing to her. I laughed this time as well. Kristen put her purse on her shoulder and put another card on the bar and slid it in my direction. It was her room key. "I fly back to San Diego tomorrow and I still have to pack. You know these airports want you there hours before you even board the flight. I'm going up to my room to take a shower. I'll give you a few moments to decide if you wanna see what I'm putting on." She smiled and shook my hand before walking towards the elevators in search of her room. I watched her walk away then looked at the key as I held it in my hand coming to grips with the proposition she had made.

CHAPTER TEN

My mother was going to pick up Evan and Michael and keep them for the weekend while I was in Atlanta. I really didn't understand why Dwayne couldn't watch his own children while I was out of town. This was his way of being spiteful because in reality he really didn't want me to be gone. It was another example of his passive aggressive bull crap, but I wasn't going to fall for it. I was just thankful that my parents lived in the same city, besides the boys loved their grandparents. With Dwayne's mom being deceased and his father being missing in action, they were the only grandparents our children had. Sometimes I felt as though Evan and Michael were missing something not having that connection with both sets of grandparents like I did as a child, but mom and dad more than spoiled them both equally. Dwayne was curt and abrasive as he prepared to leave this morning but it didn't bother me in the least. I had the boys' things prepared for the weekend and I kissed and hugged them before they left for school, knowing that it would be Monday evening before I saw them again.

It had been days since I smiled, but the thought of seeing Kennedy forced my face into a blushing grin. Moments later the doorbell rang and right on cue it was Gabby. I told her to park her car here so that we could drive down to Atlanta together in my Tahoe. There was no way that we could fit all our luggage, supplies, and materials in her convertible Jaguar. It was cute and all but we needed some room.

I often joked with Gabby that she should have gotten a Cougar since she certainly had an affinity for younger men; much younger men. When I met her outside to consolidate cars we hugged as we always do. She was wearing some leggings with a fitted Ed Hardy t-shirt and some flip flops and some really cute Ed Hardy shades that I hadn't seen before. Her hair and makeup were always on point. Guess it helped being a hair and makeup artist. To look at Gabby you would never know that she was about to turn 45. The way that she spoke you would think that she invented cursing.

"Hurry the fuck up Jacqueline! It's hot as hell out here; I don't wanna sweat with this damn makeup on. You know this Atlanta traffic on 85 is a motherfucker!" All of that just rolled off her tongue for no reason at all. This was mild for her, and I have definitely seen her get more revved up. Her bipolar tendencies were on full display. Maybe when we got to Atlanta I could see if Kennedy had the hook up on some mood stabilizers.

"Can you please stop cursing? My virgin ears can't take it." I teased. She gave me that look like she was about to start dropping F-bombs, but she didn't. I dreaded the thought of the next several hours that it would take to get to Atlanta if she didn't remain calm. I wasn't the biggest fan of marijuana usage and had only experimented in college, but it seemed to be the only thing other than sex that calmed Gabby down. Heck I'd even buy it at this point if she would just take it easy.

Once we got onto I-85 towards Georgia and Gabby seemed more even keeled we talked more about the Bronner Brothers show and our display. Although I didn't let on, I was really nervous. When you worked in marketing your successes and failures were all measured in sales. It was all about the money. With two shows annually and over 60 million dollars up for grabs I had to make sure that Genesis would get its' lion's share. Mr. and Mrs. Dillard were good people but they didn't understand that it took money to make money. I had finally gotten them to loosen their grip on the checkbook and trust my skills at making sales. Now all I had to do was back up all of the talking that I did. They each had given me several not so subtle reminders that this was the largest amount of money they had ever spent at the Bronner Brothers show. I wondered how they expected to compete with the other companies by being so darn cheap.

I couldn't quite wrap my mind around the 9 billion dollar industry that black hair had become, especially since most of the major players were Korean. It made me think that if just one third of women decided to only buy products from black owned companies what impact that would make economically on Black America. It was just another example of everyone else's ice being colder than your neighbor's was. It was too much like making sense.

Gabby and I were nearing Atlanta and it was so far so good as far as traffic went. We were moving right along with only a few miles to go before we got to downtown Atlanta. I wanted to text Kennedy but I had promised my mother that I would quit texting and driving so I decided against it.

When we got close to Peachtree Gabby said that she was hungry so we stopped at Maggiano's for a late lunch. Gabby was just like me in that she loved Italian food. After we sat down I got up to use the restroom, but more importantly to call Kennedy. His phone went to voicemail. Maybe he was on his rotation or doing one of those catered lunches that drug reps do to keep doctors writing prescriptions. I left him a message to call me later. While we waited for our order I called other members of my team to make sure that they were all in position. Everything had to go according to plan. If things went bad this would all come crashing down on me.

I picked over my Chicken Parmesan, all the while trying not to let my nervousness show. Gabby's appetite was nonstop which let me know that she had taken her medication. Gabby was a chronic weed smoker and it was obvious that she had slipped away and indulged in her drug of choice without me even knowing it. I cringed at the thought that she had illegal drugs and paraphernalia in her possession while riding in my car. Call me a scary cat, but I was not about to get arrested for her bad habit.

After Gabby scarfed down her entree and dessert we were on the way to check into our hotel rooms. I had to lecture her about not smoking inside of the hotel rooms. Even though I knew that it would go into one ear and out of the other one, at least my conscience was clear. She would have to suffer whatever consequences would come as a result of her getting caught. Inside I prayed that she would at least make it through the show. There was so much riding on our display and Gabby was a huge part of that. Like it or not I had to put up with her unpredictability, drug usage, and mood swings all because she had talent second to none. In this business, talent supersedes everything.

Once I had finally settled into my room I decided to take a hot bath and luxuriate in one of their $100.00 dollar robes. It was still early, but evidently I was more exhausted than I thought because in no time I dozed off. Kennedy was embedded in my conscious and unconscious mind. In fact he was the ruler of any thoughts that I had. I inhaled him with every breath I took and he had become a part of my being. Our connection was undeniable and scary at the same time.

I knew that I was in trouble when Kennedy and I met for a weekend trip to some remote cabins in Helen, Georgia. It was somewhere that I had begged Duane to take me for years, but he always had some excuse why we couldn't go. Helen was absolutely beautiful, especially the time of year that we went. It was in the middle of fall so the leaves had begun to change colors and although the temperature was brisk it wasn't too cold. It was just right. The view of the mountains was absolutely breathtaking. Aside from this being the home of Cabbage Patch Land, most people didn't even know that Helen existed except for the people who lived there. It was somewhere we didn't have to worry about running into anyone we knew.

We drove my truck for the 4x4 capabilities and mountainous terrain that we'd encounter getting to the cabin. Kennedy made such a huge fit because I insisted on paying for the whole trip. It was my idea, plus I wanted to do something to show him how much I cared for him. I knew that I had fallen for him and at the time it had only been about 6 months since we were involved. I wanted to know what it would be like to make love to him all night and wake up with him holding me. To that point we had only existed for small moments of time inside the four walls of hotel rooms, but never overnight.

Kennedy and I went shopping for groceries at the local Ingles supermarket. It was their version of Publix or Kroger and was definitely overpriced, but served the purpose anyway. I wanted to prepare my special seafood Alfredo. He insisted on paying for something so I let him buy the groceries when we checked out. Men and their egos I thought to myself. The cabin was everything I thought it would be and with the temperature dropping by the minute would make for snuggle weather.

We weren't even there for five minutes before we began making love. Our attraction was undeniable. I was so lost in him. It was as if he knew every inch of my body which naturally fueled my attraction towards him. When we were done we toured the rest of the cabin. The pool table made me think of using it for more than billiards, it would make a great prop for later on. There was modest furnishings including the bed, but overall we had everything we needed to hibernate for the next few days. Knowing us we could feed on each other for weeks.

The view of the wooded area behind us was serene and eerie in the same breath. On one hand it was comforting to take in the natural beauty that was offered, but scary because you couldn't see your hand in front of your face at night.

Kennedy was like a kid on Christmas trying to contain his excitement when he saw the Jacuzzi outside. The water was the perfect temperature, so we both got inside. He bought a few beers with him for hydration purposes. He offered me one and without hesitation I gave it a try. I wasn't much of a beer fan but this was further proof of the power of suggestion that this man had over me. Duane had insisted several times that it was an acquired taste, and for some reason beer never tasted the same with him as it did with Kennedy. Being stuck in traffic for hours or having a migraine headache didn't seem like such bad prospects being in Kennedy's presence.

Minutes gave way to hours as we sat inside a Jacuzzi in the middle of nowhere all the while neither of us wanted to be anywhere but there. Kennedy had always been open with me but never in this way. He shared stories from his childhood and his difficulty dealing with his parent's divorce. It made me understand his personal struggles dealing with the possibility of repeating the same cycle. He wanted to prove that he was a better man than his father and secretly feared suffering the fate of splitting his family. I understood this man more in a few hours than I understood my own husband after years of marriage and two children. I knew what his fears were. I knew what his dreams were. It made me confident that I could bare my soul to him, so I did the same thing. I told him about my guarded upbringing and my limited experiences thus far in my life. I felt as though I hadn't really lived. I was envious that Kennedy had visited so many countries and seemed so cultured on so many fronts. Heck, I didn't even have a passport.

"What's keeping you from doing the things you really want to do Jacqueline? Why haven't you traveled outside of the country? There is a huge difference between merely existing and truly living. Anyone with a pulse is alive, but it doesn't mean that they're living." Kennedy made me pause and think about his questions. I wasn't offended; instead I felt the exact opposite. I was glad that he challenged me to think about things that otherwise troubled me. The truth was that I didn't really know. Maybe sometimes in life we put our dreams on pause so long that they just stopped playing altogether. I had made every excuse in the book including Duane, Evan and Michael. While those were reasons deep down they were not excuses. I chewed on those thoughts as I drank Heineken with the man that I swore God had placed on Earth just for me.

At the time I could have existed for the rest of my life inside of that Jacuzzi with Kennedy, but the prospect of wrinkly skin made us exercise better judgment and we got out. Just when I thought there was nothing else that he could do to amaze me, Kennedy joined me in the kitchen and in his own sweet way insisted that he help. He told me that he helped his mom cook as a child all the time. This was the most caring man that I had ever met, far from the cavemen that I've encountered in my father and Duane. The two of them didn't know how to boil water and couldn't care less. There was something very sexy about a man that knew his way around the kitchen and it didn't hurt that he was wearing jeans with no shirt on. I thought about using his washboard abs to chop the onions but there was no way I was wrecking that hot body.

Over dinner we continued our deeper level of exploration. I realized that he was a Libra to my Gemini. We were both air signs. We both thrived on balance and were innately pleasers which made perfect sense. This was why he couldn't allow me to do for him. I didn't bring it up at the time but it made more sense as to why we were so compatible. I have always found something fascinating about astrology. It explained so much about a person's characteristics. Some people just fit together and there we were as living proof.

Kennedy insisted that he wash the dishes, so I allowed him to do what I knew came natural to him. I just sat back and enjoyed the view. Later on we made love all over that cabin from the kitchen counter, pool table, living room sofa, and the bathroom sink. This was sick I thought to myself. I have never felt an attraction like this and it was obvious that it was mutual because when we were holding one another in the afterglow of ecstasy he told me that he loved me. His words served as confirmation that not only mirrored what I was feeling, but also to let me know that I was in big trouble because I felt the same way.

CHAPTHER ELEVEN

If last night was any indication as to what my reality was as a soon to be divorced man, then I would give anything to have a time machine to go back in time and right some of my wrongs. There are a number of things I'd change. Heck I might even go back to my childhood so that I could warn my mother of the eventual hurt that my father leaving would cause her. Maybe I'd send myself a better father while I was at it. One thing is for certain; I would have inserted myself in Jacqueline's life before she met her husband. I would have been the one to meet her right after she finished college instead of Duane. I even hated saying his name. I know that I shouldn't have animosity towards him but I did. How could you truly love someone if you didn't resent the person who they chose to be with over you? Reality was that sometimes no matter how much you wished some things; they'd never come true. Fate had its own destiny to fulfill whether you liked it or not.

At this point of my life I had sworn that one night stands were a thing of the past, but obviously I was wrong about that to. I decided to take Kristen up on her offer for a number of reasons. She was very attractive, I was horny, and I doubted if Jacqueline was saving herself for me. I needed it; needed to feel good. Needed to forget why I was feeling so bad in the first place.

I can honestly say that Kristen did not disappoint. In fact she exceeded my expectations. Just as promised she had slipped into something more comfortable and she was waiting on me as if she knew I couldn't resist her offer. Once again proving that women always determine how these situations played out. Maybe this was the way she concluded all of her business trips. When I entered into her hotel suite I cautiously stirred around not knowing what to expect. I shrugged away any anxiety that lingered when I took notice of her sprawled out on the king bed clothed in nothing but her birthday suit and red stilettos. She was making me develop an instant affinity for Brazilian waxes. It made me dig her taste in attire as well as her boldness in communicating her wants. Too many people played games and "beat around the bush" as my mother would say when it came to expressing themselves. That made me even more aroused; made my pants grow. My manhood was letting me know that it wanted to take the lead in this scene. Who was

I to argue once my blood flowed south quicker than the economy during the Bush administration?

She put her wine glass down and crossed her legs in a smooth seductive manner. It reminded me of Sharon Stone in Basic Instinct. Jacqueline or any other woman not named Kristen was the furthest thing from my mind at this point. I was a prisoner to the moment, but I was enjoying my time.

"Why the hell are your clothes still on? They say southern people do things slow but geesh! Come on Mason Dixon." She teased as she crawled to the foot of the bed beckoning me to meet her there. Kristen exuded sexiness in her every movement. She moved her flowing blond locks from her face as she sat up on her knees and began unbuttoning my shirt and unloosening my belt.

My shirt and pants fell to the floor and I stepped out of them removing my socks and shoes. I hated seeing the guys in the porn movies with their socks on. It looked so tacky. She kissed my neck and ran small circles over my nipples until they became stiff. Kristen pulled my boxers down and stepped up to the microphone like a Grammy award-winning singer. She was no stranger to this stage; in fact it was well within her comfort zone. As she gave me head, it made my eyes roll back and I was damn near on the verge of a major release that she must have sensed when my body began to tense up. Her lips were about as tight on my manhood as OJ's hand was in that glove. If they gave college credit for fellatio this girl would be on the PhD level; heck she'd be teaching the advanced courses for sure.

Kristen let go of her oral vice grip and eased back on the bed. She tossed me a condom from her nightstand and watched me put it on nice and slow. I was glad to know that she believed in safe sex; at least safe intercourse. There were still risks in having unprotected oral sex, but some people chose to plead the fifth in acknowledging that fact and not talk about it. We just applied the Nike motto "Just Do It." Kristen looked at her clock and then at me. With her eyes she was telling me to hurry up and get this show on the road because she had a plane to catch. I felt like a glorified escort; felt cheap and insignificant. Felt all of the feelings related to sex that I haven't felt since I was probably in my teens or twenties when I didn't wanna feel anything at all. Call me old fashion but maybe these were feelings that I didn't want to have. Maybe I wanted to lay with a woman that I actually adored and wanted to hold as the sun came up; or at least be next to her.

At the end of the day I was what I was, and that was a man. In typical man fashion I was not in the business of letting an opportunity for no strings attached sex go by the wayside. Kristen was a beautiful California blonde with a nice rack, nice tan lines, and an unexpectedly shapely body, who wanted to end her trip to Atlanta with a little southern hospitality. Who was I to ruin that for her? She said that she wanted me to have my way with her, and so I did. She said that I needed to bring it, so I did. In fact I bought the thunder and the lightening. I took out my frustrations on Kristen in the form of pure unadulterated headboard banging, no strings attached, multiple orgasmic, "I didn't know you could do it like that," "I'm coming to Atlanta more often," "once you go black you never go back," "don't stop get it get it,"" you the best I ever had," "ohh…ooooowe I'm cuuummmin again," "how much do I owe you?," "damn…damn……damn… sex!"

When we finished we were both drenched in sweat. It felt like I'd run a 10K at a sprinter's pace after doing P90X my heart was pounding so fast. We had both gotten more than we bargained for. She was a good lay. Her reaction to me during and afterwards let me know that she thought I was pretty good too. Okay she thought that I was damn good. I couldn't act or sing or do a lot of things that famous and wealthy people do, but if there was one thing that I was born to do it was pleasing a woman. It came so innately to me. They said that Libras made the best lovers partly because we were about pleasing our partners and not just getting ours. I absolutely loved pleasuring a woman. It was like taking a finely tuned automobile on the highway and shifting gears until it got to top speed; hearing the engine purr ever so gently. I knew when to down shift or when to really open it up.

Kristen had purred enough in the early hours of what was now Saturday morning that she had probably reached her quota for orgasms in one month. She was breathing harder than I was. Her body had red areas that looked like bruises. The dankness of her skin made her pull her wild mane into a pony tail. I went to the bathroom to rid myself of the semen filled condom and built up urine that needed to flow as both a result of the alcohol and the orgasm that I had as well. When I returned, she wiped away dampness from my body as if I was royalty. Moments ago she was rushing me; preoccupied with her flight itinerary that now all of a sudden didn't seem as high on her priority list. There was something about hitting the right spots that would make a women respect you more and actually want to tolerate a man and linger in his presence.

"Kennedy, I must say that I didn't see that coming...no pun intended. I have never had that many orgasms during one encounter. Heck not even with several encounters. Are you on something? I laughed and then sipped more water.

"Of course I am not on anything. I just take care of myself. It's all about blood flow. Not everyone in the south has diabetes and high blood pressure." I teased with her this time. She smiled and popped me with her towel. I was on a roll and had her laughing so I kept on. "My standard fee is $500 just to show up, and that includes at least two positions of your choosing, along with a guaranteed orgasm. I charge $100 for each additional orgasm. That would bring your total to around $1000." She pursed her lips into a half smile and raised her right eyebrow as if she was considering it. "You take credit cards? I would definitely pay for that type of performance all jokes aside. Kennedy you could have a very bright future in the escort business. You're good looking, charming, got a smile like Denzel, a body like Adonis, and you fuck like a porn star." I took her compliment in stride and laughed it off all the while knowing that it was nothing that I would consider.

We made small talk while she came to grips with the fact that she wasn't going to get any sleep with a 6:00 a.m. flight back to Cali. Kristen began packing her things in preparation for her exodus from Atlanta. Somehow I figured that I'd be getting calls when she was in the area. Heck I might even call her the next time I was on the west coast. Kristen was pretty cool, and besides I suddenly didn't have what you'd call a committed relationship these days.

She asked me if I would give her a ride to the airport. Said that she really didn't want to take a cab all alone at this hour; it was the least I could do considering the fact that she helped me to temporarily forget about Jacqueline. Besides her head game was a force to be reckoned with. That thought made me laugh inside.

There was something about having sex with someone that made people wanna ask questions that they probably should have asked in the beginning. Kristen asked me about my status; married or single. Perfect timing after the fact I thought. I told her about my pending divorce after 14 years. It gave her just enough information without going into intricate details. I didn't bother bringing up Jacqueline; figured that some things were left better unsaid.

She had nearly gathered all of her things. She had two suitcases, one to be checked and one to carry on. These airlines were raking in the dough charging for bags after they charged a hefty rate for the ticket itself. What would they think of next? Kristen combed the hotel suite to make sure she had everything. What she did next was both eye popping and a telling sign of the times that we were now living in. Kristen slipped her wedding band back onto her finger. Wow!

I was certain that she didn't have one on when we met, and deep down inside it probably wouldn't have changed much. Maybe she was just doing what men did when they went on business trips. Either way, who was I to judge anyway? Technically I was still a married man albeit on the brink of a divorce. To further complicate matters I was madly in love with a woman who was herself married. I didn't even bother to let her know that I had seen the ring. I didn't wanna hear her rationale for mixing business with pleasure. People could convince themselves that they were right in doing just about anything. At this point I didn't see how anything would change between us.

After Kristen showered away my essence, she dressed very low key in some GAP jeans, sneakers, and some sort of sorority shirt that I wasn't familiar with. It started with Delta, but wasn't the brand that I was used to at Norfolk State University. We headed to my car en route to the Hartsfield-Jackson Atlanta International Airport with plenty of time for her to make it through security and board her flight back to San Diego. Kristen treated me to coffee at the Starbucks counter in the hotel lobby before she checked out. I took her luggage to my car. I hoped that she didn't mind my dated Honda Accord, but really couldn't care less. She asked me for a ride.

When I pulled to the curb Kristen got inside and we headed to the airport. She seemed to perk up after several sips of her black coffee. Her talk game was non-stop. We weren't even halfway there and I knew everything that I could possibly know about someone I had known for less than 24 hours. Kristen was a Cal-Berkley grad; summa cum lade; no desire for kids. Her husband Terrance was 12 years older than her making him 53. According to her there wasn't much heat in their bedroom and hadn't been in some time. She was there because they had shared business interests, and they hadn't been married long enough to void the pre-nuptial agreement entitling her to half of his mini fortune. At least that was the version she fed me with a long handled spoon. Again, who was I to judge?

I asked her for her flight information to determine her correct terminal. This was a huge airport and could have you turned around for days if you didn't know how to navigate it. When we pulled up to the curb for passenger drop off we both got out. I removed her luggage from my trunk and wheeled it towards her. Kristen thanked me for the ride both to the airport and for the one that took place inside of her room at the W-hotel. She kissed me on my cheek. It felt warm on my chilled face. She winked at me with her blue eyes as she turned to walk inside of the airport. I turned towards my car and walked away from her in the same way that she walked away from me. "Mason-Dixon…." I literally laughed out loud pulling away in search of my dwelling all the while beginning to embrace the changes in store for my life.

CHAPTER TWELVE

I yawned and stretched myself awake from my slumber. Still caressed by the ultra-soft bath robe compliments of the Westin Hotel I struggled to find my bearings. My exhaustion had gotten the best of me; and the August heat in Atlanta wasn't helping much. I really wasn't in the mood for hanging out late with the early start of the show tomorrow, but I didn't wanna be alone in my hotel room.

Since Kennedy hadn't called me back I decided to call Gabby to see if she wanted to get a drink. I called my mother to see how my angels were doing. The hardest part of my job was being away from them. They were my heart and soul. In fact I sometimes would take a second and pause just thinking how I contributed to something so perfect.

"Hi Mom, I was calling to check on Evan and Michael and to see how things were going." "Everything is fine sweetheart. Remember that I am your mother...I raised you." She chuckled. "Your father is reading to them and they have already had their baths." I remembered when daddy used to read to me; made me feel so special. He could be sweet when he wanted to. Pig headed most of the time, but sweet when he needed to. "Well, I was just checking. You know that I worry sometimes." I struggled to get that out. "Well if you'd like it darling, I could call you every time one of the boys has to potty or needs something. Would that help?" My mother was such a smart ass when she wanted to be. "No Mom that won't be necessary. I will try to call less and worry less. How's that?" We both laughed. "Goodnight, I love you Mommy." "Goodnight Jacqueline, I love you too." We never hung up or parted company without saying that we loved one another.

My mother had a way of making me feel like a little girl at times, no matter how old I was. She had a way of reminding me that she would always be my mother; that she'd know more regardless of how much I knew. She has made it known on more than one occasion that she despises me even working, let alone traveling and being away from the boys and Duane as frequently as I am. I didn't have the heart to tell her that I had no desire to be a homemaker or stay at home mom or whatever the hell they called it these days. I had gone to college, gotten a good education and I wasn't gonna waste that no matter what. Those June

Cleaver and Florida Evans days were about as ancient as rotary phones. I was more determined than ever to not be like her in that regard. It was bad enough that she and Duane agreed, which only made me more determined to ignore them both.

I threw on a sundress and some flat sandals to meet Gabby downstairs for drinks. Figured I would rest my feet in preparation for an all-day affair with the 4-inch heels that I'd be wearing for the Bronner Brothers show.

When I made it to the lounge I looked around for a moment searching for Gabby. I noticed her engaged in deep conversation with a guy; a much younger guy. It was obvious that she was on her game. I took a seat at the bar leaving a few spaces in between them, not wanting to seem intrusive. I ordered a Pomegranate Martini. It was my favorite. The guy working the bar even put a few gummy bears in it. He leaned on the bar and waited until I sipped it to give him my approval. It was good; really good. I nodded my head and he showcased a very modest smile dimples and all.

In typical bar fashion he broke into a conversation that seemed more like a mini interrogation. I told him that I was in town for the show and that I was here with Gabby. Decided to keep it light and not divulge too much information. People were crazy these days. He was very attractive and kinda put me in the mind of a younger more buff Blair Underwood minus the nice hair. I never told him my name and didn't ask him his.

I was onto my second martini while I continued to wait on Gabby and exchanged verbal pleasantries with the wannabe Blair Underwood. This man was so gorgeous I thought; his complexion, arms, smile, even his mustache were so sexy. I bet he had his pick of women in Atlanta. We continued to chit chat as time passed on. It was nice to just flirt sometimes knowing that there were no intentions of taking things any further, at least on my end. I was sure that he got plenty of practice in his line of work. Blair told me that he had a semester to go before he finished his degree at Morehouse. He had aspirations of becoming a doctor one day. I told him that I had gone to Florida A&M University and graduated in 1997.

I saw him doing the math in his head trying to figure out my age so I beat him to the punch and told him that on my next birthday I would be 37. He gave me that look that said you don't look that old. "WTH?" I thought to myself. I didn't know whether that was an insult or a compliment so I didn't bother asking. Suddenly his company didn't seem all so great anymore.

Gabby introduced me to her new beau. His name was Antonio as if I really cared. From what I could gather, she had taken more than a few back, which was not good, but typical. I reminded Gabby in a subtle but serious manner what the real business at hand was. We were here for the Bronner Brothers show and not here for young hot guys. I could tell that she was not in favor of my approach and she wore that look on her face. The power struggles had grown all too common with Gabby when it came to being professional and meeting deadlines. I didn't have any problems separating our friendship from our business relationship like she did.

"Look, don't get all mad with me cuz your lil boyfriend ain't call you back and shit! Now you are sitting here pouting and trying to ruin my evening wasting your time flirting with that faggot." She was referring to fake Blair Underwood. No not Blair I thought to myself, a fine gay man; what a waste. "That's beside the point Gabby. You know that there is a lot riding on the success of this show. You know that I personally have a lot riding on this, and so do you. Could you for once stop thinking about yourself and consider other people?" She rested on my words. I know that it took lots of restraint for her not to have a venomous reply, but she did not. Instead she smiled.

"Your ass is lucky I love you like a younger sister. Otherwise I would be slapping the black off you about now." Now I was smiling. I leaned closer to her. "Is FBU really gay? How do you know?" "Who the hell is FBU?" "Fake Blair Underwood." She burst into laughter. "Girl....don't ever insult Blair like that again. FBU is as gay as the day is long; you better turn your gaydar on high, especially in Atlanta."

On that note I decided to retire for the evening. I reminded Gabby of our early start for the show in the morning and left her and Antonio at the bar getting drinks from the suddenly not so attractive FBU. I couldn't help feeling that I owed the real Blair Underwood a huge apology for such an awful comparison. Maybe I'd buy his novel series as a way to make it up to him.

I don't even know why I set an alarm, because I didn't even need it to wake up this morning. Let's just say that anxiety was having its way with me and it would until the show was officially over. I hadn't been this nervous since I did my first recital as a kid. I had taken my shower and I was drinking a cup of coffee that I ordered from room service.

Since our theme this year centered on sexy, I knew that I had to look the part as well. I had to be on top of my fashion game even though I basically stayed behind the scenes. I was waiting for Gabby to come and do my hair and makeup before she began styling all the models. I wanted my hair pulled back away from my face so that the eye lashes and make up would really stand out. My lashes were so long that they would make great air conditioning for anyone close enough to feel the breeze while I batted them.

Gabby told me all about her encounter with Antonio and how she had to kick him out because he wanted to cuddle afterwards. "I don't even like cuddling with my own man for what it's worth. His shit wasn't that good anyway. Can't stand these men trying to be all close and sensual. That shit is played like cassette tapes. Ain't nothing worse than a man that can't lay pipe. Shit I could have just pulled BOB out and had more fun." She ranted on and on referring to her battery operated boyfriend or commonly known as a vibrator. I just laughed inside thinking how things have changed so much. Gabby was a man trapped inside of a woman's body. She could detach herself in an instance from any emotional involvement when it came to sex. It was just something to do; literally. She seemed as if she was incapable of investing emotions whatsoever.

When we got to the show it was business as usual, in that everyone was putting their last minute touches on their respective displays in anticipation for a huge crowd. There was nothing ever done at Bronner Brothers that came as a surprise after you had done a few. I was pleased to see our display coming along as I had outlined. It was my idea to go with a sort of Sex and The City theme. Genesis needed to break out of the box and get some attention without the huge budgets of our competitors. I had an idea for a way to bring attention to our product all the while being tasteful. We had a huge round shaped plush bed and a few bar tables. Our models were men and women in their early twenties with hot bodies that would be strategically placed in various poses exuding both sexuality and sensuality.

The models would be made up using body make up to give the appearance of some nudity. During the model call I hired several models because I knew that the statuesque poses would require great endurance over the course of the entire show. We posed the models on the bed to appear engaged in a ménage à trois, two girls and one guy. Having Usher come through, as our celebrity talent didn't hurt any either, especially with his latest hit "Climax" almost being acted out through our display. The models at the bar tables appeared to be in deep and steamy conversations that bordered on sensuality and an animalistic attraction between a man and a woman. Sure it had nothing to do with hair or beauty, but it would grab attention. That's what we needed the most. Attention was what sold.

Everyone knows that despite all the other events at the Bronner Brothers show it is about moving product by making sales. I knew that our display was risky and that we were taking a huge chance, but when you were the small fish you had to take whale sized risks to compete and even be noticed. With immense pressure from Mr. and Mrs. Dillard and the weight of the entire brand of Genesis Hair and Beauty I anxiously sat back to watch things unfold throughout the day. Our display looked even better than it did inside of my head once it was finished. I wished that Kennedy were here to see it, I know that he would be proud of me. We were getting the attention that we needed to get like I had prayed; everyone was talking about our display and how good the models all looked. Some people even thought that they were statues, because of the makeup and they didn't move.

The most impressive part was the way we moved product at such a rapid rate. We even drew the attention of some of the bigger brands that for years dominated in sales without even lifting a finger. They were just used to showing up and standing on the brand they had built. Today was our day and by the time the day was done we had sold our entire inventory on hand. We even had product on back order for weeks, which was major for a company of our size. The Dillard's were ecstatic and so was

I because today's sales tripled any previous show they had done. That news really made me feel good.

In typical Bronner Brothers fashion and I guess sales in general your competitors always took notice of what made you successful. Without any shame whatsoever I had been offered several opportunities with other companies for more pay. This was a dog eat dog world and I realized that. That's why I didn't believe in burning bridges or limiting my options. For today, I'd celebrate the success with Genesis. Tomorrow I'd figure out my next move. The Dillard's realized it as well; because they insisted that we have a face-to-face once I got back to Charlotte next week. Mr. Dillard was mumbling about new responsibilities with more money. He gave me his black card and told me to make sure everybody celebrated tonight. "Spare no expense." He did not have to tell me twice. We were going to hit up some of the nicest places that Atlanta had to offer.

CHAPTER THIRTEEN

I ignored my body's call for immediate rest following the conclusion of the show mainly due to the sheer enthusiasm that correlated with an extremely successful show. It served as a stimulant that allowed me to celebrate and enjoy the moment. After Gabby and I returned to our rooms and showered, and changed clothes we were off in pursuit of a good time. I put my black Capri leggings, gold sequined top, so that I could wear these killer gold sandals with the four-inch heel that wrapped around my legs. They really showed off my calves and I knew they'd bring lots of comments and attention. That was the real reason people bought things anyway. Plus I knew that Kennedy would not be able to resist me in this outfit. He was a sucker for a woman in leggings, especially me. I smiled with that thought.

Since my phone died while I was at the show, once it was charged I saw where he texted and even called. "Finally", I thought to myself with much anticipation and excitement to see him again. Gabby and I met downstairs since her room was on the 60th floor. She wanted to be as close to the top floor as possible. The girl loved being high I guess. Gabby had on some skinny jeans and another of her trademark Ed Hardy t-shirts. If only Christian Audigier knew Gabby, he would personally thank her for promoting his label I thought. She looked cute all the same. We exchanged pleasantries and waited on the stretched limo to take us out.

Most of the models opted for younger venues, which was fine with Gabby and me. It ended up being a smaller crowd of myself, Gabby, a few of her stylists and makeup artists inside of the limo. We enjoyed fine dining at Spondivits Seafood and Steaks restaurant. The ambiance was really nice and for a minute I thought that I was at an aquarium with all the live fish swimming around. There were sharks, eels, and even octopi, which made me, rethink my menu selection slightly. I was all for fresh seafood but I wasn't really into seeing the before image of what was coming to my dinner plate. Suddenly a nice steak was not sounding all that bad, so that's what I ordered. I told everyone to get what they wanted. It was a very small token of my appreciation for a job well done, and an even smaller token on behalf of Mr. and Mrs. Dillard. After all we lived in a society where money talked and bullshit ran faster than a crack head with stolen merchandise.

Our table was filled with appetizers, entrees, and drinks that many spectators looked on and wondered what we had going on. I had even succumbed to the juvenile dares that Gabby and the others offered and began taking shots of Patron. I wasn't a fan of tasting my liquor, but I had to admit they went down smooth one by one. It was a good thing that neither of us was driving. Then I remembered why I haven't taken shots since my college days at FAMU. That all of a sudden seemed like ages ago. Now I began to question a number of things in my life. It was funny how diminished inhibitions could sometimes make you really see things for what they were. I wanted to share my accomplishment, but I knew that Duane wouldn't really be happy for me. He would find some way to down play and minimize me even working. Maybe deep down he was a little insecure or even jealous. He was nothing like Kennedy. How I wished that he was mine and I was his. That's when I noticed that I had missed the call that I was waiting for. It was Kennedy.

I didn't even remember what happened afterwards because I became captive to the strong hold of one too many shots of alcohol. When I came to I was lying in my hotel bed wrapped in that plush robe. My clothes and shoes were lying on the floor and I didn't even remember taking them off. When I looked around I saw Kennedy glowering at me from across the room as if he were my father. His look was both judgmental and angry. It wasn't warm and inviting the way that I have come to know and love him. He let me have it for what he referred to as my "reckless decision making." It was obvious that while heavily under the influence I acted in a way that was not like me. "Big fu@#ing deal," I wanted to say.

According to him he picked me up from the restaurant and we went dancing at the Opera Nightclub and I became too flirty for his taste. I was dancing with some guys when he came back from the bar. I didn't even remember, but he obviously didn't forget. Wow, I didn't even know that he cared so much. This was a different side of Kennedy. The more he talked it became similar to Duane which was not so attractive after all. Okay, so I got a little drunk and let loose more than I normally would; nobody got killed. It's not like I slept with someone at least I didn't remember doing so. Kennedy reminded me that I gave the guy my number and at that point I slowly started remembering bits of my evening. I remembered enough to know that it was totally Bronner Brothers show related and not what he was thinking; not even what the guy probably thought. I had listened to enough of his chastisement and decided to respond.

"You haven't seen me in weeks and this is how you greet me? No hello Jacqueline. It's good to see you Jacqueline. I really miss you Jacqueline. Any of those would have sufficed. Instead I get your condescending tone and harsh judgment. Good morning to you to Kennedy." I snarled as I jumped out of bed to go to the restroom in an attempt to make myself more presentable. He had me on the verge of cursing, which I don't do unless I am really pissed off.

Kennedy and I have never really argued or been at serious odds before, so this was unchartered territory as far as we go. I brushed my teeth and washed my face before I took a quick shower. I couldn't believe that he picked me up and bought me back to my room, took off my clothes, put me in bed and didn't even try to take advantage of me. He was a true gentleman in spite of his present standing as an asshole.

When I returned to the room Kennedy had gone downstairs to buy a toothbrush and two cups of coffee. He handed me a cup and I sipped it without hesitation. Kennedy knew that I sweetened my coffee with Splenda and I only used half and half. It was just the way that I liked it.

He was quickly earning his way out of the doghouse with that act. After he brushed his teeth he came out more like himself.

I apologized for my actions that he found offensive. I told him all about the success at the Bronner Brothers show and how we were the talk of the entire show. "You would have been so proud of your girl." I boasted as I drew closer to him. He didn't respond quite the way that I thought he would which let me know that he was concealing his thoughts from me. "I am happy for you. I know that you worked really hard on that." He fed me a half-hearted congratulation like a hurried person feeds a parking meter. I deflected my emotions in pretty much the same way that he did and we began kissing.

We offered each other our coffee laden tongues all the while pressing forward and denying that differences rested among us. Never before has there been a problem with our chemistry; until this moment we had existed in that rarified place where only true soul mates exist. This felt like being with Duane. It scared me to think in those terms, but it was true. I had never been at a point that I had doubts that Kennedy and I were reduced to simply a physical act. There always seemed to be more of a spiritual and mental bond that made the physical that much more pleasurable.

Gabby's words crept into my head, "There's no such thing as a damn soul mate.... Dick is just better from some people than others." I tried my best not to subscribe to her outrageous philosophies on relationships.

Right now I didn't feel the hands of a man taking his time with me; touching me gently in all the right places as if he were my creator. I didn't feel like he was painting a masterpiece; his life's work while using my body as the canvas. This felt like some rough sketches by an angry artist. I refused for us to be reduced to this level of despicability and even surprised myself when I asked him to stop. I acknowledged and confronted his coldness towards me.

"Something's not right Kennedy. I can't put my finger on it, but I know what having your undivided attention feels like and this isn't it. What's wrong?" He attempted to downplay my intuition and insist there was nothing different. "What are you talking about? Everything is fine." I gave him a look that told him that I was serious; it told him that I knew him better than that. The one thing that I have come to love the most about him is that we have never existed in a place of dishonesty and I was glad that he wasn't about to change that. "I am extremely frustrated over what we've become Jacqueline. Neither of us planned to be here. We didn't plan to fall in love, but here we are. I just don't think that I can continue to play on your second team while Duane gets starter minutes. Sometimes in life we have to make choices. We have to choose who we are and we have to choose who we want to be with. Everything comes down to choice." He said that as if he was waiting for this moment in time to release those words.

I exhaled with great frustration that communicated my disgust with this topic. "You know that I would like nothing other than being with you Kennedy. You know that my situation is not the same as yours. I have so many more factors to consider mainly Evan and Michael. I can't just blindly make decisions without considering them and you know that. Your situation with Marlene is clear cut." I could tell that my words stung him which made me feel hurt and deeper frustration. It was hard to hurt someone you loved, but in this situation somebody was going to be a casualty in the war of love.

He moved to the edge of the bed and grasped his head with both hands as if he was searching for answers to his life's biggest challenge. I moved towards him and wrapped my legs around him while I caressed his back. I wished that I could take away his hurt and eliminate my frustration as well. Kennedy told me that he loved when I wrapped my legs around him, and I reminisced on moments in the past where I had done the same. Only now my doing so didn't seem to provide the same magic. We were both hurt and frustrated.

He broke my embrace as he moved towards the window and gazed down 46 floors towards Phillips arena and Centennial Park, which housed the 1996 Olympics. Kennedy looked like a man in deep contemplation over what he was about to do next. I felt myself becoming emotional and I didn't want him to see me cry so I went in the bathroom to hide my tears in the shower.

When I got out I began my hair and make-up in preparation for the second day of the show. Kennedy was dressed in jeans, no shirt or shoes sitting in the chair with an even more solemn tone. I was kinda past the point of reconciliation as far as this trip was concerned. He had really pushed my buttons. This was the first time I was really angry with him. There wasn't much peace between this Gemini and Libra at this moment. We were two cerebral people which made existing easy, but under these circumstances things became difficult and neither of us had any viable solution.

Then in typical Kennedy fashion he knew how to tame me and smooth out all the rough edges. He simply grabbed my hand and pulled me towards him the way that a man pulls a woman that he loves close to him. My body simply melted in his forceful embrace. He kissed me with a passion and fervor that wasn't present before. It made me perk up and my whole body was tingling. Kennedy picked me up and put me on the counter top and loved my body the way that he always had before.

I thought that I would scream when he took my legs and spread them apart as he put his mouth on my pleasure center. I felt the heat from his breath where it felt good the most. He used his tongue to apologize without uttering a single spoken word. He was using a language that I was very familiar with; that I preferred. It made me scream his name over and over. This feeling is what people search a lifetime to find. Once you have it, you never want to let it go. Before I knew it he had taken me to another muscle tensing, pleasure filled monogasm that rang out and filled the four corners of the room. He kept his mouth firmly attached to my lips and pulled them inside of his mouth drawing more blood to that area. I was damn near shrieking at that point.

Kennedy wasn't done and neither was I. We had a lot of catching up to do. I opened the curtains fully exposing our love fest for anybody that was high enough to see. He gave it to me from the rear as I looked down at what the view offered. I thought of the medals that were handed out over a decade ago to deserving athletes at Centennial Park and how Kennedy deserved a Gold medal for vaulting his pole deep inside of me. I begged for more as he made me cum again and again at a record setting pace.

I could barely stand because my legs were trembling and I felt like I would fall. We moved to the bed and I mounted Kennedy like a wild woman fresh out jail. I was so turned on; it was like I couldn't get enough. I wanted to make him cum so I rode him hard and rugged the way he told me he liked it. When Kennedy came, we came together. I had lost count for me, but for him it had only been one time. This man had crazy stamina especially approaching 40 years old.

We fell into a warm and dark embrace gazing deeply into each other eyes both in search of unanswered questions regarding our destiny as lovers. I was searching him and he was searching me. We were so much alike that some things didn't even need to be said between us and we'd still know. We were both wondering if this would be the last time that we made love to one another. I fought back what I knew would be a rush of tears when I thought that. He held me tight and looked me in my eyes when he told me that he loved me and that he always would. I told him the same in the sincerest way that I knew how before we parted company.   It was one of those moments that you wished could last forever.

CHAPTER FOURTEEN

One thing was certain after I left Jacqueline in her hotel room and it was that I have never loved anyone the way that I loved her. I would even perform criminal acts if it meant being with her. No matter how much you wanted someone if they didn't reciprocate the action then it would never be. You just couldn't will certain things to happen and Jacqueline and I being together was one of them. I swallowed that bitter reality pill with the same ease demonstrated by BP in stopping the oil leak in the Gulf. It was hard as hell to do.

My cell phone vibrated its way back to life when I turned it on. I neglected it all night while I was in Jacqueline's room trying to preserve the remaining battery life it did have. I missed several calls and text messages. Kristen texted and called to let me know that she was safe at home in San Diego, and there were about a dozen calls from Marley. What the hell did she want? What was so urgent that she was blowing up my phone like the world was ending? The last time we spoke she was less than thrilled to hear from me. Then I thought that maybe something was wrong with Miles.

I immediately returned the call apprehensive about what might be going on. When I called she answered the phone and it was obvious that she was in sparring mode. "Hey Marley, I see I missed a few calls from you. Is everything alright? How is Mil..." She interrupted me before I could finish saying Miles. "First of all it's Marlene to you...and if you were so damn worried about Miles your ass would have picked up the phone long before now!" She said some other things in her native tongue that I didn't want a translation of. I have found out first hand that you didn't want to be the focal point of a Caribbean women's fury. It was like being caught in the eye of a category 5 hurricane. It wasn't a safe place to be. I was suddenly thankful for the distance that my move had created.

After minutes of her verbal tantrum she just gave the phone to Miles. I could hear her in the background spewing her dislike for my existence. Let's just say that if words were weapons, I'd be dead and buried and probably suffering in the afterlife. Miles picked up the phone. "Miles is everything okay?...At least with you?" He sounded worried, not like himself when he spoke. His voice owned uncertainty and hopelessness. I began to naturally worry and fear the worse. "Dad…I …uh..need to talk to you, but mom can't know. She's already mad you hear her." I knew that he was troubled which concerned me. "What is it son? You can tell me anything you know that Miles." I probed so that my anxiety would lessen, hoping it was something a good heart to heart talk could fix. "I can't talk about it over the phone. Dad I need you!" There was so much desperation in his voice. I knew that it was serious. How serious was the only question that I had. "I am on the way son." He hung up.

I clenched my phone tightly as I clung to Miles's words. I rushed home threw together some clothes in a small suitcase and headed back to the airport where it seemed that I had just literally dropped Kristen off to. His timing could not be more off as I thought about my important sales meeting scheduled for the next morning; the one that was earmarked as mandatory. Emergencies didn't seem to factor in the element of convenience and they rarely if ever factored your readiness into the equation. They just happened without rhyme or reason.

I parked in long term parking and caught the shuttle to the nearest terminal. I knew that I would be on a stand by flight to get me anywhere close to Northern Virginia. I couldn't even be picky between Reagan and Baltimore

Washington International. I would have to rent a car either way and pay a nice grip of cash to get there ASAP. I didn't mind paying extra for the straight flight because I hated connecting flights, especially for such a short distance. After the woman at the AirTran desk surveyed numerous flights she booked me for a 12:15 p.m. departure into BWI which normally costs around $157 dollars. Today, since I was last minute and despite the fact that there was more than enough room I got to pay close to $500 dollars. What a reward I thought to myself but charged the ticket to my Visa anyway. The one hour and forty-six minute flight was departing in about an hour which meant I had to hustle to the security checks in order to catch this plane. Since I had a carry on I ran through the haze of people who strolled through the airport like they had all day. I had to see what was going on with Miles. I knew that he needed me.

By the time I waited and was processed through the rigorous security checks to include the emptying of pockets, removing my belt, and shoes I was at the gate. Timing couldn't be better because the plane was already boarding which was fine for me. It seemed like more and more people were carrying on their luggage and opting not to pay these ridiculous fees to have their bags checked. These brainiacs booked my seat at one of the emergency exits. Now I couldn't complain about the extra legroom, but I didn't think they wanted the person least likely to assist anyone other than himself responsible for helping others evacuate in an emergency.

Despite my fatigue associated with the hectic last several days I felt my mind racing as I processed at least a million "what if" scenarios. I was worried about Miles, my job, this meeting about my book, seeing Marley, and most of all Jacqueline weighed heavily on my mind. Seeing her again only served as confirmation that I couldn't deny what I felt for her. She claimed that she has never felt what she feels for any other man. It made it hard to believe her words considering that she wasn't going anywhere anytime soon. "How could she stay with someone who treated her like he did; someone who didn't cherish her the way that I did?"

I couldn't deny that she had feelings for me. I just wondered why they weren't strong enough to make her act on them. Maybe what I felt was greater for her than what she felt for me. Maybe she was going through a rough spot in her marriage and I helped smooth things over for the time being. I didn't have the answers to the questions that recurred over and over in my thought process. I just knew one thing, and that was no matter how hard I tried I just couldn't stay away from this woman on my own. I knew that it would take a force far greater than me to keep us apart; things would have to end badly. She would have to leave me alone because I didn't have it in me to walk away from her completely.

As the plane leveled off to its cruising altitude I reclined back in my chair and attempted to make the most of this opportunity of uninterrupted rest. I remembered the conference I attended in Tampa, Florida on pharmaceutical regulations for erectile dysfunction drugs that I attended nearly two years ago. Not that the conference itself was great, but the fact that Jacqueline tagged along made it the best conference I had ever attended. It wasn't the first trip we had gone on, but the first trip where we were really able to get away from the watchful eye of others. To say that we were able to be ourselves was like saying that ice was cold; some things didn't bear mentioning.

Jacqueline was wearing a sundress and to my delight nothing underneath but goodness and mercy. She wasn't very fond of panties, which was fine with me as well. We were like two newlyweds on their honeymoon; free to showcase what we felt for one another. Inhibition and uncertainty were both left behind and weren't invited on this trip. We must have lip locked the entire flight, but didn't manage to work up the nerve to join the Mile High Club. When we landed in Orlando there was about a 60 mile drive up highway 4 to get to Tampa. The flight seemed to serve as foreplay because we both found it damn near impossible to make the commute to Tampa without releasing in a major way.

Jacqueline was all over me as I attempted to keep the rented sedan on the road and not kill us both. This woman had me stirred up in the worse way and there was only one way settle this and we both knew what that was. I pulled over on the nearest exit trying my best to find some obscure location for us to handle our business in the middle of the day. We were like two horny teens. It was one of those times when I really didn't care who saw us. We were both having a Janet Jackson "Anytime, Anyplace" moment.

No sooner than I pulled over we were going at it fast and furious totally oblivious to the world outside of the car we were in. Our attraction was undeniable. It was as if we were soul mates or kindred spirits. There was such a familiarity for someone that at the time I had only known for less than a year. Being with Jacqueline lent credibility to theories and perspectives that I have never subscribed to in the past. When you felt that way about someone it made the physical even more intense and meaningful. It just wasn't one of those empty lays between two people that didn't have much substance. It made me consider thoughts of there only being that one true love for a person, and I even considered that maybe we were lovers in another lifetime. I thought of things that would make someone like Marcus laugh himself to death if I ever shared them with him. He believed that there was no such thing as being destined to be with one person. Sometimes you couldn't deny what you felt for someone no matter how it defied all rational logic. Maybe he just hadn't met the right one.

When I climbed in the back seat where she was awaiting me we went at it fast and furious. It bordered on a primal act between two people with chemistry that rivaled the greatest lovers this world has seen or will ever see. Once we both released we were back on track headed to the Sheraton River walk in Tampa. Jacqueline remained in naughty mode as she distracted and teased me by masturbating as we traveled along highway 4. It was all I could do to keep the car in between the lanes and not swerve or run into any other car. Despite the cool breeze of the air conditioning, she had my temperature rising like a phoenix. My pulse was quickening and it seemed as though blood had taken up permanent residency in my loins. In retrospect it was probably the most difficult stretch of road that I have ever covered; definitely the hottest. I probably made record time in bridging the distance between Orlando and Tampa just to be inside of her.

Knowing that I had her all to myself for the next three days was bittersweet. On one hand I didn't have to worry about her leaving or being pressed for time, but I knew that these days would fly by and then I'd be back to existing in secrecy the way most affairs did. What was the point of having such a great love if it had to be concealed? I intended to make the most of the limited time we would have this weekend. I guess it was kinda like going to Disney. You could go there and exist in a way that was magical and enjoy all that there was to offer, but at some point you would have to put your back to their gates when you left. I told her to remind me of the number 20 by the time we headed back home. With a puzzled look on her face she assured me that she would.

I really didn't remember much pertaining to my conference and rightfully so it was the most boring thing I have ever endured, but I do remember becoming more open when it came to Jacqueline. Just when I didn't think that I could feel anything more, I did. Part of it scared me due to our respective situations but there was a part of me that held so much intrigue as to what we could be without the limitations. It crystallized things for me concerning my marriage to Marley. I just knew that if I could feel what I felt for Jacqueline that there was no way that I could honestly exist being her husband. I knew that I needed to leave the situation for both of our sakes. Marley needed someone to give her what I no longer felt I could; maybe never did. Those thoughts rang loud in my mind and forced me to confront things that I had been in denial about. I tried hard to break the cycle of my parents' divorce pattern and swore that I would do what it took to keep my family intact. I guess some cycles repeated themselves no matter how hard you tried to stop them. I could and would make sure that Miles had a better transition than I did, that much I could promise.

We ventured into Ybor City to explore the best Tampa had to offer. Ybor was rich in culture mostly comprised of Spanish, Cuban, and Italian influence from its rich architecture to its fine dining and overall appeal. There was something here that would appeal to almost anyone from college kids to tourists looking for something to get into. Jacqueline and I could have a blast in a cardboard box, so we were definitely feeling the vibe and going with the flow. The thing I liked most about Jacqueline was that I could truly be myself and not pretend to be someone else. She even thought my jokes were funny. Maybe Marley's culture had some influence, but it was safe to say that there was so much difference in the way that we saw things. Maybe opposites did attract, but having similarities was what made relationships really work. Things that I thought were funny she didn't, her overall lack of appreciation and experiences were counter to mine. Jacqueline and I had so much in common that it was insane. It took little effort at all to appeal to one another.

After enjoying a fine meal at Columbia Restaurant we walked the busy streets and took in the beautiful scenery. It was paradise. The inhalation of smoke from the many cigar shops almost made me want one, despite my dislike of smoke. We bar hopped and had everything from beer, frozen drinks, and even shots of Tequila. Jacqueline and I blended in with the rest of the crowd and it was obvious that we shared the "I could be like this forever sentiment." We had our picture taken which I kept as a tangible keepsake of a perfect time in my life. I knew that she couldn't keep it without the consequence of her husband finding it. My space from Marley allowed me to be a little more liberal.

It was after 10 so most of the night spots had already put out the velvet ropes in anticipation of huge crowds of people ready to have a good time. We decided on a club called Prana because they seemed to be playing the most familiar music that we liked dancing to. Clubs lined both sides of the streets playing everything from Techno to Hip Hop. Prana had five levels including VIP and roof top access. The crowd was a good blend of cultures all focused on having a good time. It was good to see people put down their burden of prejudices all in the name of having a good time. It made me wonder why our everyday existence couldn't be done in the same way; too much like making sense I thought. Jacqueline and I danced and drank and drank and danced, all the while growing closer to one another. Once again she had a way of making me block out any and everybody around me. The Matrix feeling had returned and everyone else seemed to be in slow motion around us; she was all that mattered and this was one of those moments in time that I could have remained in for eternity.

In typical fashion time flies when you were having fun and it was time to leave the lover's paradise that Tampa had provided us. Jacqueline and I reminisced on the trip and the memories that we had created in such a short time. Our epic lovemaking over the three day trip reminded her to prompt me about the number 20 and its significance. I asked her to count the number of times that she had climaxed since our trip began in Orlando. She told me that she had cum 19 times all together. I told her that I owed her one more to make it an even 20, and we both smiled. I loved pleasing this woman; it seemed as though we just fit together perfectly. Even though the trip was over I remained a mile high in love with Jacqueline Tate.

When my plane touched down in Baltimore I snapped back into what my present circumstances were and began to focus on my son. I was determined to be better to him than my father was to me. After exiting the plane I was at the rental car desk to secure a vehicle to conclude the rest of my journey to Lorton, Virginia to check on Miles.

CHAPTER FIFTEEN

It was bad enough that I didn't know what I was walking into as I headed to Lorton, but thanks to a shortage of cars at Avis I would have to get there in a P. T. Cruiser. What else could go wrong with this day I thought to myself? It was after 2, but closer to 3 in the afternoon so I called Miles to let him know that I would be there shortly. Once again I was greeted by his voicemail because he didn't answer. I hung up because I just wasn't very entertained by his greeting that followed the latest Soulja Boy song about his morning swag. Maybe I was getting old or maybe today's artists weren't artists anymore. They just said some lame ass phrase over and over to a catchy beat and called that music. Who was I to judge considering I grew up on NWA, and Two Live Crew? I am sure my mom didn't appreciate me singing some of those vulgar lyrics either. I guess every generation has what they considered to be good music.

Although it was still hot there was a huge relief being away from the awful humidity that the Deep South owned.

The temperature was in the mid 90's but it felt so much more tolerable. I couldn't deny the huge knot of nervous energy forming inside of my stomach as I drew closer towards my old place of residency. I didn't exactly know what I was walking into. There was a huge sense of being overwhelmed with years of history between Marley and me; the times that were good and the times that were not so good. Nonetheless those times and that period of my life were about to be a thing of the past. We would both be facing new futures. I just wasn't certain as to what mine would look like.

I would be lying if I said that there wasn't a lot of ambivalence regarding my future. It would be so easy to stay in a bad marriage to have all of the securities that a marriage provides, rather than diving into an ocean of uncertainty. A part of me understood why people stayed and weathered the storm even though things didn't get better, but I couldn't bring myself to do it. I was a person who prided themselves with a balanced life and the truth was that Marley and I had simply grown apart. I had come to grips with that reality, although she probably had not. She had been raised to weather the storms of life in marriage no matter how bad things got. She didn't believe in divorce under any circumstances. She was resistant to change and stubborn which was in her nature as a Taurus. She viewed broken promises as a sign of betrayal and didn't tolerate disappointment easily. Marley would rather hold on to the fallacy of a relationship on life support than to face the reality that it was over and ending it.

I was all about peace and harmony in a relationship; strife and conflict was not my deal. Being that change was foreign to her it made me unbalanced and balance is what I desired most, maybe it was the Libra in me. It made me withdraw all of my efforts to make things work. I didn't have it in me to be to her what she was not to me. I was all about reciprocity and it was impossible to give what I wasn't getting. It didn't mean either of us were bad people, it just meant that our relationship had run its course plain and simple. It just wasn't in my nature to pretend. I was not that good of an actor. I needed to feel a certain connection that I truthfully hadn't felt for Marley in a very long time. It was the type of connection that I felt for Jacqueline. It was what made me want to truly pour my whole self into a relationship and not just be on pause. It was the difference between being alive and living. The more that Jacqueline gave of herself, made me give more of me. I didn't know what to do with this thing that we had created.

When I pulled up to our townhouse I contemplated using my key to unlock the door and enter, but decided not to. I rang the bell instead which was probably the most perplexing thing to me in recent memory. I knew that I had to begin to see Marley separate from me and realize that there were no more us. Miles answered the door and we embraced like it had been years since we saw one another, although actually it was only about three weeks. It made me feel good and he seemed comforted as well. It made me wish that I could have at least one moment like this with my own father. He was so damn cold and rigid. I swore that I would never be like that with Miles. I wanted Miles to know that it was okay to show emotions, and that it just proved he was human.

Before I could put my bag down and inquire about Marley, she sashayed from the kitchen to the family room where Miles and I were. She spoke with her eyes and seemed less agitated and a little friendlier. Marley was wearing some running shorts, sneakers, and a sports bra. She was perspiring which let me know that she had just run on her treadmill. Her locks were pulled back and bound by a black and green scrunchy with her iPod attached to her arm. There was slight perspiration on her top lip and lower back leading to her shorts; made me focus on her tattoo and bought back memories.

My mother told me that when people sweat on their top lip that they were mean. Marley was no exception to this rule. This was one woman you didn't want to piss off. In one of her angry tirades she could be about as pleasant as an agitated bull.

That beautiful plum colored skin was on full display. She looked sexy as hell. Marley's abs was ripped and her hips and thighs rivaled Serena Williams. It was good to see she was still into taking care of herself. I would be lying if I said I wasn't still attracted to her. She didn't bother removing her headphones and continued to sing along with Rihanna's "Rude Boy" song.

It was funny, but I felt like a stranger inside of my own home; old home now. Looking at the pictures throughout the house bought back memories of the early years when we were newlyweds and of Miles in every stage of his life. There were pictures of us being married on the beaches of Negril in Jamaica, back when we took vows of "till death do us part." In some ways we exceeded that because we had died a thousand deaths inside of our 14-year marriage.

Miles calling me broke me out of my trip down memory lane and alerted me that he wanted to go into his room to talk. I followed his lead up the stairs into his bedroom. Although I had climbed these stairs thousands of times today seemed like the first time. Entering into Miles's room made me fully aware that he was not the little boy I remembered when I moved to Atlanta. Gone was his interest in Nickelodeon, now it was replaced with pictures of Alicia Keys, Beyoncé, and Rihanna. The boy definitely had great taste in women. At least he was normal I thought to myself.

I began to question what was so important that I had to drop everything and come to his aid. "Are you okay son, this had better be pretty darn important." I insisted. He hesitated and his eyes surveyed the floor as if he was searching for something important. Maybe he was trying to frame his otherwise unclear thoughts. "It is important dad. I had been feeling kinda weird lately." I prompted him to pick his head up and insisted that he looked me in my eyes; the way that I taught him when communicating. Miles was beginning to make me feel uneasiness that I didn't want to feel. Part of me felt like shaking him until he spilled his truth, but I knew that would only complicate things more. "I think that there is something wrong with me down there." My face claimed a very puzzled look. "Son, what are you talking about? It's just you and I and you know you can tell me anything." I said that with the confidence that a father should have when talking with his son. I just hoped that it was something that I could tolerate. Miles went on to tell me that he has been experiencing pain when he urinated along with a discharge in his underwear. This had been going on for nearly two weeks. The one thing that became certain to me was that either he was having a bladder infection, or my son was having sex. This should not have been the way that I found out that Miles was no longer a virgin.

"When did you start having sex? Why in the world did you not use a condom?" I really tried to keep my emotions contained, but I was really disappointed in his decision making as I immediately owned an accusatory tone with him. He replied, "About six months. She said she was on the pill...that it was okay." "Miles I don't care if a girl is on the pill, has foam, an IUD, and a tubal ligation...never have sex without a condom! Didn't I tell you this over and over? Didn't I tell you that when you felt like you were ready to just let me know?" I felt myself getting worked up the way parents do. I felt myself judging him so I backed off. I stood up paced around his room looking at pictures that took me to a simpler time in life. They took me to a place where Miles was an innocent kid whose only challenges consisted of eating, sleeping, and pooping. Now he had contracted a venereal disease and hadn't considered the totality of his actions.

"Dad every time I call you, you're busy or you need to call me back. By the time you call back I lose the nerve to tell you what I want to say. It's not the same since... since you're not here anymore." Miles's words stung like a thousand wasps protecting their nest. His words bought everything back into perspective. The very thing that I had tried to protect him from was the thing that I had failed in doing. I had become just like my father in that I wasn't there for Miles when he needed me. I felt like such a failure; felt just like my father. That was a feeling that I didn't want any part of whatsoever.

I sat beside him on his bed and put my arm around him. I explained to Miles that I was still disappointed in his failure to protect himself, but that there was nothing he could do to make me stop loving him. I told him that we would take care of this and made him agree to always use condoms, no exceptions. Miles did as I said and took a shower and changed his clothes. That gave me a chance to put a call into a doctor that I knew who agreed to see us at their office. I dreaded emergency rooms and didn't feel like waiting till dooms day for him to be seen. If a person wasn't bleeding or flat lining there wasn't much of a chance of them being seen.

Now it made sense why he didn't want Marley to know what was going on. It was difficult for a boy to talk about sex with his mother. I never talked about it with my mother and even to this day considering that I've been married 14 years and Miles is her grandchild, she doesn't know that I'm not a virgin anymore. For some people not acknowledging something meant that it didn't exist in their minds. Sex was not one of those topics that a parent could ignore. It was only a matter of time before kids figured out how things worked whether you talked about it or not. The truth was that somebody was gonna talk about it with them.

Miles and I hopped in my unsightly rental and headed to the doctor's office. I told Marley that we needed some father/son time and that we'd be back. She appeared attentive, but never really broke from the trance that her Lifetime movie had her under. Just as well, because less was more in this instance. Miles didn't need her overreacting.

True to his word, my good friend Dr. Dennison met us at his office. I caught him up to speed on what Miles was presenting symptom wise. I was no doctor myself, but had hung out in enough medical settings to suspect Chlamydia as the culprit. I was praying that was it, and nothing that a Z-Pak couldn't cure. Dr. Dennison informed me that he would have to screen Miles for everything and that blood would be required in addition to samples of his discharge. I told him to do what he had to do to give us both peace of mind.

I watched Miles and Dr. Dennison go back into his examination room while I waited alone in the reception area. I couldn't recall a time when Dr. Dennison's office was not full of anxious patients. His office was a part of my rotation while I was in Virginia before all the cuts sent me to Atlanta or the unemployment line. Maybe it was the fact that I hooked him up with ample amounts of male enhancement drugs, but he really seemed to take a strong liking to me. He acted like it was no big deal to come to his office on a Sunday just to accommodate Miles and me. Whatever the reason, I knew that I couldn't put into words what it meant to me.

I must have paced back and forth at least a mile, had read every magazine in his office, and surveyed every channel awaiting word on my son's condition. It was at that moment that I first considered among everything else whether or not this girl could be pregnant. The last thing I needed was to be some kid's grandpa before 40; heck 50. It was not a thought that was growing on me. "Lord please let this situation be nothing that an antibiotic can't cure!" I pleaded silently in my moment of divine desperation as I sat with my head in my hands.

Nearly two hours later, Dr. Dennison called me back in a room separate from Miles. He reassured me when he said that Miles had only tested positive for Chlamydia and nothing else. He said that he gave him a shot to get some antibiotics in his system and wrote an additional prescription as well. I was so glad that he wouldn't have to wait two weeks for results like some of the old tests used to take. I didn't think that I could stand the suspense. Now my only challenge was to conceal this prescription from the ever-curious Marley who was always looking for something. I thanked Dr. Dennison for his act of kindness and told him that there was no way that I could repay him. He brushed it off and we all left his office in the same manner in which we had entered.

Silence blanketed the car as we rode away balancing relief with awkwardness. I wouldn't be much of a parent if I hadn't explained to Miles the nature of his actions. I explained to him the emotional and mental aspect of sex that teens often overlook. I reminded him of things that he hadn't considered, such as fathering a child, losing his life, and how to tell her. He seemed most frightened by telling her about his status of having a flaming penis, which is what Chlamydia felt like, so I've heard. I told him that sometimes females don't feel symptoms the same as males, and that she needed to get herself treated before there was long term irreversible damage. Hopefully she wouldn't put any more people at risk. It was one of those realities that he hadn't considered. He was still so innocent and naïve in his thinking that he hadn't considered that she was obviously making her rounds. Miles assured me that Amber was the only girl he had been with. If only she could say the same thing we wouldn't be having this conversation. Among everything else he was processing mentally, was his first disappointment associated with females. I wished that I could take that hurt away, but some pain we had to experience firsthand to learn those tough lessons in life. I just hoped that this wouldn't be one of those things that scarred him for life and made his heart turn cold to women.

While I would trade this problem for the ones that ice cream always made better, I wouldn't have it any other way than to be here with him in his time of need. I was grateful that Miles did finally come to me when he didn't have anywhere else to go. It made me see some sort of silver lining about this whole situation. I couldn't remember a time that I have ever been able to count on my father for much more than being a disappointment. At least I was not like him after all, which was a huge relief. As we rode away I knew that somehow things between us had to improve in order to strengthen our bond as father and son for both of our sakes.

CHAPTER SIXTEEN

The Bronner Brothers show was behind me and I was mentally, physically, and emotionally drained as a result. My mind and body were not on the same page because I felt like falling into the type of slumber that was closer to a bear in hibernation, than a normal sleep wake cycle. Gabby had fallen asleep shortly after we got back on I-85 headed back to Charlotte from Atlanta, which I didn't complain about because I didn't want to hear her negative feedback. Normally I would have stopped for coffee or an energy drink just to keep my eyes open, but I thought of Kennedy instead. It was as if I was drawing energy from this man and he was nowhere around.

I could still feel his breath against my body; its heat that warmed me and made me melt like the sun does the snow. He knew just how to touch my body as if it were his own creation. In a crazy way he even touched my soul. Our spirits co-mingled as if we were destined to find one another because there was nothing that felt quite the way being in

Kennedy's company felt. In fact it was the only time that I ever truly felt alive. Before I met him I had simply been existing, but the two years of knowing him I have never felt more alive. He makes me feel like I can do anything; like no barriers existed. That was confirmation that what we felt was not only mutual, but it was one of a kind.

Seeing him also reminded me of the painful reality that despite what we feel for each other we have some very real obstacles in our way; at least I did. His situation became simpler when he separated from his wife and moved to Atlanta and now they are divorcing. My life was not that simple. On one hand Duane is "jerk of the year," but he is the father of my children and I did promise before God and several hundred witnesses that I'd be his wife for better or worse, till death do us part. That was such a frightening prospect. It made me wonder if that was a literal death because I have been dying a figurative death for a number of years now. I wondered if God would grade me on the curve and not judge too harshly for excusing myself from my marriage to be with the man I truly loved with everything inside of me.

I could tell that Kennedy was growing more and more inpatient by the day for me to decide what I was going to do. His situation had become crystallized and mine was about as hazy as the Los Angeles skyline. I just didn't think that Kennedy understood where I was coming from and what I had to deal with. It just wasn't like I could break up my family and put Evan and Michael through changes that they didn't sign up to be a part of. Duane did love his boys and I would have no justification in turning him into a part-time father no matter how much I loved Kennedy. I knew that if I reinvested emotionally in my marriage that things would improve to some degree. I would never feel for Duane what I feel for Kennedy, but maybe something would be better than nothing at all. There was just way too much to consider and someone was bound to be hurt no matter what I did.

I wrestled with those thoughts while I navigated us safely to Charlotte. The Queen City had never looked better through my weary eyes. All I could do was crave a hot shower and several hours of uninterrupted sleep inside my own bed. Gabby magically sprang to life as soon as I pulled into my driveway. It was as if she had some internal GPS that alerted her when we arrived at our destination.

We exchanged very tired and brief pleasantries as she hauled her luggage from the rear of my SUV. I didn't bother removing mine. I just opted for the inside of my house through the garage entry. I was relieved that Duane was at work and the boys were at school. Evan and Michael never ran out of energy and they would expect me to match their efforts when they got home so I had to prepare. As much as I missed them, I was probably missing sleep a bit more.

I peeled off my clothes, put on my shower cap and entered the shower. The steam had totally consumed the shower stall and over flowed throughout the entire bathroom. Despite the fact that it had been over 24 hours since Kennedy and I made love his scent managed to linger all over my body. It was strong and masculine, yet sweet and gentle just like he was. I have never smelled anything like it. I inhaled deeply and breathed in my lover's essence as I lingered in the moment under his enchantment. I could feel his hands caressing me where I liked it the most and before I knew it I was totally stimulated. In reality my shower head would perform the duties that Kennedy wasn't physically able to, although he more than adequately performed over and over in my vivid imagination.

Once I had reached my Kilimanjaro sized orgasmic peak I felt myself slowly descending to my life's reality. I realized that all fantasies end at some point and no matter how bad I wanted to click my heels three times and magically appear in my own little world with Kennedy King I didn't see how it could happen realistically. That sobering reality brought me to tears. It made me question so many things in my life. Why did I have to be the one to sacrifice my true happiness to consider others? Why did I not meet Kennedy before I met Duane? Why was I so darn traditional and cared what everyone else thought of me?

Those questions only made me cry harder because I didn't have the answers. After drying off I oiled my body and pulled my hair back in a ponytail. I almost didn't recognize my own reflection and not just because I wasn't wearing any make up. It was because my face owned such much doubt and uncertainty. Let's just say it looked like I was showing my age, which didn't do a thing to lighten my otherwise depressed mood. I forced my face into a smile anyway, but my emotions were not playing along. They remained unchanged.

I carried my burden of thoughts with me to my bed to lie down. Normally I would have a fit about Duane not making the bed but right now my pet peeves would have to take a number. Suddenly the small things didn't matter as much. In fact they paled in comparison to what truly bothered me.

I nestled between Egyptian cotton trying to attain some level of comfort but it was no use. I tossed and turned for at least twenty minutes if not longer. I decided to call Kennedy. Somehow he always has a way to sooth me by saying just the right thing. That was what I needed. After ringing twice, his phone went straight to voicemail which was strange. I was already having uneasy feelings about him going back to Virginia even though I know he has to see his son Miles. I just knew that he'd also see his soon to be ex-wife as well. Even though he told me that things were over between them I have sense enough to know that men will be men.

I guess you could say that I was jealous. As crazy as that sounded being a married woman and sharing the same bed with my husband every night, I was feeling a little territorial. I was guarded when it came to my feelings which made my existence with Kennedy even more bizarre and puzzling. As irrational as it was I had invested my entire allotment of feelings into him and there was no more to give. When you feel that way for someone you don't want anyone in their space whatsoever regardless of their title. Knowing that we were so in tuned with one another I recognize his struggle with my home situation which is why I really go over board to show him that I am completely into him when we are together. Even if you had to read using brail, you could see that as far as I was concerned Duane and I only existed on paper.

I didn't even realize that I had fallen asleep until I was awakened by my two favorite guys not named Kennedy. Evan and Michael were so elated to see me and I reciprocated their sentiment. I hugged and kissed them both. It was the only drawback from my job when I had to be away from them. I could see Duane staring at me out of my periphery. He was towering over the bed posts at the foot of our king sized bed. His tie was already loosened and he was holding his suit jacket in his right hand and a bouquet of red roses in his left hand. After all of these years he still didn't know that wild flowers were my favorite and I didn't see now as the time to inform him of that. A bouquet of flowers that nice should make any woman gush with emotion and gratitude, but that wasn't the case. In that moment I realized that the gesture was only breathtaking when the man you were into gave you flowers.

I manufactured the most insincere smile all the while convincing him that I was appreciative. I didn't know that I was capable of such impromptu acting capabilities; it was academy award nomination worthy if I must say so myself. "Daddy bought mommy flowers." Michael said to Evan. "Do you like them mommy?" Evan inquired. "Mommy loves them just like mommy loves her babies." "Does mommy love daddy?" Duane inserted. I hated when he used the kids to deflect otherwise serious issues. I played along for the sake of harmony and hopefully to put an end to this ridiculous inquiry. "Mommy loves all of her handsome men." Duane leaned over and kissed me. He was aiming for my lips but I slid my head to the side so he ended up kissing my cheek. The truth was that I didn't feel as though he deserved my lips. I didn't want to send any mixed messages as if we were on good terms.

I busied myself with the boys as a means to both reconnect with them and to avoid having another awkward conversation with my husband. To my surprise he didn't make a big deal. Instead he took the flowers and said that he would put them in some water. I released a huge breath when Duane exited the room and concentrated my full attention to what mattered the most in my life and that was Evan and Michael.

After the boys caught me up to speed on every single detail of the last several days since I left, it was time for their baths. I was off my game a little in terms of their daily structure due to my fatigue and hadn't even given a thought to dinner, but was pleasantly surprised that Duane had taken care of that. Pitching in and being considerate was not the norm for him in the least bit. He was very traditional when it came to roles within our relationship. I thought that he would need therapy once I decided to return to work after the boys were born. In fact if he had his way I would be barefoot and pregnant all the while slaving over a hot oven all day long just waiting to perform fellatio at his command.

Considering his thought process it was encouraging to see that he had gotten take out from P F Changs, which I absolutely loved. I had to give him credit for trying. He even insisted that he give the boys their bath while I simply eat and relax. How could I refuse? Heck, I even wondered to myself what this man had done with my husband. I enjoyed a serving of Sesame Chicken, brown rice, and steamed veggies along with two glasses of Chardonnay. Now I was feeling more like myself.

The boys were in bed sound asleep, I was full and very relaxed under the influence of two glasses of wine. Sitting on my sofa with my legs pulled into my body I glanced at the flowers that Duane had given me. He had them in one of my vases made of crystal. They were gorgeous and the petals were still tightly wound which indicated their freshness because they hadn't opened up yet.

I tried to refrain from thinking of Kennedy but it was no use. He penetrated every mental fortress I could think of and somehow became front and center in my consciousness. I just couldn't stop thinking about him no matter how hard I tried. Part of me wishes I could simply walk away from him and focus my efforts towards fixing what was wrong with my marriage. I just couldn't bring myself to making that happen. I knew in that moment Kennedy would have to walk away from me because I could never let him go.

I was meditating on that thought when Duane walked up behind me and began massaging my shoulders. I jumped because he startled me; caught me off guard. "Relax baby." He implied as he continued trying to help me unwind. Duane began kissing me on the back of my neck as he slid my mane to the side. It dawned on me that he had done all those things earlier because he wanted to get some. Normally I would have played along but there was something that didn't feel right; something that made me feel uneasy. I tried to repress feeling like I was committing some sort of criminal act by being with my own husband but it was no use.

It felt like Duane was a stranger and not like he was my husband for all these years. I felt so conflicted; so ambivalent. I felt like I was betraying Kennedy by being with my own husband and those thoughts even frightened me. I couldn't go through with it, so I pulled away. "What's wrong baby?" "It's nothing, I am just kinda tired.....you know?" "You seem really distant Jacqueline and there is always some excuse. You know I can't go long without having sex. I think that I have been extremely patient here. That's why I didn't want you working that crazy job anyway." Duane had become angry at this point, but I was glad that he had begun to show his true colors. He had given me the ammunition that I needed to cease his little sex games tonight.

"Duane I am not your little puppet. You can't pull my strings and expect for me to perform for you at your word. My "crazy job" as you called it is what makes me happy okay. You are not the only one with goals and ambitions in life. I am sorry that you didn't marry some lame ass woman who wanted to have your babies, sit home all day, clean your house, and suck your dick on demand, but I am not her and never will be! You need to get over yourself." "Listen, don't act like you're doing me any favors being with me Jacqueline. You ain't the only damn woman I could be with. Your ass needs to recognize a good man when you see one. I wouldn't exactly go begging for bread without you. A lot of women would love to be in your position trust me." Now I was really pissed off. "Save that shit for a woman with no damn self-esteem Duane. Do us both a favor and go fuck the women who would love to be in my position. In fact you can go and be with them right now. I am not in the business of keeping someone who doesn't want to be kept, so don't bring that shit up again. I think that you know it works both ways."

We both starred in each other's eyes as if we were fierce competitors and not husband and wife. Our chests rose and fell at a feverish pace as we spewed insults back and forth; words were our weapons in this war. He fired back and so did I, round for round and shot for shot. I could tell that he had been holding back his true emotions and so had I. Even though it wasn't right deep down it felt good to let go of some things that I had otherwise hidden from Duane regarding how I truly felt.

Everything that we had been taught in our pre-marital counseling discouraged fighting like this and emphasized appropriate ways to vent, but it was safe to say that tonight the sun would set on our differences. None of that Dr. Phil made for TV crap was gonna work tonight. If only I had the courage I would have pleaded for him to give me a divorce right then and there so I could be with Kennedy. The coward in me prevailed in that moment. We both retreated to our respective corners like two prize-fighters signifying the end of a round. He adjourned to the basement with his collection of dark liquor and dusty ass vinyl records, while I opted for our bedroom where I would be comforted by my iPod and 5,000 thread count sheets atop our king bed. That night I drifted off to sleep thinking that life had to be better than this.

CHAPTER SEVENTEEN

For most of the ride home an awkward silence consumed the car and Miles and I existed the way two people do when they don't know how to break the ice to begin communication. I was treading on thin ice because I didn't want to make him feel judged; all the while he needed to understand the serious nature of his poor judgment. I didn't want to make him feel the way most parents make their children feel when they have done something wrong, so I was searching for a way to package my words in a way that he would truly receive them and feel as if he could still come to me. I tried to put myself in his shoes first and foremost.

"Miles from this point forward I am going to need you to promise me two things. One is that you will never keep anything from me no matter how you think I will react, and secondly promise me that you will never have unprotected sex again." He looked at me with a look of shame as if he had let the entire world down and nodded his head in agreement. "I promise dad, I won't let you down again." I explained to Miles he didn't let me down he just made a mistake; the kind that could have had greater consequences than taking antibiotics for five days. I just didn't see the need of beating him up and making him feel worse than I know that he did already.

We stopped for dinner before heading back home. I knew that Marley would have her fair share of questions about where we were and what was going on with Miles. Despite the fact that he begged me not to say a word, I knew that I would have to offer something about what was going on. After all she was his mother and he was living with her while I was down in Atlanta so she should have some clue as to what was going on. I was beginning to have thoughts about whether I should move back to be closer to Miles or just talk with Marley about having him move to be with me. That would probably go over about as well as a root canal with no anesthesia.

After a few slices of cheese pizza and French fries, we were on our way back to what used to be my home. I was still getting used to the idea of referring to it as Marley's place and not our place. This divorce was going to be an adjustment for everyone involved. Anytime you did anything for 14 years good or bad, it was going to take an adjustment to do something else.

When we got inside Marley was nowhere in sight. I told Miles to go on upstairs to bed. Out of nowhere she appeared. She was wearing green and black boxer shorts and a yellow fitted t-shirt showcasing her country's colors. "Jamaica's finest," I thought to myself. She was also showcasing her deep dark complexion, toned body, and stiffened nipples. Marley had my full attention which made me second guess not getting a hotel room. It was gonna take some tremendous will power not to end up in some sort of horizontal or vertical position with her before this day ended and the next one began. "Lord, have mercy," I whispered inside.

I told her that we needed to talk about Miles. Marley sat beside me on the sofa, which made me a little uneasy because despite our differences there has never been a problem with our physical chemistry. Just being around one another would mean clothes coming off almost instantly, since we first met over a decade and half ago. I disregarded those thoughts and proceeded to discuss the fact that our teenage son had begun engaging in sexual activity himself. There was no easy way to break this to Marley so I opted for the more conventional route. "Miles is no longer a virgin Marley."

She didn't pretend to hide her feelings for what I had just told her. In fact she responded as if I told her he was in a bad accident or something. "Ohhh noo! Not my baby! He told you this? Ken...please tell me you're lying." I figured that it would be in her best interest if she didn't know about the whole sexually transmitted disease issue. "Yes he told me this Marley. He probably didn't tell you because of how you're reacting now. We had a really good talk about some things for him to consider. You have to promise not to overreact about this whole thing." "Overreact huh? Excuse me because I find it shocking and unacceptable that our 14 year old is having sex. I can't be as calm as you are." "You know I didn't mean it like that Marley. I feel like it's a big deal too, but the way we feel won't change the fact that Miles is having sex. There is no sense in making him feel like he can't talk to us. He is going through a lot as well." She swallowed my words like she was taking a BC Powder with no water. Marley hung her head on my shoulder and began sobbing. I put my arm around her and allowed her to grieve the loss of her baby boy and embrace the birth of her horny adolescent son.

In that moment we managed to put our differences aside and coexist in a simpler place. It reminded me of the way we used to be before life made things so complicated and messy. We really talked about what was best for Miles moving forward and I asked her to think about allowing him to come with me to Atlanta for school and spend summers with her. Although she wasn't totally on board with it, she did say that she would consider doing what was in his best interest.

Even though on paper our marriage would be coming to an end for what was termed as irreconcilable differences it should be duly noted that we simply grew apart. Marley knew it and so did I, she was just from a culture that didn't believe in divorce no matter the circumstances. Her parents had been together for nearly 40 years and that was important to her. I was proof that you just couldn't break some cycles no matter how hard you tried because I really wanted to prove that I could make my marriage work unlike my parents, but here I was moments away from suffering their same fate. There was part of me that wanted to be the complete opposite of my father, but in many ways I managed to mirror him and I found that repulsive.

After we had a very difficult conversation I decided that I needed to take one very cold shower to avoid acting on my physical urge to get inside of Marley's underwear like I have done thousands of times. I was calling on will power that I wasn't sure that I even knew existed.

I stood in the middle of the shower stall and allowed the water to rain down atop my head as I washed away the many thoughts that took up residence in my mind. When I turned the water off I began searching for the towel that I remembered leaving on the rack beside the glass door but it wasn't there. "Are you looking for this?" Marley was inside of the bathroom with my towel wrapped around her.

I was standing butt naked dripping water onto the bathroom rug. "You'd better hurry up and get this towel before you catch a cold Kennedy." She teased as she drew closer. When I reached for the towel she revealed that she was wearing nothing but goodness and mercy clothed in her birthday suit. Even though I had never witnessed Serena Williams in the nude, I had a hard time believing that she and Marley couldn't be body doubles. My body immediately reacted one way while my mind had doubts of its own. I felt the blood flow from one head to the other which was making me have difficulty thinking any good thought. "I'm not sure this is such a good idea Marley." "I can't tell it seems as if your dick has other plans. Besides I am a little horny." She began drying off my body very slowly and seductively planting kisses everywhere that she wiped which turned me on even more. Marley knelt down and saluted my soldier with the warm embrace offered by her mouth. She did it with so much emotion and passion. I was at the place where saying no wasn't even an option. She teased her tongue up and over my abs until she got to my nipples where she reciprocated the same to the left as she had to the right one.

I couldn't stand anymore so I began to take control and dominate her the way I knew that she liked me to. I pulled her by her locks and kissed her passionately which made her breathing intensify. Marley was really into it. She started manipulating her clitoris and her moans became louder. I was afraid that her noise would wake up Miles, but I wasn't about to stop either. Marley fed me her fingers as I suckled her essence from them.

I picked her up and put her on the counter top and entered inside her comfort walls like I had so many times before. She was in rare form as if she hadn't had sex in years. Her entire rhythm was different. Marley wrapped her strong legs around my back like a python suffocating its prey. She couldn't conceal her accent during sex and I didn't understand half of what she was uttering aside from the fact that she had cum a few times. She pushed me away long enough to get off the counter and turn to face it while she welcomed me inside of her from the back. I stroked her at a sprinter's pace just like she liked it, just like she asked me to.

Marley's strong legs began to tremble and weaken which let me know that another climax was on the horizon.

I turned her around and hoisted her into the air and entered her again this time using just my legs to support us. She continued to give and receive pleasure while gyrating her hips like there was no tomorrow. I could truly say that I had experienced Jamaica's best in that moment. I felt my own legs weaken after we shared one violent orgasm that had us both cursing and breathing hard. I slowly put her suddenly heavy frame down to keep us both from collapsing to the cold tile floor.

I sat on the edge of the tub to gather my strength and to process what had taken place. Marley didn't linger afterwards. She told me to get some rest so that we could be up early enough to get a run in before going to the attorney's office to sign the final papers. Just that quick I was left alone with nothing to console me aside from the orgasm she had left me with. I had heard of some couples that divorced and still maintained their benefits package from time to time, but didn't really know how I felt about that one. Hell, I really didn't know how I felt about anything these days. I got back in the shower and decided to try my routine again in preparation for bed.

I tossed and turned my way to sleep with disturbing thoughts of my relationship with Marley, and Jacqueline. On one hand I needed to emancipate myself from the bondage of this marriage, but there was also apprehension in giving up the securities of knowing someone existed in the world that had your back. Deep down I knew that it would be a long shot for Jacqueline to abandon her life of comfort to offer her heart to me totally and freely. At my age the prospect of being the "good time" guy was not a very attractive one. Kristen's suggestion of being an escort actually made me laugh a little and I was asleep shortly thereafter.

Hours in real time, that seemed more like moments later Marley and I were stretching along the shore of the National Harbor. I was dressed in my signature black tights and a Norfolk State University T-shirt, while Marley wore very short runner's shorts with a white sports bra that concealed her modest allotment of breasts. Her ripped abs and pronounced legs were on full display. Running was how we both connected and it was something that neither of us has abandoned. She told me about the little over 5 mile run that would take us from the harbor until we were atop the Woodrow Wilson Bridge. The things I let people talk me into was what I thought, but I didn't put up a fight.

The run started out fine, mostly because the sun hadn't begun to blaze the way that it was forecasted to do by mid-day. Unlike Marley I wasn't much on talking while I ran so I chose to keep my answers short and sweet and pretend like I wasn't afraid of falling off the very high bridge that we were approaching. About a mile into it, my breathing adjusted as we began the series of inclines that would put us atop Woodrow Wilson. Out of nowhere Marley asked, "So are you seeing someone special?" Talk about awkward, she didn't even ask if I was seeing someone. She specified "someone special." Her probe had me a little off guard so I deflected a bit. "Isn't this a bit of a weird line of questioning, especially for a couple that hasn't even officially divorced yet?" She hissed like a cobra. "Don't play cute with me Kennedy. I know you don't think that I think you are sitting your ass in Atlanta jacking off. Give me more credit than that. You know that I haven't been sitting on mine either."

I can't say that it didn't bother me to know that she was moving on because I'd be lying, but it didn't sting the way I thought it would. Maybe this wasn't such a bad conversation anyway. "I am not exactly jacking off as you put it, but there is nobody special that I'm seeing." That lie rolled off my tongue easier than I imagined it would. I knew that no matter how tough she pretended to be she didn't want to know the truth about me being in love with another woman any time soon.

By this time we made it to the bridge and I was encouraged to find out that there was no vibration and it was wider than I imagined which made me feel a little less anxious. I wasn't the brightest person but I wondered how a bridge could start in Maryland and by the time you got to the other side you will have crossed D.C. and end up in Virginia in a single stretch less than 2 miles. It made me wonder who was drawing state lines.

Naturally my pace quickened atop the bridge because I didn't want to be on it for longer than I had to and before I knew it we were coming back across. Now we were running into the same direction that the cars were coming towards us. Despite the thick glass and cemented barricades I was not very comfortable, but I kept running. This time we were leaving Virginia headed to Maryland by way of D.C.

The sun had gotten a little brighter, there were more cars speeding by, and more people were walking, running, and riding bikes to and from the harbor. I thought seriously about taking someone's bike to hurry things up but wisely decided not to. By the time we made it back to the shore where we began we were both winded, and had worked up a good sweat. Marley told me about a guy that she has been dating from her office and shared her fears about dating as well. I was glad that she was moving on. It was one of those sobering moments that life was full of.

We dried off with the towels that she had in the car and stretched again before leaving. I tossed Marley one bottle of water and I drank the other. I thought to myself how running had bonded us years ago at a college track meet, and now even through our differences it seemed to still be our common denominator. I guess it was one of those full circle moments that helped to define our lives.

CHAPTER EIGHTEEN

That night I slept on a bed of anger that was about as comfortable as having a tooth extracted with no anesthesia. I tossed for most of the night mentally replaying my argument with Duane. I was surprised at my tone towards him. There was so much hate and venom that covered my words. I'd be lying if I said that part of me didn't feel good; even justified in telling him how I felt about him while the other half felt callous and hallowed. The truth was that I was angry at Duane because he wasn't Kennedy. I wondered why my own husband didn't know me the way that Kennedy knew me. Why didn't he know what to say to make me smile, or when to just listen to me? Why didn't Duane know how to touch me the way Kennedy touched me? He didn't even know that I hated roses after all these years.

Being consumed with those thoughts didn't leave much time to get anything that closely resembled a good night's rest. My anger towards Duane stewed overnight like an over cooked meal that was poorly supervised. I didn't know what to do with these emotions, because everything was so fresh still. The last thing that he could expect from me was a "good morning" salute. It would probably be closer to "go to hell Duane."

When I stumbled into the bathroom and began my morning routine of examining my face while pleading that Father Time would grant me mercy, I became even more despondent. My face revealed worry and anguish. I hadn't even removed my makeup and my eyes looked like a rabies infested raccoon. Mascara was not supposed to look like this. I turned on the cold water and cupped my hands to wash away my outer flaws wishing all the while that I could erase what bothered me on the inside. There probably wasn't enough water in the four oceans or the seven seas to make that happen.

By the time I finished bringing myself back to some form of decency I heard Duane rustling around preparing himself for another work day. The reality was that in spite of our differences, the world wouldn't stop spinning on its axis. Time truly waited for no man or woman. I was somehow comforted knowing that he looked like hell and that it was unlikely that he got any real sleep either. At least we were both miserable. There was nothing like fighting and having your spouse somehow feel better while you felt worse. We didn't even exchange pleasantries, only eye contact that communicated more hate and very little love. These were the moments that we agreed to when we repeated the vows that signed us up for the "worse" part that came after "better." I was regretting that verbal contract with every growing moment.

I ignored him and he ignored me. Finally we agreed on something. I sashayed past him to check on the boys to get them ready for school. Years ago that seemed more like ages ago I used to lay his clothes out and even iron his shirts for him. Part of that was because he wasn't the most fashion savvy man; the other half was because I was in love with him. Now that was merely a memory tucked into a very remote place within my memory's museum never to be called on again; at least not for him. Kennedy on the other hand, could get me to iron his drawers if he asked. Unlike Duane, Kennedy was very conscientious where fashion was concerned. It was just another way that he proved to be in a class by himself when it came to any man that I have ever known.

I dressed Evan and Michael, made their beds, and helped them brush away the cavity creeps. They seemed to grow overnight and both of them insisted on doing things for themselves. My babies were no longer my babies it seemed. My love for them was the only reason why I was enduring this living hell of being married to Duane Tate.

I fixed Evan grits and eggs, while Michael only wanted oatmeal. They could not be more complete opposites in personality despite physically looking the same. Normally I would have made Duane coffee and even cooked him breakfast to make sure his day got off to a good start, but that part of me was long gone. I didn't have it in me to be kind to him whatsoever. That was a side of me that was new. It was a cold and dark place where tenderness and kindness had been smothered to death by coldness and spitefulness. Those were the only feelings that I was left with for my husband. I felt like I needed to go and sit on someone's couch simply for my own regard, not for Duane's.

When I thought of all the romantic feelings that I had developed for Kennedy and how I had fallen deeper in love with him even after I didn't think that feeling more was possible, I resented Duane more and more. It was all that I could do to mask my negative emotions from the boys and maintain some type of civility towards him. A woman could go to jail for a very long time for acting on some of the thoughts that I was contemplating for Duane. In spite of what I was feeling I was calm until he came into the kitchen and released my emotions like a pressure cooker.

He leaned into me and looked me into my eyes and said, "I don't know what your problem is exactly, but it better be taken care of when I get back home." When he finished he walked away as if I were some over-zealous teenager that he had taken into his office and threatened to discipline them with a suspension or a call home. At that point I gave no regard for Evan or Michael and even less for Duane. "You are my problem Duane. You are what is wrong with me. So unless you don't plan on coming home tonight, then I will still be dealing with "what's wrong with me." Despite the boys being young they knew that this was not a pleasant conversation between us.

With every ounce of restraint that I could muster I swallowed my ever-growing hatred for Duane and kissed my boys and hugged them before they left. I didn't even watch them leave out of the house. The garage came up and then it came down letting me know that they had left.

That morning I cried so much until my allotment of tears had reached their expiration. There were officially no more tears to cry, and to be honest I was tired of crying about a situation that I knew deep down was not going to get better.

Despite how I felt I managed to press on and prepare myself for something better. Mondays were always hard after coming off a weekend lull. This Monday took on even more of a solemn tone than usual. I remembered my meeting with Mr. and Mrs. Dillard following the Bronner Brothers show. Even though it was customary for us to meet and review following any show this meeting had me more anxious than I normally would be. I had to start thinking about realistically being able to support my boys and myself and begin to think of life without Duane. Even if that meant exploring other career options that didn't involve Genesis. Despite my love for the Dillards, I loved my boys and me a lot more.

I managed to pull myself together at least on the outside and put on my best face literally and figuratively before I left home. It was comforting to know that even though I felt like hell, that I could still look beautiful.

Looking at my phone out of habit made me a bit disappointed because Kennedy hadn't called or texted me. Talk about the things that make your day and never missing something until it was gone. I didn't even want to imagine what he was doing in Virginia the last couple of days with his wife. The more I thought that thought, the more I realized how complicated our relationship was. How could I have fallen in love with a married man when I was married myself?

Sometimes life left us with more questions than we had answers for. Instead I just shook my head as I dismissed the thought. I was pulling up to Genesis for the meeting in the same fashion as I had hundreds of times but this time just felt different. It felt like my life was about to change one way or the other.

In no time at all my meeting was over and I was back in my car. I had to admit that I didn't know what to expect, but not on my best day of negotiating did I expect what they told me.

Mr. and Mrs. Dillard had always maintained that I was appreciated and even a time or two they called me an asset, but never did their money and their mouths speak at the same time. They not only met my salary demands to put me in six figures, they also offered me stock in Genesis as well. Mr. Dillard said that he couldn't risk me going to one of their competitors in the beauty industry.

As excited as I was, there was only one person that I wanted to share this news with. Kennedy was the one person that not only knew how hard I worked, but also would be happy for me. I called Kennedy to tell him all about what had just happened. He picked up on the second ring. "Guess what baby! You are not gonna believe it. Your girl just got a huge raise. I'm sooo excited!" I managed to get all that out on one breath before I paused to breathe and hear his reply. His tone was muffled and he spoke as if he was otherwise occupied; like he wasn't really concerned.

"That is really good Jacqueline...I am glad for you. You deserve it." It wasn't the normal way he talked to me which was pissing me off by the second. "Are you busy or something Kennedy?" He paused.... "I umm, it's not a good time. Can I call you in about five minutes Jacqueline? I am finishing up a meeting." I hung up before he could say anything else. Now I was pissed all over again. This time it was not only Duane, but Kennedy too. Maybe all men were stupid. Either way I was fed up and other than my raise there was nothing else that could make this day get any worse.

My phone rang and I thought it was Kennedy so I answered without looking at the screen. He was calling to apologize and told me that he had just gotten out of a meeting with his divorce attorney. It actually made me feel kinda bad for screaming on him. Kennedy told me all about his son's emergency. Suddenly I didn't think that my fight with Duane compared to what he must have been going through and it made me feel selfish for the way I acted earlier. This was one of those times that I wish I could have been there to hold his hand and let him vent. Here he was going through some emotional hardships with the divorce and growing pains with his son and I was bragging about my raise. It was a little difficult to see how the two compared. I could honestly say that I wasn't looking forward to Evan and Michael hitting puberty ever. Divorce impacts everyone involved, especially the children. I wondered how my two would be impacted, because Splitsville was on me and Duane's radar and it was fast approaching.

We talked for about an hour about this and that but really nothing major after that news. It was light but flowed. He and I could talk all day and not grow weary or run out of things to discuss. My voicemail was getting a good workout taking messages because I didn't click over and there had been multiple calls from people who probably wanted nothing at all. There was nobody other than my boys that I considered more important than Kennedy King. I was completely in love with him.

My mother had called me at least a dozen times which even for her was unusual. I just kept on talking with Kennedy while I drove around killing time with no particular destination in mind. I was right where I wanted to be; where I needed to be.

He told me that he was flying back into Atlanta later in the day from Virginia. I talked to him all the way to the airport and despite switching from both ears a couple of times and my phone feeling like it was on fire I kept on talking to the man that I adored; clinging to his every word. When he had to go through the security check we regretfully ended our conversation. While talking with Kennedy being several hundreds of miles away provided an escape from the realities of my world, it didn't mean that the world and its problems stopped existing. Since Gabriel hadn't begun blowing his trumpet, life went on regardless of who took notice or even decided to participate. That statement had never been more apparent in my life until I got the call that would change it forever.

There was nothing in the world that could have prepared me for the news that I had avoided for hours by talking to Kennedy. The time that I was living in a fantasy world the landscape ceased to remain unscathed in my world. I was immediately taken over by an avalanche of emotions and I didn't know whether to cry, scream, or yell which probably meant I did all three. "Oh my God!" Please tell me you are lying!"

CHAPTER NINETEEN

Being in Virginia the past couple of days had served its purpose. Shortly after running with Marley and getting a quick shower, I went by the attorney's office to sign my part of the divorce papers. She had already done her part so it was left to me. My legs always felt heavy after a run and today was no exception, I felt every single mile. Despite the nagging pain and discomfort, there wasn't much that compared to the high I feel after a good run. Nothing could compare to the weight of the thoughts that burdened my mind. There was Miles and his issues, Marley and our transition, and always front and center was Jacqueline and our existence. I knew how Atlas felt because it seemed as though I was underneath all of the world's massive weight.

Sitting in the conference room waiting for my divorce attorney, Elise Harrison, had given me time to get better acquainted with thoughts that I would rather divorce myself from metaphorically. She entered into the very plush and chilled confines of the Richardson, Steele, and Peterson law firm. Judging from the seasoned, European influenced faces of the partners that were pictured on the conference room wall told me that Elise Harrison hadn't quite climbed that high in her firm's pecking order. Before today she had only existed through phone and email, so I had no clue of what she looked like. Elise was less than 5 "3" from where I was sitting without her 3-inch heels that she was wearing. Her complexion boasted the hue of honey, her hair was wavy and jet black, her skin was beautiful; not a blemish in sight, teeth were perfect. She was "do a double take" beautiful. Judging her from the bottom to the top told me that she was making a pretty penny as an attorney despite not having made partner. She was wearing black pumps, a gray skirt with a classic navy blue blouse with a white collar and her hair was pulled back into a bun. She boasted modest breasts and deceiving curves that made me do a double take. "Wow," I thought to myself. Not even moments like this could mute my instincts as a man. I was what I was and there was no denying that. She was fine.

I met her right hand with a right hand of my own as I stood to greet her. She had a smile that while it was business left me wondering thoughts that I was embarrassed to admit. "It's nice to meet you Mr. King." She said that and proceeded to get things underway. "It's nice to meet you as well Ms...Mrs. Harrison," as I hesitated uncertain of her marital status. She interjected, "I'm not married if that's what you mean, but you can call me Elise. I am not that formal." She smiled. "I will call you Elise if you call me Kennedy." She nodded in agreement and began to go over the forms that I was about to sign.

I thought to myself about how complicated it was to get out of a marriage compared to what it took to get into it. All you had to do was ask someone and have them agree and after getting a license and repeating some words then you were married. Heck even a Notary Public in some states could perform a marriage ceremony. Getting out of one was altogether more complicated. Provided both parties agreed to go their separate ways there was still the matter of hiring an attorney to consider dividing property and other assets, even children. I didn't see why it should cost more to exit one than it did to enter one. I found myself grateful that Marley and I called it quits before we grew to hate one another.

The forms seemed pretty straight forward. She and I would both have joint custody, she got to keep the house, and we split our savings down the middle. I stroked my John Hancock as if it were my first time writing in cursive; made sure my "e's" looked like "e's" because I didn't wanna have to do this again. I slid the forms back towards Elise Harrison and like that it was done. Once the state of Virginia reviewed it, I would officially be a single man. That was not the thought that I expected to have when I vowed to be Marley's husband till death departed us. In reality some promises could not be kept. Our right hands met again to signify not only the close of our meeting but also the end of my 14 years of matrimony.

On my way to the airport I thought about Marley. Thought about her dating someone else. Thought about how weird that thought was. Deep down I was glad that she was moving on because I had moved on about two years earlier with Jacqueline. The guilt was devouring me and I just didn't have anything left to give as her husband.

In typical Jacqueline fashion she always called when she was heavy on my mind. I told her that I was in a meeting with my attorney and had to call her back. When I called back she told me all about her promotion with her job. I was really thrilled for her in spite of my vacillating feelings of sadness and relief about my own life and its problems. I wanted her to know that I was genuinely excited for her and I didn't want my issues to contaminate her so I buried them in a place to be dealt with later. I masked my emotions and existed as the person she had always known me to be. It was a place that was more idealistic and less realistic; a place that allowed me to listen to her for hours while she yapped about her hard work, and her being "deserving." She never once pretended to consider that I might need to process what I was dealing with and that planted a seed of resentment in the pit of my belly.

We talked up until it was time for me to go through the security check points in the airport. Walking through the Thurgood Marshall airport better known as BWI afforded me the opportunity to confront some realities that I had been in denial about. Here I was a single man and the woman that I loved more than any woman I have ever loved didn't love me enough to give us a try. I know that neither of us signed up for this when we met, but here we were and where we were was not a place that could exist much longer. Either way something had to change.

I had to end our call as I prepared to practically strip down before I went through the security scans at the airport. After showing my identification and boarding pass I emptied the contents of my pockets into the plastic bin along with my shoes, and belt. They had my wallet, loose change, iPod, and my watch being scanned to ensure that I had the best interest of safety in mind as I traveled back to Atlanta. While it was a bit frustrating I was all for making sure nobody wanted to heat up their crotch to take down a plane filled with Americans in the name of Allah with the reward of several dozen virgins waiting for them in the afterlife. What good would you be to any woman void of what made a man a man in the first place? Maybe that was the part Al-Qaida left out in the suicide bomber training, or maybe you would grow a new appendage once you crossed realms. Either way that thought served to make me smile and brighten my otherwise dull mood as I proceeded to gather my things and move towards my terminal shaking my head.

I thought about calling Jacqueline but decided that a drink sounded like a much better option. The truth was that since I didn't wanna rain on her parade that I'd much rather sulk in my own misery with reservations for me, myself, and I. In fact after touching base with Miles I turned my cell completely off to ensure that lonely would be my only company. I surrendered my burdens to the liquid spirits better known as tequila. It was one of those days.

By the time I was finished with round one on my way to round number two I had overheard my share of conversations at the bar about optimistic republicans hell bent on "sticking it" to Obama than I cared to listen to. I was rapidly losing any faith I had that people had any sense whatsoever these days the more they talked. Together they didn't have a pot to piss in or a window to throw it out of, yet they were vehemently against accepting any help that came from the suddenly tanned version of Uncle Sam. I gritted my teeth, held my tongue, and sipped more tequila. It was all I could do to keep from having a not so peaceful demonstration inside of the airport that honored our nation's first black Supreme Court justice. In some ways I guess he was the only one, because nobody regarded Anita Hill's ex-boyfriend in the same way.

Before I knew it I was in my window seat slightly behind the right wing of the aircraft awaiting take off. I prayed that there wouldn't be anyone next to me only to find that my prayers went unanswered when this young couple sat beside me. They looked mid-twenties, she was blonde, slender frame, and wore a sorority t-shirt with ripped jeans and average features. He had dark curly hair that stuck out of his baseball cap and must have thought not shaving was a religion he took seriously. They were young and neither one was probably out of college. Their whole lives were ahead of them. I wanted to warn them that all relationships are great in the beginning, and then the bottom falls out with no warning. Sanity prevailed and I decided not to rain on their parade just because my love life had more problems than Charlie Sheen had stints in rehab. I placed my headphones in my ear and turned my iPod up instead, both ignoring Romeo and Juliet and the captain's advisory to turn off portable electronic devices. Today just wasn't the day that I really cared about complying with anyone's rules.

Shortly after we had taken off and somewhere before we reached our cruising altitude I succumb to the influence of overpriced airport tequila and mental fatigue and I slumbered while nestled beside strangers.

I was in Charlotte, North Carolina on my way to surprise Jacqueline for her birthday. It had only been a couple of months since we had been seeing each other, but I just couldn't get enough of her. I took a chance by coming up to see her. Luckily it worked out because she didn't have any concrete plans. A modest room inside the Aloft hotel would serve as our private getaway to celebrate 33 wonderful years and one of the best creations ever crafted by God's hands.

Since I was going pretty much without a script I only packed bottled water, fruit, and my laptop for music. Under normal circumstances I would have sent flowers to her with an invitation to dinner later on at her favorite restaurant. It was clear that these were not normal circumstances, which was why that couldn't happen. Only these four walls would bear witness to what we felt for one another.

I wished her happy birthday with everything in me. After hours of making love to her the way a man makes love to a woman that he loves made me both tired and thirsty. I fell away from Jacqueline after we had both had too many orgasms to remember and retrieved us both some water. Sweat covered our bodies and our chests expanded and contracted with reaction to intense pleasure.

It felt like I was back in my teens again whenever we made love; there was such a youthful exuberance. Jacqueline was like a drug and I was definitely addicted, in fact I didn't even want rehab. This was a high that I loved to feel. Maybe it was how addicts felt about their drug of choice.

When I returned to the bed I couldn't help but stare at her. It was as if it were the first time that I was seeing her. If a person's eyes were the window to their soul, she bared it all. Her eyes communicated her fears and uncertainties. They told me that she didn't mean to get here, but that she also didn't have any plans of leaving. They told me that she had never felt this way about anybody and that included her husband. Her eyes told me that if she could she would give it all to be in this moment with me forever. Jacqueline had communicated all of that to me without so much as parting her lips and involving any of her vocal functions.

In those moments that followed epic lovemaking our intimacy had grown exponentially. Jacqueline seemed to open up like a flower in full bloom. She began to talk about her feelings towards her husband and how she never thought she'd end up breaking her vows of fidelity. Her words possessed so much regret and sincerity. She was disappointed that her husband had not lived up to his full promise and as a result neither could she. The more she talked the more I could truly relate to what she meant. It was eerily similar to what I had been coming to grips with in my own marriage at the time. This was the part that made relationships so difficult in the first place. Falling in love and actually remaining there were two completely different entities.

In hindsight that was the moment where we both crossed into territory where we probably should not have. It was one thing to be having an affair in the first place, but it was a totally different scenario when we began forecasting a future that involved us in an exclusive manner. Jacqueline and I both journeyed to an imaginary place ruled by idealism one where realism had no jurisdiction.

Looking back on it, that was when things really changed and began to get complicated in hindsight. Despite the obvious chemistry and compatibility we shared it would have been wise to stay away from all the "what if?" thoughts that we began referencing. It only served as a measure to further complicate things. What if I left my husband? What if I left my wife? What if we were free to be with one another? What if we didn't have to hide our love for one another? It went on and on and we became further tangled in the sticky web of delusion.

Our reality had become a fallacy which began to cloud both of our judgments moving forward. Our perception of what could be or what might be was our new reality and that was how we governed our world from that point forward.

A slight tap from the flight attendant bought me back to the present and disturbed my trip down memory lane letting me know that my trip from Virginia was over. I yawned, stretched and secured my carryon luggage in preparation to depart the aircraft in search of long-term parking and the comfort of my vehicle.

It seemed like I had been away for weeks with all of the drama that unfolded while I was home. I was still trying to familiarize myself with the fact that I was no longer married as I manipulated my wedding band in a circular motion out of habit. It was what I had done since Marley placed it there on our wedding day. Now all I knew was that I'd have to do something different, but the something was less clear than Sarah Palin's thought sequences. I didn't have a clue. I left the Hartsfield –Jackson International airport with feelings of defeat and extreme uncertainty.

CHAPTER TWENTY

For moments that seemed more like a lifetime I struggled to get my mind wrapped around the words my mother had fed me. Despite the few semesters of Spanish that I studied in school, English was the language that I was fluent in but still she made no sense. "Your father was rushed to the hospital!" There was so much desperation in her voice; so much uncertainty. My mouth was open but I wasn't making a sound; at least not any sound that made sense. She told me that he was at Presbyterian Hospital on Hawthorne Lane. I was about 15 minutes away , but in this traffic it was no telling how long it would take.

I got off the phone with my mother and hurried in that direction. There was very little regard for the speed limits set by the city of Charlotte where I was concerned. Thoughts began to process rapidly in my head as I conjured up countless scenarios of what could have happened. The suspense of not really knowing what was wrong with my father gave me a sense of fear and panic unlike anything I've ever felt. To my knowledge he had never been sick a day in his life, and he probably hasn't been to a hospital since he was born.

My eyes were blinded by the abundance of tears and the bright glare of brake lights that I was facing in this bumper to bumper traffic. I wiped my face and did my best to remain calm under the mounting pressure of simply not knowing. I thought of calling Kennedy; he always knew what to say to make things right. Then I remembered that he was probably 35,000 feet above the Earth on his way back to Atlanta. That made me realize just how dependent I had become on the man that wasn't my husband. It really wasn't his place to begin with. It should be my own husband that I thought of calling, but that thought only served to complicate my emotions and make me more upset.

Then I realized that the hours I spent chatting away with Kennedy and ignoring my mother's phone calls that my father may have needed me the most. Maybe there was something that I could have done. The load of my guilty thoughts grew heavier as I approached Hawthorne.

When I got to the hospital I parked near the emergency room in search of answers. I wasn't even sure if I'd locked the doors, or even if I parked legally. I just knew that none of that mattered right now. Walking past dozens of nameless faces that all owned anxiety and fear that weren't familiar to me as I pressed on deeper until I reached the nurse's station. Before I could ask for information about my father I felt a tap on the shoulder. When I turned in its direction I saw the first recognizable face. It was my father's sister; my aunt Rhonda. We embraced in gladness and in sorrow because neither of us wanted to have a family reunion in the emergency room.

She stared at me with a stare that said she was astonished at how long it had been since she'd seen me. I reciprocated her expression because those were my exact sentiments. My family was not exactly what you'd call connected and loving by any stretch of the imagination. She told me that my mother was waiting on me, but really didn't provide any other news. Part of me was glad because not only was no news good news at this point, but I didn't really want to hear any news about my father from his least favorite sister.

I followed the ER Nurse who guided me in the back where my father was. Each step made my legs feel as though they would give out causing me to collapse where I stood. My breathing picked up, my heart raced, and it seemed like I would be the one needing emergency care. It was my first time being in an ER since I was a kid and had to get stitches after I fell off my bicycle when I was 7. I didn't remember things looking quite this way. People were literally clinging onto their lives and all they were afforded was a wide open space separated by hospital sheets that served as partitions and a mobile twin bed. There was no privacy to speak of. Family members would have to process bad news about their loved one's prognosis in the face of everyone. Where the decency and human compassion was that everyone should be afforded?

The nurse speaking made me focus more on her words and less on my thoughts. She obviously sensed my apprehension over what I was walking into and tried her best to ease what was uneasy. Looking at her name tag told me that her name was Erin. Erin told me not to be alarmed by the tubes that my father was hooked up to both in his nose and mouth. So far her attempts to calm me had done the exact opposite because I became more anxious. Erin grabbed my hand and told me not to worry; that everything would be fine. In that moment I was grateful for her sincerity that went beyond a mere job function; it was personal and heartfelt. I only hoped that she was a clairvoyant because right now things didn't seem fine at all.

I saw my mother sitting at my father's bedside holding his hand and rocking back and forth as if she were praying. When she saw me she seemed a little calmer but disappointed that I hadn't been there sooner. I was disappointed in myself as well. We both embraced as she caught me up on everything that had taken place to this point.

My mother told me that shortly after supper that my father was resting and watching television in the den. She grew concerned after he hadn't stirred around like he normally does. After calling him she tapped his shoulder thinking he had fallen asleep. My mother became afraid when she noticed that he had wet himself. Since my father had no bladder problems she immediately thought there was something wrong and called 911. He remained non-responsive and hasn't gained consciousness since. The paramedics began CPR and rushed him to the ER. She told me that she had been calling me for hours once she called 911. I felt worse by the minute.

When my father needed me the most I conveniently disregarded my mother's telephone calls to linger in a fallacy with Kennedy while this was my reality. I wept like I had never wept in my life. I disregarded the tubes connected to my father and I hugged him like a scared child holds their father. He had always represented my security blanket regardless of the insecurities present in my life. Right now all of that was in serious jeopardy and all that made sense to me was now senseless. I didn't care about Genesis and my raise, or my problems with Duane, or even my twisted relationship with Kennedy. I would give all that I thought made sense just to see my father open his eyes and be okay. Aside from Evan and Michael, my parents were the most important people in my life.

I prayed to God in a way that I've never quite prayed to him before. It was the type of prayer born out of desperation and sincerity. There I was bargaining with God and making promises to do what I should have been doing all along in exchange for my father's clean bill of health. It was funny how moments of desperation helped to crystallize what was otherwise hazy. I just hoped that God was in the mood to make a deal. I hoped even more that he'd truly consider my offer.

The ER doctor joined us behind the curtain. He carried a cold demeanor and seemed as though time was his only concern. Bedside manner was not his attribute. Numbers were his game. "Mrs. Turner," he said more in a tone of discernment between my mother and me. Even though Turner was my maiden name, I knew that he was referring to my mother. He directed his statements toward her where she remained seated as I stood and looked on. "Mrs. Turner I'm Dr. Tillman and I'm the ER Dr. that treated your husband when he came in. It appears that he suffered a major heart attack. The paramedics stated that he may have been unconscious for an undetermined amount of time before they arrived. We've tried to do everything that we could, but I'm afraid that even if he regains consciousness that there could be significant brain damage already done. There is no telling how long his brain has gone without oxygen. At this point it's really hard to say. The machines are pretty much the only thing keeping him alive at this point. I'll leave you two alone to decide what you feel is in his best interest." He said all of that without even blinking his eyes. He said that like he was saying that everything would be just fine. My mother and I wept as we embraced. We wept like the two Marys' weeping at Jesus' empty tomb.

There was no way that I could fathom giving up on my father so even if there was a chance that he would live I was willing to take it. I figured that my mother would echo my sentiment, but when she spoke her words confirmed the exact opposite. "Jacqueline...sweet heart, we have to do what is best for your father. You know that he wouldn't want to live if living meant that a machine would breathe for him. We both promised each other that we would let go and give way to God's will if something like this happened." She spoke with so much certainty in her words as if there was no other consideration. "Mother, how can we just give up on him like that? We don't even know if any of what that son of a bit@# said was true." I almost cursed in the face of my frustration. "I can't just give up on him like that until I know that we've tried everything possible." By now the tears were really coming at record pace.

My mother stood and embraced me the way that a mother embraces their child when they need it the most. When she pushed me away her face owned a strength that mine did not. "I know this is hard, but my mind is already made up. I am honoring my husband the way that he would want to be honored. I have to do what I know is the right thing to do. Sometimes we have to do what's difficult even when it doesn't feel good." Right now her words were about as pleasant as a bed of needles. I couldn't accept them. I had never been more against her judgment than I was at this moment. Although my face pleaded for her to reconsider I knew deep down that my mother was a woman of her word. She had her mind made up whether I liked it or not.

"I'll give you some time to say good bye to your father Jacqueline." In that instance I was left with moments to try to cram my 35 years of existence with my father into. My mother had been saying her goodbyes and now it was my turn. How do you say goodbye to someone who means so much to you? How do you prepare yourself for never seeing the first man that you loved ever again in life? It was pretty hard having a one-way conversation that you weren't even sure they heard to begin with. I just didn't know where to begin and I certainly didn't know what to say. I was consumed with a rush of memories of my father and how he'd always been there for me. I remembered him picking me up anytime I fell and scraped my knee or had faced any type of adversity. He always knew how to make me feel better. He always told me that I was the prettiest girl in the whole world. It was my father who taught me how to ride a bike, drive a car, and he was the one who taught me how a man should treat a lady. So many memories and so little time.

I wished that I could have said those words to him while we looked each other in their eyes followed by a tight and long embrace, but it didn't seem as though that was happening. Instead I cried tears of regret that this would be the last time I would lay eyes on him while he was still alive; even if it was courtesy of life support. I rubbed his curly mane and took in his handsome and rugged features one last time. I stared into the face of the man that my mother fell in love with. I stared into the face of the man that always made me feel loved and protected and never judged. I told him that I loved him with everything inside of me and that I was truly a better person because of him. I told him that I'd miss him and that I would never forget him. I told him that I'd make sure that his grandson's would know how much he loved them. Lastly, I told him that one day I'd see him again and that I'd take care of my mother just like I knew that he would want me to. I kissed my father on his wrinkled forehead in the same manner in which he has done to me throughout my life each time before we parted company. I watched one last time as my tears fell upon his face trying to embrace our final goodbye on this side. With great sadness, tremendous regret, and a bountiful disdain for the shortness of time I let him go as I turned to walk away and join my mother in the hallway.

She gave the doctors her consent to remove my father from life support and moments later he was gone. No signs of a heartbeat and there was no rise and fall to his chest. I watched as he faded from this world into the next one. His face owned a restful peace that he didn't have moments earlier. The Dr. called his death at 9:03 p.m. Although my heart kept on beating I knew that it would never own the same rhythm. Just like that life, as I knew it had forever been altered.

CHAPTER TWENTY-ONE

The last two days I struggled trying to get back into my routine of legally distributing government approved and regulated drugs to the various doctors that I was assigned to. I had to work extra hard to make up for all the missed visits last week due to my son and his emergency. The bright side of my trip back home so far has been improved communication between Miles and me. We talk every morning while I am on the way to work and he is on the way to school and again each evening.

Marley seems to be open to allowing Miles to start the school year in Atlanta with me next year considering all that's happened. The extra work has served to take my mind off of the things that bothered me the most and gave me something to focus my attention towards.

After I finished my 5-mile jog around Stone Mountain I had never felt better. Not only did it feel as though my stamina had returned, but there was also a mental clarity that I hadn't felt in quite some time. My mother had always taught me that there was always something good born out of every struggle. I guess that if divorcing Marley meant that we'd both be happier apart, Miles and I would be better than ever, and I'd have peace of mind then it was worth the hassle.

The one thing that hadn't resolved itself was probably the single most perplexing dilemma that I had and it was my relationship with Jacqueline. There was nothing more frustrating than knowing that there wasn't anyone in life that made you happier; knowing that they felt the same, yet you couldn't be together. Everything about it bared no resemblance to rationally sound judgment, but sometimes you couldn't help what you felt. I felt as though Jacqueline Tate was the one woman that was made for me, but she wasn't with me because she was married.

I tried to call her a few times but my calls went unanswered so I figured that she was otherwise occupied with her new job duties and that she'd call me when a better time permitted her to do so. No big deal. It was the nature of operating in secrecy. We'd have to wait until convenience prevailed. I carried on my grind of traveling from office to office, appeasing doctors and their staff, getting signatures to satisfy the DEA, delivering drugs to satisfy my company, scheduling lunches to take care of office staff all so I could get taken care of on payday. It seemed like a fair enough exchange and everyone got his or her needs met with the exception of the patient. They were the ones that absorbed the burden of "business as usual" politics in this world. It had become the American way to place the biggest burden on those who could least afford to pay it.

When I arrived at Felicia's office I took my time a little because it was my last stop for the day and I really enjoyed being in her office. It was a friendly environment and her staff made me feel really welcome. It was a big reason why I didn't mind the long drive just north of Buford, Ga. Felicia practiced internal medicine and she really appreciated samples and discount coupons for anti-anxiety/depression medication because she served a very high underinsured population. That was a nice way of saying, "overlooked" or just "flat broke" in my book. Some people didn't understand the need for quality access to healthcare in this country. I found it very admirable that she went out of her way to treat that population with the same dignity and respect that the wealthiest among us would expect to receive. It was a big reason I made sure that she got the most our company had to offer.

While making my way from Felicia's office all I could do was think of how good my bed would feel once I got back home. Marcus called to check on things with Miles and to play catch up concerning my manuscript. He had been trying to set up the meeting with a producer to begin negotiations and other technical stuff that he was trying to explain over the phone that sounded more foreign than trying to order sushi in Japanese at a restaurant. Whatever he was trying to say let me know that it would have more involvement than a handshake and a smile. I could honestly say that although I was excited, I really hadn't given much thought to writing. It wasn't that I didn't take it seriously; it was just that sometimes in life personal conflicts could interfere with creative pursuits.

Marcus and I yapped and yapped and covered just about everything from Miles, Marley, and even Jacqueline. He even wanted to know about Kristen, which really let me know that it had been a minute since we talked. Since Marcus was closer than a brother we didn't have any secrets. I knew that I could tell him anything, so I did. He got to hear everything about my evening with Kristen that followed a good morning with Jacqueline and ended with a hell of a good night with Marley. "Damn man that's one hellified 48 hours! Eddie Murphy would be proud of that." His attempts at humor were eventful at best, but I laughed anyway. I guess since I said it out loud it did sound crazy.

It was proof that I was all over the place emotionally which meant that my decision-making was not the most sound.

I knew that I was over Marley and sex with her was just living in a moment in time marked "past," sex with Kristen was a reaction to my present marred with thoughts of an unattainable future with Jacqueline. I was a wounded man that needed healing in the worse way; there was no denying that. At this rate I'd be going through lots of condoms.

A call was coming into my phone from a number that wasn't in my address book, which normally wouldn't get answered, but this one had a (704) area code. That was a call from a Charlotte, NC number and I thought it might be Jacqueline so I answered without hesitation. "Hey Marcus, I have a call I gotta take. I'll hit you later." "Call me so I can tell you the rest of the details. King, don't drop the ball on this. Handle your business." I didn't reply or bother to see if he had hung up before I switched over. My voice owned mild uneasiness because Jacqueline had never called me from any other number. " This is Kennedy." When the voice on the other line responded I knew immediately that it was not Jacqueline. "Hi Kennedy, this is Gabrielle.....Jacqueline's friend. Anyway…I was calling you to let you know that she's had a situation." Now I remembered her girlfriend Gabby. I'd never heard of her being referred to as Gabrielle which threw me for a second. "Gabb....Gabrielle, what kind of situation are you referring to?" I was beginning to get tightness in my stomach and my heart was beating overtime. She paused. "Her father passed away rather suddenly last night."

Now I was speechless. It made sense why I hadn't spoken with her at all today. I thought that she was busy with work or something, but I had no idea. I felt like crap. There she was having the biggest crisis of her life and here I was probably the last to know. "Wow, is she okay? How's she doing? What happened?" Those stupid questions kinda flew off my tongue before my brain could reel them back in. Of course she was not doing well I thought to myself. Gabby told me that he died from an apparent heart attack and that Jacqueline was in total shock. She had been by most of the day after getting the news and said that Jacqueline tried to call me but got my voicemail. She asked Gabby to reach out to me and let me know.

It made me feel really bad to know that I had purposely made myself unreachable because I didn't want to be bothered with anything and the person I loved the most was going through this type of ordeal. Of course I couldn't call Jacqueline myself or stop by as if we were in a normal relationship. This really magnified the true limitations of our affair. We may have meant the world to one another, but the people in this world couldn't know. The only other people who knew about us were Marcus and Gabby.

I told Gabby to keep me posted with arrangements for Jacqueline's father and I asked her if I could send correspondences through her to Jacqueline. A part of me wanted to do a serious U-turn and head north up 85 until I got to Charlotte and drive directly to her. This situation truly made me regret our existence probably more than any other point. I felt so limited; so helpless. The best I could do was to send her an email to let her know that I'd gotten the news and that she could call me anytime day or night.

When I got home that evening Jacqueline remained heavy on my mind. I was responding as if I were grieving a loss. My appetite deserted me, and it was truly difficult to fall asleep. I guess when you truly care about someone their problems and worries become your problems and worries. I knew that I would not truly be satisfied until I could see her face and hold her in my arms to comfort her. That was the only way to right what was suddenly wrong with me.

The next couple days were torture for me. I resumed my normal activities of peddling pharmaceuticals, attended meetings, talked with Miles, my mother, and I even ran to clear my head. I dodged Marcus's calls because I was not in the place mentally to deal with what he wanted to deal with. Gabby told me the name of the funeral home and she even gave me Jacqueline's home address so I could send flowers to both locations. She told me that Jacqueline wanted to talk to me but she was really depressed and that her husband was off work the entire week.

That thought sickened me to the pit of my stomach even though it shouldn't have. He was after all her husband, even if only in title. I telephoned a local florist and had flowers sent to both locations. For the funeral home I selected a nice arrangement of carnations and sprays that no doubt would fit right in with the peace lilies that people usually sent. I was sure that Jacqueline and her mother would have enough peace lilies that they could open a floral shop when this week was over. For Jacqueline I sent the type of flowers that I knew or hoped would cheer her up. I sent her an arrangement of wild flowers that were her favorite. I decided that a personal message was not necessary; figured she'd know my work.

The funeral was scheduled for Friday at 2:00 p.m. I had to clear a couple of meetings and lunch dates, but it wasn't anything that she wouldn't have done for me. I would have given just about anything to be able to look into her eyes and tell her that I was there for her however she needed me to be.

I thought back to a conversation we'd had during pillow talk when Jacqueline told me about her family and growing up as a single child in a very traditional home. Her father served in the military where he was wounded in the Vietnam War, but nothing life threatening. She told me that her mother thought that her father was dead because he neglected to return any of her letters for a period of time. His reasoning was that thoughts of home could keep a person from returning there the way he left.

Jacqueline told me that her mother was the submissive type; never confrontational when it came to her father. Jacqueline was raised to be the same way, but she has rejected many of her mother's teachings. That is why she is so driven in her career and it's why she strives to be at the top of her game. She told me that despite her love for her mother that she wanted to be nothing like her except for being a great mom. I could totally relate to that because I wanted to be nothing like my father with no exceptions.

One major difference between Jacqueline's father and mine was that she actually had someone who was there for her; someone who gave a damn and didn't just give some sperm. I truly couldn't imagine what she was going through because in many ways my father was already dead even though he wasn't the one lying in a funeral home about to be put into the ground. His death was more of a voluntary withdrawal from my life years ago when he and my mother split up. I never knew divorcing your wife had to include your child as well. A big part of me would rather trade places with Jacqueline because it would seem easier to say that my father died of a heart attack rather than saying that my father was born with no heart in the first place. Maybe she was lucky and I was the one mourning a loss of something that I never truly had to begin with.

On the day of the funeral, Gabby texted me the name and address of the church so I could pull it up on my GPS. I decided that I'd leave earlier to allow myself time to make a few wrong turns here and there and to ensure I arrived before the family. I'd be lying if I said that my nerves were the least settled or that I didn't have doubts about going. I just knew that Jacqueline would have done the same for me with no questions asked regardless of our less than complicated standing. I wasn't the biggest fan of funerals and avoided them whenever possible, but today I'd make an exception. Whoever said love could make you do things you never thought you would do, might have coined the saying of a lifetime. Here I was traveling to Charlotte, North Carolina from Atlanta, Georgia to attend the funeral for the father of the woman that I was desperately in love with. The only thing wrong with that scenario is that she happens to be married and her husband will be there too.

Thoughts of Jacqueline jostled inside of my mind the entire time I commuted to her father's funeral. They weren't the normal thoughts that occupied my mind that were flirty and led to mental fornication. These thoughts were more or less about her well-being. It truly bothered me that I couldn't make sure that she was okay. It was so not protocol for us to be out of the communication loop, but I understood that this was unchartered territory where she and I were concerned.

I decided to make small talk to ease my anxieties and take my mind off of what I'd eventually encounter when I got there. I returned missed calls and did some readjusting to my schedule for next week. I returned every call except for the dozens that Marcus made. I texted him instead and told him that I was swamped with work and that I'd call him later. I didn't feel like hearing his vocal judgment for the way I was responding to Jacqueline's emergency. I really wasn't in the mood to hear him say that it wasn't my place to be there and that she had a husband for that. Those were things that I had already said to myself so I didn't need to hear an encore. I knew with everything inside of me that it was wrong for me to be there, but nothing about our situation was right so I didn't see now as the time to cave in to my morals. I just knew in my heart that she would do the same. I knew that she needed me in the same manner that I would need her if the roles were different. That was the rationale I chose to abide with.

Turn for turn the GPS had guided me all the way from Atlanta to Charlotte hitting every major stretch of highway and even some roads that were secondary to secondary roads. I was surprised the satellites even registered them, but thankful that they did because I couldn't have found them on my own. I had ridden with storm clouds from south to north but only now had the drizzle of rain begin to fall. This was the type of weather that only served to dampen the mood on a day that needed no cosigner; grief and misery would always own this date for Jacqueline.

I secured a park in short walking distance of the medium sized Baptist church parking lot nestled on the outer banks of Charlotte when suddenly the skies opened up and released an out pour of rain sufficient to remedy drought conditions that forecasters complained of for weeks. It was as if God was mourning the loss of Jacqueline's father as well in his own way, taking and still giving. I decided to say a prayer for her and her family in their time of grief. I prayed that in her own way Jacqueline would gain peace through losing her father and that she would understand he had fulfilled his destiny in this world and that it was time for him to go onto the next one. I knew that death affected everyone differently and that it would definitely affect her. I was hopeful that she'd be better for going through it. When I was done with my prayer the storm clouds had lifted and the gray skies gave way to radiant beams of sunlight. If it weren't for the water atop my windshield you never would have believed that there had been a torrential downpour moments earlier. I exited my car and put on my jacket as I approached the front of the church.

CHAPTER TWENTY-TWO

I didn't remember much that happened moments after watching my father pass from this world into the next. It was as if the last several days were fast forwarded like images from a projector that ran too fast. My body felt numb and none of my senses seemed to work the way that I remembered them. All I tasted was heartache and bitterness, which destroyed my appetite. I didn't feel like eating despite everyone's attempts at getting me to do so. If I had a dollar for every piece of chicken that I saw or for each Peace Lilly that came into my mother's house, I could probably eliminate America's debt problem. I guess in times of grief everybody had the same thoughts when it came to comforting a family. The only problem was that none of it was working; at least not with me.

Each time I tried to fall asleep it was like fighting a fight in which I was grossly overmatched. The only thing that I could manage to do with regularity was shower and dress, which had suddenly become major milestones. There was no denying that depression was having its way with me.

Duane had driven me home from the hospital and put me in bed the night that my father died. He had fallen asleep fully clothed while he embraced me, tears, smeared make up and all. Just days ago we were at each other's throats and here he was providing me comfort in my time of need. I found myself grateful for the mini truce that my father's death suddenly provided us. He and I decided to keep Evan and Michael on their normal routine as much as possible in spite of what already happened, so they went to school for most of the week as we helped to plan my father's funeral. I was thankful for his presence and sound decision-making in a time like this. Duane had taken the rest of the week off and assumed the lead on things that I normally did.

He reached out to Mr. and Mrs. Dillard and to Gabby to explain what happened as best he could. I honestly didn't feel like having to rehash the story and didn't think that I could without having some serious emotional breakdown. The one call that I knew he couldn't make was to Kennedy. Somehow it would make me feel reassured knowing that he knew. I wasn't sure why, but it made sense to me. I wondered if somehow Kennedy knew how much pain I was in. He told me before that I had always communicated with him without even parting my lips. That thought provided me with a little comfort.

Gabby stopped by immediately after hearing what happened which was what I needed. Times of grief helped to put into perspective things that needed to be considered, such as relationships and how people truly regarded you. She was showing me that despite our sometimes bizarre existence that she valued our friendship. Let's face it, Gabby never missed the chance to make a dollar and would even open her salon on Christmas if she thought people would come. The fact that she left work to be by my side in my single greatest moment of need was truly priceless. I didn't have the words to express to her what her presence meant to me. In between our moments of simple chatter to keep me distracted from my pain, I would sob like a disappointed child. My pain was unbearable. It seemed as though my pain had its own pain. Why me?

After having several long hard cries, sandwiched between some gut bursting laughs several hours came and went. Gabby really did a good job listening to me tell her how I felt instead of her telling me how I felt. I had grown sick of people telling me that they knew how I felt and what I was going through when I didn't have a clue myself. It made me rethink my tone for comforting people who endure bereavement in the future. Two people could experience the exact same thing and wouldn't experience it in the same way; that much I knew.

Gabby told me that she had contacted Kennedy and that he sounded concerned. She wasn't really Kennedy's biggest fan, which had less to do with the fact that we were in an affair, and probably more to do with the fact that she really didn't believe in love. She graduated with honors from the school of "love is for dummies." Her thesis was, "screw em then dump em before they hurt you." Her heart had been used as a doormat one too many times, and she had the type of dirt that couldn't be cleaned. It was no use describing what I felt because to her it was a foreign and complicated concept. In spite of her feelings she thought that Kennedy truly felt helpless and wanted to be there for me. He had been calling her since he couldn't call me. My cell phone's voicemail was full and I turned it off since I got the news at the hospital about my father. I would give anything to curl up in his arms, with my head on his chest and take up residence in his suite of comfort and bliss.

Although people meant well I had already grown tired of the well-wishers that came and went, came again, and went again as the time drew closer to put my father in the ground. I could see that things were really hard on my mother so I did my best to swallow my grief and put on a good face for her. I didn't want to be selfish in that regard because although I had lost my father, she lost not only her husband but also her best friend. My mother was the one who would ultimately go through the biggest adjustment of living alone.

By virtue of subtraction our family had been reduced in number and it ended up being me and my mother to execute my father's final wishes for his funeral services. In death, just like life he was detail oriented and had all of his business in order. He wanted a simple service and not some over the top spectacle of grief and misery that in the end did nothing but make people feel worse.

My father's VA benefits as a retired officer were more than enough to take care of his funeral expenses. Our family wasn't that big, so we only needed two limousines. One by one my father's former co-workers, military comrades, friends, neighbors, and of course extended family dropped by my parent's home to pay their respects and reflect on his life and how they knew him best. I never needed a reason to be proud of my father, but as I listened to those long and sometimes repetitive stories I grew strength and some level of solace in knowing that he affected so many people's lives. It was further proof that despite my personal biases, that he was indeed a good hearted person.

I looked at my mother and she even seemed comforted by the many acts of kindness, whether it was flowers, food, or company. I had seen my share of first and second cousins the last couple days. It was shameful how some families only got together after the grim reaper swooped in and collected his ransom. Regretfully so, I belonged to such a family.

My emotions fluctuated in the same manner as a bipolar person's mood swings; without warning. Just when I thought I had cried a lifetime of tears, I cried even more. Even my laughter felt like I was crying only without the tears. I felt like I was at my lowest point and I even considered having my physician call in something to make me feel numb. That's when I noticed the bouquet of flowers in the midst of lilies and sprays. They were an arrangement of wild flowers. The card attached read "Wishing you and your family comfort in your time of need." It wasn't signed but it was his handwriting. It had Kennedy written all over it. I was really crying now, but these were not tears of sorrow, but tears of joy. He was letting me know that although things were limited between us that he was there for me in the best way that he could be.

After getting Kennedy's flowers I felt a small glimmer of hope that things would be okay even though I had convinced myself that the world as I knew it was over. Minutes turned to hours, which gave way to new days and inched me closer to the finality of this very horrible encounter. It was time to bury my father.

Gabby lent me support with making up my face and doing something with my hair, which was an absolute mess. She had to pull off her best styling job to help me look normal and conceal the grief and anguish that was etched all over my face. I was waiting for someone to wake me up from this awful nightmare but they never did. As much as I prayed and bargained with God that he had made a mistake and that perhaps it wasn't too late to correct it and make things the way they were I realized that this prayer would go unanswered when the family limousine pulled up to a very crowded church parking lot.

The sun's rays had broken through an overcast sky and the North Carolina heat was soaking up every bit of moisture that had fallen minutes earlier. I clutched Duane's hand as I looked at both of my sons who sat beside me. I was concerned how they would respond and even thought about leaving them home, but Duane insisted they would be okay. We were all adorned in typical black to signify that we were mourning. I wondered who chose the darkest colors to wear as the official colors of death. Not only was it too hot, but it also made me more depressed.

The car was blanketed in silence as we sat behind the hearse containing all that was left of my father's earthly remains. I think that reality hit my mother with more than she could even handle. Gone was her look of solidarity and in its place was her sobering reality that this was real. My mother's scream, which was more like a tone deafening shriek was soon followed by a flash flood of tears. She was no longer able to contain the hurt that she had managed to conceal up to this point. I hated seeing her in pain and knowing there wasn't a thing that I could do. Before I knew it I was crying myself, which made the boys cry as well. The only dry eyes in the car were Duane's and the guy driving the limo. I simply couldn't help myself.

Duane had to be growing tired of trying to comfort me, my mother, and the boys so he got out and gave them to Gabby who was standing outside of the limousine. When he returned to the car he fanned me while the driver fanned my mother. It was no use we were both emotional wrecks and their arms would fall off before we could compose ourselves.

Seeing the pallbearers carry my father into the church was too much to handle and I knew that my mother felt the same. Arm and arm we managed to garner enough strength to face our major fear by walking into the church. My shades not only blocked the beaming rays from the sun, but they also concealed my swollen and weary eyes. My mother wore a black hat with a vale and gloves to match.

My legs felt like rubber and I thought that I would collapse from the tremendous amount of pressure that this journey had become. Nonetheless we pressed on. As we drew closer to the church entrance I could hear the sound of the organ and I could feel the extra humidity from the packed sanctuary. There were too many eyes staring back at us, each one extending their deepest sympathy meanwhile not one of them willing to take our place or feel our pain. I never knew so many people loved and adored my father. It was somewhat comforting to know that I wasn't the only one.

It seemed like it took twenty minutes for us to make it to the front of the church with all of the "I'm sorry for your loss" embraces extended to my mother even before we sat. Sad song after sad song, followed by more tears, and more wretched sounds from the organ seemed to be how the rest of the service would go. I took one final look at my father in his eternal state of rest. I looked at his lifeless face, looked for his rugged good looks and charismatic charm but they were gone. There was nothing that resembled the man that I had known and loved since I could remember. I kissed him on his cold, lifeless forehead and touched his stiff dead hand. It was more than I could handle and my legs nearly gave way. Duane had to help me back to the church pew. Unfortunately this would be one of those moments that I would never forget, no matter how much I wanted to. I didn't think my life could get any worse.

CHAPTER TWENTY-THREE

Once I was inside of the church I found myself nestled between strangers who made it clear that they weren't giving up the last seat of that pew. It was as if they were pew guardians or something. When I sat down I naturally gazed around my unfamiliar surroundings and quickly noticed that all churches pretty much looked the same and that I didn't know any other person here so far. I took advantage of the solitude that the moment provided and familiarized myself with the obituary of Jacqueline's father provided to me by the usher. My disdain for organs grew by the second as the musician played note after note of death tones. It was as if he wanted everyone in tears. I wasn't sure how any of this was aimed at lifting anyone's spirits.

From what I could gather Stanley Michael Evans lived a good and plentiful life. He had served his country in the Vietnam war, been married to his wife for nearly 40 years, raised a child and has even seen two grandchildren. I never realized that Jacqueline named her boys after her father before now. She had managed to leave that part out despite our numerous in depth conversations. I thought that it was very admirable. That was an honor that I would never have bestowed on my father; neither an insult that I would have given to my only son. After Mr. Evans concluded his military duties he served as a plant manager at a local textile plant near Fort Mill, South Carolina where he retired after over 30 years of service. The man worked the majority of his life and had accomplished things that most people could only dream of. His greatest accomplishment in life according to his own words was being a husband and father. Simple, yet profound I thought to myself.

My concentration was broken when the family processional began and all eyes turned in that direction. The spotlight was on Jacqueline and her family. No matter how much people felt sorry for them, I seriously doubted if anyone would trade places with her family. Nobody wanted to be burying their loved one on this or any other day. I thought seriously if it was me and not Jacqueline and we were burying my father instead of her burying hers. I wondered if I would even shed a single tear or if a part of me would secretly rejoice. It bothered me to realize how cold I had become to my own father. I seriously doubted if this many people would come out of their way to pay respects of any sorts to my father the way hundreds had turned out for hers.

I watched as the family marched inside of the packed and stuffy sanctuary stopping every few feet as hugs and well wishes suffocated them. The front of the church couldn't have been more than 20 feet away, but it took nearly 10 minutes for them to make it. It was amazing how much Jacqueline resembled her mother; it was as if I was looking at her 25 years into the future. She had Jacqueline's eyes, her complexion, her nose, and even her lips. I guess that she owned them first. Judging from the many pictures of her father, it was clear that her mother's genes had been supremely dominant in that bout of sperm vs. egg. There wasn't much of a resemblance to him whatsoever.

My heart nearly sank in the pit of my stomach when I saw my beloved Jacqueline as she came into view; unblocked by the heads of other onlookers. She was even beautiful in the face of grief and sorrow. I couldn't see her eyes to read her expression because they were concealed by her designer sunglasses. Whenever I looked into her eyes I could always gain a more true sense of how she felt. The view was blocked out like a total eclipse when her husband came into my sight as well. It was like being confronted by your worse enemy. He was the person who stood in between me and Jacqueline's happily ever after. He was the man that until now had only existed through conversation and now he was walking within shouting distance from me, embracing the woman that I loved; his wife.

My eyes remained glued to Duane's back as they were all guided by the funeral home directors to gaze upon the departed one more time before the service officially began. I searched him to see what she saw in him. I began comparing what he had that I didn't, have besides her. I watched helplessly as Jacqueline said a goodbye that nobody ever wants to say. Her body language spoke a hurt that resonated with the entire congregation, because dry eyes were in short supply. I fought my tears back with everything inside of me. Seeing someone you cared about in pain made it difficult not to get emotional. Knowing that she was hurting and not being able to comfort her made me envious of Duane's existence and that envy was growing in leaps and bounds. In fact hate was on deck.

I prayed for strength to get through this ceremony and even questioned whether I should have even come at all. It was clear that Jacqueline and Duane were slightly better off than she led me to believe. In between their shared misery and frequent arguments lied some level of genuine care and adoration that until now, I had been naïve to. In affairs people always had a way of making their spouse seem like the worse person ever, yet they stayed. I had always heard my mother say how answers always came out of death. Through Jacqueline's father's death I was seeing some tough answers to several tough questions that I was having about our future. I felt like such a fool. How could I have allowed myself to feel what I feel for her? I have had friends that I'd known for years and I wasn't sure that I would have driven all the way here to see their father buried. Deep down I guess I had to see things for myself; had to see if we had a future or if this needed to be buried as well. The selfish part of me wanted to see her family and people from her past as a way of connecting the dots to the otherwise fragmented existence that we shared. That thought sounded crazy as it played aloud in my mind.

Several songs and reflections later Jacqueline stood and addressed the crowd of mourners to deliver some words about her father. I feared that she wouldn't be able to emotionally get through it, but she had garnered a tremendous inner strength. She didn't speak words written down, as she obviously had prepared to do so. Jacqueline folded the papers and spoke from her heart instead. She removed her sunglasses, inhaled and visually surveyed the mass that had gathered to say farewell to her father. Jacqueline spoke of her fathers' many accomplishments and honors and her unique relationship with him. Her words made me feel as though I'd been cheated out of a father/son relationship. A part of me was envious, but I guess you couldn't miss what you never had. When she finished her words were met with a thunderous ovation, and many "praise the Lord" utterances.

Just before she took her seat, her eyes met mine. I could tell that she was caught off guard by the look of uneasiness that transformed her expression. Jacqueline had a way of making me feel like I was the only person who existed despite being in a room full of people and today was no exception. I wanted to leave my space in that crowded pew to embrace her the way that I have hundreds of times. I wanted to be the one that she was seated beside at her father's funeral, but I wasn't. She had her husband for that and it was Duane's job to comfort his wife. I was nothing more than a well-kept secret that nobody would ever know about. Right now my truth was hurting in a way that I didn't think was possible.

My mind was sending me the escape I needed; the one that I couldn't get physically. I had gone to that happy place where Jacqueline and I shared so many times. The place that problems didn't exist, there were no arguments, bills, toothpaste tubes squeezed from the middle, toilet seats left up, or drama with in-laws. We shared all that was good with relationships before they turned bad. I was remembering every single moment that I had spent with her since we met. It made me wonder seriously about fate and things being destined to happen. I knew ultimately that we had free will to choose whatever we felt that we could, but maybe some encounters were planned whether we wanted them to happen or not. How else could our encounter be explained? It was the most ironic thing that has happened, yet it made perfect sense. I was giving serious credibility to the whole notion of "soul mates," in the sense that some people were just naturally more compatible for you than others were. I was proof that anyone could get married, and I was also proof that things could go south quicker than the Dow.

The rest of her father's service would remain a blur to me. What I did remember I wished that I could forget, but it was no use. The image of seeing Jacqueline's husband embracing her was something I'd remember for as long as I lived. That drive back to Atlanta seemed much shorter. Maybe it was because I tussled with random thoughts of what needed to happen next with us. Sometimes knowing in your mind what needed to happen versus feeling what you feel in your heart was not always aligned. As much as I knew it would hurt to let her go, it would hurt more to hold onto half of her. When I made it home that evening, after stopping at a Quick Trip for some over-priced gas I had come to grips with what I had to do for Jacqueline and what I had to do for me.

CHAPTER TWENTY-FOUR

The moment my eyes met Kennedy's I felt relief in the midst of my suffering; a measure of joy in the company of all of my pain. I couldn't believe that he actually came to my father's funeral considering our very private existence. If I had ever doubted how he regarded me he showed me with his actions that he adored me. He had said on many occasions that he wasn't big on talk, because anybody could say anything. He was big on actions. His actions had spoken a language that I desperately needed to hear on what had to be the worse day of my entire life.

I was attempting to process so many thoughts about what was going on with the finality of my father's life. I was glad that I got through the service and that I was able to honor him in my own way. Duane kept asking me if I was okay and I lied by saying yes, because the truth was not one that he could handle. The truth was since my father died, that seeing Kennedy in that mere glimpse was the only relief that I've had. Just when I didn't think it was possible to love someone more completely than I loved Kennedy already, was the moment I loved him more. Despite all of the support and kindness shown by Duane recently I knew that I would never feel that way about him and that honestly terrified me. I haven't loved him in that way for seven years, and I wasn't gonna start now. It was what it was. That was the type of truth that not even Jack Nicholson could handle and I didn't think Duane could either.

Suffering through my father's burial was probably worse than the funeral itself. Seeing his body lowered into the bowels of the Earth before being covered by dirt was a level of pain that I didn't know was humanly possible. It hurt even more to see the pain that my mother was enduring despite her attempts at being strong. She had masked her feelings all week and hid behind smiles faker than Mitt Romney's. Despite her attempts of being strong, even her armor began to crack and her vulnerabilities became exposed; she was breaking down. I felt like I had to be strong for her, so I swallowed my grief so she wouldn't have to swallow hers. Right now she didn't have the one person that she could count on to shoulder her huge load, so I had to be that person for her. My mother was all I had as far as close family went. There were no siblings, just me. I was all she had as well, which suddenly began to worry me. I never had to worry about my mother's well-being until this moment.

Death had a way of leaving a gap that needed to be filled by someone else. It now would require our circle to tighten considerably. My father had very large shoes to fill and I was determined to do my part, whatever that meant.

A couple of days had passed by which made it over a week since my father passed away. It was becoming increasingly obvious that although this was a nightmare, it wasn't the type that I could wake up from and realize that it was all just a dream. This was the type of horror that was now my reality. My father wasn't about to walk inside my mother's front door like he had so many times before, no matter how hard I prayed, bargained, or pleaded with God. Whether we wanted to or not we were going to have to begin the business of moving forward and not looking behind or standing still. I had to begin embracing a life that no longer included having my father in it.

Duane was back at work and the boys were in school, so that gave me some much needed time to help my mother pull a few things together. I packed all of my father's clothes in some boxes. They were sorted and labeled for Goodwill, storage, or trash pick-up. I had seen my mother break down too many times looking at his clothes hanging in the closet as if he were still alive, so I had to act fast.

Once the boxes were loaded inside of my truck I had taken them all to their respective destinations and just like that there wasn't a shred of physical evidence aside from pictures to remind my mother of her now late husband. I had even taken the death certificates to a few destinations to provide proof to my father's debtors that he was in fact deceased. Who knew that it took this much to prove a person's demise?

I had to give him his credit; he had all of his affairs in order and didn't leave my mother with any debt. In fact she would now become the beneficiary of his death benefits from several insurance policies. Even in his death he was continuing to take care of my mother.

When I returned I found my mother taking a well-deserved nap in the den with the television now watching her. For a moment I took notice to see the rise and fall in her chest. I didn't need any more surprises after last week. I was all too familiar with the pattern of one spouse soon following the other into the afterlife with no medical reasoning whatsoever. I guess a person could die from a broken heart. I'd have to make sure to keep my eye on her; couldn't imagine having no parents at this point in my life.

Losing my father forced me to look at my own mortality in a way that I never had prior to his passing. I always knew that death was possible, but when it hit this close to home it had a way of grabbing my attention.

I was sorting through all of my father's policies and other paperwork making sure that everything was in order and where it needed to be, so that my mother wouldn't have to bother with anything. There was his military paperwork and most recent results of his annual physical exam, which stated no health problems aside from some arthritis, which was not uncommon. It made me wonder how this otherwise healthy man could drop dead from a heart attack with seemingly no notice at all.

It seemed as though everything was in order with the business of death, and everything that was left would classify as the grim reaper's version of collateral damage. I had all the policies categorized and I was getting in touch with the respective agents to ensure that my mother didn't have to. That was when I noticed a letter addressed to my mother that looked like it had seen better days. The envelope was addressed in the same manner that my father addressed letters to my mother back when he was in Vietnam fighting Sam's War. I would have dismissed it, if it weren't for the name on the letter. It was from a man named

Lionel Jackson. My interest was definitely piqued so I opened it up and read it.

My Dearest Clara,

As usual I will keep it short. I don't get many opportunities to write so I take advantage of them when I can. I won't lie and pretend that being over here fighting Sam's War is a picnic, but at the same time it is the job I chose, even if the job really chose me. So right or wrong I have a job to do in commanding these troops. There is not a day that I don't think of you and miss you. For some men emotional attachment is a distraction, but for me it is the very air I breathe. When you told me in your last letter that you were pregnant I have never been so excited in my whole life. I have already been bragging about looking down on Little Jack's face. I just know it's a boy, even though everybody is taking bets that it's going be a girl. Private Stanley says if it is a girl I should name her Jacqueline. That's okay; I will love her just the same. Everybody knows how excited I am about being somebody's daddy. That has a nice ring to it. Ever since I saved his life he has been going on and on about owing me something. Over here it's us against them. We are each other's family trying to make sure we all get back to see our family. As usual, don't you worry about me; instead tell my unborn child I love 'em. Be strong and I'll see you real soon. I love you.

Jackson

My face owned a twisted expression that mirrored confusion and disbelief. I wasn't quite sure what I had just read even though it was written in the only language that I fluently spoke. A man named Jackson was referring to my mother as if they were romantically involved and he even mentioned my father. This was a head scratcher. What baby was he talking about? I needed answers and I needed them now! I stormed into the den in search of my mother, but she wasn't there. During my brief search for her she turned up in the kitchen over a steaming pot of hot water as she was preparing some tea.

Mother turned to face me as I cried out for an explanation of what I had just discovered. She was crying too which made me feel as though my timing was off and that there was a better approach, but I kept on. It was as if she already knew the question that I had before I could even ask it.

"I saw you reading the letter when I got up to check on you after I dozed off and I understand how you must feel." Tears rose in her eyes and cascaded down her face. "Have a seat Jacqueline, I can explain." I didn't feel like sitting, or drinking tea as I let that be known when I nodded in response to her gesture. "Just explain to me what is going on Mother. I am a grown woman, so just give it to me straight." This was the first time I ever spoke to my mother in this tone and I still found myself leery that she would introduce her backhand to my face, but she didn't.

When she spoke her voice owned a hesitation in which I wasn't familiar with. It was a far cry from the woman who never bit her tongue or minced her words until now. What was different? My mother explained that Lionel Jackson was the author of the letter. He was also married to my mother. I quickly found the comfort of the nearest chair as my knees became weak. She told me that they were married prior to his deployment to Vietnam and apparently she got pregnant on their wedding night. My mother was the biggest abortion critic and made me promise to never have one, so I wasn't expecting her to be a hypocrite after all these years. "What happened to the baby that you were carrying? Why did he mention my father? Were they friends? I rolled those questions off like an inquisitive child.

She reached for my hand as if she wanted to protect me from imminent hurt. "The baby that I was carrying is you Jacqueline." I wished that I hadn't asked so many questions, because I hated the answers that I was getting. "You mean to tell me that my father is not really ....my father? I was speechless; there were no words to do this moment any justice.

"Jacqueline, your real father was my first husband and his name was Lionel Jackson. He and I were married and planned to live a long life together raising you. He was killed in combat two days after writing that letter that you read. Lionel always talked about how much he wanted his children to have a good father in their lives because he didn't. He and the father you know, Stanley were really good friends and they met in Vietnam. Lionel saved Stanley's life while they were in combat and he never forgot it. When Lionel died Stanley made a promise that he would do his best to look out for you. He finished his tour and came to find me. He knew how much I loved Lionel, and that I didn't love him but he wouldn't take no for an answer. He was there for me and he was there for you. I eventually grew to love Stanley and I have never regretted doing so. Stanley fell in love with you from the moment he gazed upon you. Due to his war complications and Agent Orange exposure he could never have his own children, and I never once heard him complain. I know this is overwhelming at once Jacqueline, but you have no idea how this has bothered me for all these years. I hope you understand."

The only thing that I was capable of feeling at this moment was confusion and shock. My emotions were over worked and out of order. I only felt numbness. Maybe that was my best defense until I could figure something else out.

"Mother, I don't understand a lot these days. This is a bit much considering all that's happened. I need a minute. There were no "I love you" exchanges. Just like that I was driving off with my back to my mother and the lifetime of lies that I have been led to see as my truth.

CHAPTER TWENTY-FIVE

My emotions were scrambled worse than a satellite signal during a rainstorm and I was an emotional wreck. I was seriously contemplating the need to sit on a therapist's couch to process the disaster that my life had become suddenly. Aside from grieving the father that I did know, I was now grieving one that I had never met at all. How crazy was that? I wondered how my mother could have kept something like that from me for all these years. Then I wondered if I even wanted to know at all. I was regretting that my curiosity had gotten the best of me. I should've just left well enough by its lonesome and totally disregarded that letter.

When I got home Duane was giving the boys a bath and he had even cooked dinner. It was funny that it took my father dying just to get my husband to pitch in around the house. Not only was I confused about who my real father was, I was confused about who my husband really was. Was he the cave man that lacked sensitivity towards my feelings, or was he this thoughtful man that recognized my worth as a woman? There is no way that I would have ever cheated on this version of Duane.

Naturally I thought of Kennedy and there was no denying that I was in love with him. I couldn't shake that reality even if I tried. If his love was a drug, then I was a happy addict with no plans of an intervention or a trip to rehab. I have never loved someone so completely and I don't think I ever will again. Not even sure if I wanted to be this vulnerable again, especially after the hurt that was just dished my way through death and discovery.

The four of us sat down to a hearty meal of spaghetti, French bread, and salad prepared by Chef Duane. It was simple, but good. Simple was just what I needed right now. I mostly played with my fork by twirling noodles after only taking a few bites. There wasn't much of an appetite where I was concerned. Seeing my boys went a long way in taking my mind off what was wrong in the first place. They were just that perfect to me. I began to realize the things that really mattered in life, at least in my own.

After tucking them in bed, story time, and prayer we said our good nights to one another. It was our customary routine. I found a kitchen full of dirty dishes left by my husband that required immediate attention. There was no way I could rest if my kitchen wasn't clean. It was one of the many habits passed down from my mother. He did cook dinner, so washing dishes was an even trade off. The more things changed the more they stayed the same and Duane was living proof. His trail of clothes led straight to the basement where I was met with melodic tunes of hits from yester year.

When I opened the door he was in his favorite chair with his feet propped upon the leather ottoman stripped down to his under shirt, slacks, and socks. Gone were the dress shirt, tie, blazer, and shoes because they were all left upstairs. Duane had taken down the majority of his dark colored beverage of choice. Judging by the hue of his liquid spirits, he had another long day as a high school principle and it was his way of coping. I appreciated the extra that he had taken on since my father died and as much as I need to be held and listened to I decided to leave him asleep in the company of John Coltrane's best. I decided to shower and attempt to sleep on my own.

After being in mourning and trying to get a handle on the business of death and dying I craved the distraction that getting back to work would provide. I arrived to work earlier than normal desperately needing to immerse my energy into something that I could understand; something I could control. As good as it was being back I could honestly say that everyone from Mr. and Mrs. Dillard, the receptionist, distributors, custodial staff, and even the damn mail man were getting on my nerves with the delicate treatment and acts of sympathy. It was as if they didn't know how to approach me. I had been told everything from, "I know just how you feel," "Don't worry baby, God don't make no mistakes," "It will get better by and by," and "It was simply his time to go." I tried to remain polite and resist the temptation to tell everyone to back off and stop treating me like a 6-year-old child who lost her favorite teddy bear. I simply wanted to be treated normal. I wanted to be treated like none of this ever happened. I wasn't the one who had a heart attack. I wasn't the one who died. In spite of my father dying there was nothing different about me. There was no use whatsoever. To everyone at this office in their mind they were doing what they felt was helping me. Only in my mind they were doing the exact opposite.

After a few days of the "you poor thing," treatment from everyone affiliated with Genesis Beauty I needed an escape in the worse way. I was literally about to lose my mind. I couldn't seek the comfort that I'd normally get from my mother, because she was a big part of what frustrated me the most and to be honest I simply needed to get away from it all. I arranged to do some work in the field away from the office and even away from my home. There was so much that reminded me of all that I was trying to forget and I needed an escape in the worst way. I needed Kennedy. I needed his arms around me, his breathe against my body, his lips against mine, his tongue exploring my intimate places. I needed him now!

Normally when I left my home to work it was extremely difficult but this time it wasn't. As much as I adored my boys I needed to detach to sort some things out in my life. I just didn't feel like the person I thought I was my whole life. I felt as though I was casted to play one role for my entire life and suddenly the script had changed without warning. I needed some understanding of what I wanted to do moving forward.

Kennedy said that he would meet me in Helen, Georgia when I spoke with him a few days ago. It was the place where he and I first truly connected and shared some very magical moments. I was hoping for an encore at this point.

Before checking into the cabin I stopped by the local grocery store to make sure that we didn't have a reason to leave our love nest. I shopped for the ingredients to prepare his favorite meal. Shrimp, scallops, fresh spinach, angel hair pasta, bottled water, fresh fruit, two bottles of cabernet, a few herbs and spices and I was on my way. Arriving before Kennedy did allow me a chance to settle in once I checked on the boys, my mother and Duane.

Making sure that everything was somewhat normal allowed me to focus one hundred percent on Kennedy. I didn't want the burden of caring about all the wrongs that had suddenly consumed my life. I was tired of wondering whether or not I'd finally walk away from Duane and end my marriage, or when my mother and I would be back on good terms. I was also tired of wondering why my parents kept me in secrecy about my real father for so many years. On top of missing the only father I've ever known I secretly wondered about the man who was my biological father. I wondered what he looked like and thought. Wondered what his mannerisms and habits were. The weight of those thoughts nearly bought me to tears and I fought hard to repress them and embrace this moment that Kennedy and I were about to create.

I wanted to be as close to perfect for Kennedy when he arrived so I showered and made sure I was at my best. I had just the outfit that would let him know that he could have his way with me.

Time had a way of being cruel. It seemed like frozen molasses traveling uphill when you were waiting for something to happen, but more like freight falling from a sky scraper when you wanted something to last forever. In this moment Kennedy couldn't get here fast enough and we couldn't be together long enough.

CHAPTER TWENTY-SIX

When I got Jacqueline's call I dropped everything to go and be with her. I sensed the desperation in her voice; she needed me. Things hadn't been exactly stable concerning my affairs lately. Although I was producing good numbers as a drug rep and making my visits there was so much uncertainty with territories being shifted, and positions were getting axed left and right. It seemed like no matter how much these greedy CEOs made they always wanted more. Then there was Miles and his needs, not to mention my status as a divorcee. To say that things had drastically changed since meeting Jacqueline would be putting it mildly. It would be like saying Hitler had no love for Jewish people. I put all of that behind me, jumped in my Honda and drove to meet Jacqueline because she had a lot on her mind. Once again I was putting her needs before my own.

She was dealing with her father's death and I knew that although she was trying to act strong, she needed a friend in the worse way. I was on my way to Helen Georgia to meet her. She had already driven out there just to get away from a world she no longer understood; a world that didn't understand her anymore. Helen was the site of where we truly became intimate in more ways than one. I replayed those memories over and over in my mind as my car drew closer to the cabin. It was the place where I fell in love with another man's wife. It was the reason why I was returning to the scene of the crime, all in the name of love.

Part of me was excited about seeing her and reconnecting. It seemed like several life times since we enjoyed each other's company. I hadn't seen her since we caught eyes at her father's funeral several weeks ago. Those weren't exactly ideal terms. The other part of me was nervous and it wouldn't allow me to embrace the moment for what it was. I only saw what it used to be, or rather what I wanted it to be.

In my mind I played about one hundred scenarios of what would happen when I first gazed upon Jacqueline's beautiful brown eyes. Wondered what I would do. Wondered what she wanted me to do. I didn't have exact answers for those questions. There was a part of me that wanted to simply embrace her to let her know that I was there for her. Another part of me wanted to disrobe as I entered the cabin and ravage her body like a sex-crazed beast.

My mother would tell me that life had a way of providing answers to our questions in its own time. Whether or not we liked the answers would be a different scenario altogether.

Upon arriving I was greeted at the door by Jacqueline's signature fragrance, candle lit background, soft melodic tunes courtesy of her iPod, a glass of red wine, and most importantly I was greeted by her beauty. Jacqueline was dressed in a black French maid's outfit, fishnet stockings, red bottom heels and enough cleavage showing to ignite my erection at a record pace. Her skin was glistening and permeating with aroma that had me in a hypnotic trance. She held me as her prisoner and there was no escape possible. Her eyes beckoning me to come closer, so I did.

I took to her like a moth to a flame. Our lips met and stimulated our respective passion towards one another. I felt her energy charging throughout my entire body. Jacqueline unbuttoned my shirt and placed kisses on my neck and chest where they felt best. She kneeled and unbuttoned my jeans and pulled them down, taking my erection inside her warm and wet mouth. I was about to lose my mind as she pleasured me orally making my lower extremities tense and tremble as she bobbed her head up and down. Slow and then fast. It was perfect. In that moment Jacqueline made everything better. She managed to right every wrong that I had and nothing else mattered.

A trail of my clothing lie in wake as we made it from the foyer of the cabin into the living room face to face, lip to lip, tongue to tongue our embrace was relentless. I unleashed her bountiful allotment of breasts and pleasured her already stiff nipples with my tongue, which made them stiffer. She moaned louder and breathed heavier whispering my name in a seductive tone. I stroked her legs, enjoyed the feeling of the thigh high fishnet stockings against her skin. It excited my erection even more. I turned her back to me, moved her mane to the left to expose her neck and I began to plant soft kisses on her neck and back. She grew more and more excited as she braced against the back of the sofa and arched her back. I entered Jacqueline's walls of ecstasy and stroked her gently and then I stroked her with authority. She was on the brink of orgasm when she propped her right leg on the sofa and cried out for me to go deeper and harder. So I went deeper and harder. I went so deep and hard that her body tensed and jerked its way to a violent orgasm. Her words became less clear, yet I clearly understood what she meant. We spoke the language that lovers do when they are in perfect harmony. She was totally satisfied, but I hadn't cum.

Jacqueline led me to the kitchen counter and hoisted herself upon it. She walked as though her legs were weary from the intensity of the orgasm. We kissed intently. Lips embraced and tongues mingled like distant relatives reuniting after a long hiatus. By this time I removed her maid outfit and all that remained were the stockings and pumps. She wrapped her thick thighs around my body and ushered me into her walls of pleasure. Jacqueline's nails dug deeper into my back and I thrust every inch of my manhood inside of her. With every stroke I pretended to right every single wrong between us. I was convinced that I could make her mine.

"Oh Kennedy……..I miss you so much baby." She insisted. My name rang out through the four walls of the tiny wooden cabin that served as our private love den. Although she told me time after time that she loved me it just didn't quite convince me given our circumstances, but it did feel good to hear it every time she said it.

With her red bottom heels pointing to the sky I was feeling like this moment was a piece of heaven on earth. I grabbed her right and left heels, as her legs stood tall like redwood trees. Her back was flat to the counter as she lay back looking at me with lover's eyes. I stroked her as if the survival of humanity depended on me taking her to that happy place lovers go. She felt so good to me. Felt as if she were mine. We had both reached the mountaintop of ecstasy and had succumbed to the forces of a spine tingling, toe curling, leg trembling, and speech stammering orgasm. Her once stiff legs slowly fell, as we lay in a warm, dank embrace chest-to-chest and heartbeat-to-heartbeat.

Moments later once I mustered enough energy I pulled away from her in search of some water for hydration purposes. When I returned from the fridge I handed Jacqueline bottled water and I drank one myself. She was standing which gave me a chance to gaze upon the beauty that her body was. I didn't see the evidence of bearing children and approaching forty when I looked at Jacqueline. All I saw was sheer perfection. Suddenly my apprehensions had dissipated and it became crystallized why I always dropped everything the moment she called. No other woman had ever made me feel the way that Jacqueline did, and despite the vulnerability and the limitations it was a feeling that I didn't want to ever be without.

CHAPTER TWENTY-SEVEN

The jets were on full blast and steam arose from the water, as we sat in the hot tub. It was the perfect temperature and seemed to provide the ideal distraction from a reality that we desperately wanted to escape. Neither of our lives mirrored what we wanted it to. After hours of love making we both needed a moment to recover.

I clenched her feet and massaged each of them as I pleaded with Jacqueline to relinquish her problems and give them to me. I knew enough about her to know when she was concealing things. She didn't have a very good poker face and it was obvious that she was not doing particularly well. Under the circumstances of her father's death I could only imagine that she had a lot on her mind.

Our less than perfect existence didn't allow adequate time for intimate conversations in person so there was nearly a lifetime that we needed to catch up on. I listened intently as Jacqueline unloaded some heavy things on me that undoubtedly would be difficult for even the strongest among us.

She told me about the details leading up to her father's death that I was sure she had rehearsed a thousand times. Then she told me about discovering that her biological father was not the man who was recently funeralized. He wasn't the man that raised her, had shown her how a woman was supposed to be treated, or the man that walked her down the aisle to be married. She explained the letter that she discovered while going through her father's insurance policies and other important documents. Jacqueline told me about her biological father whom was her mother's first husband being killed in Vietnam and never being able to gaze upon her unborn face. His joy of fatherhood would never be fulfilled in this lifetime. Instead the man who raised her felt a sense of duty to ensure that Jacqueline was raised and cared for the way that he knew that Lionel Jackson would have wanted. All because he felt he owed a debt he could never repay, Stanley Michael Evans did his best impersonation of both father and husband. Until his death Jacqueline was never the wiser. He never made her feel as if she wasn't the most important thing in his life. Even though he could never have any children of his own it was next to impossible to love a child any more even if it were biologically linked to you.

As Jacqueline talked I sat and listened, all the while we grew closer. I wished that I could take away all the pain she felt. Wished that I could make everything right, but I couldn't. All I could do was listen. Jacqueline hadn't been able to share her most intimate thoughts with her own husband. She was too busy trying to be strong for too many people and never had the opportunity to grieve the loss of both fathers.

It made me think about my own situation. Made me think of how useless my father was even though he was still alive and I could pick up the phone or see him whenever I wanted to. In many ways he was dead as well. He died the day that he walked out on my mother and I became collateral damage. I found out the hard way that divorcing your wife sometimes included your kid as well. I was realizing in this very moment that my resentment towards him was deeper than I cared to admit. In fact it resided deep within the bowels of hatred. If that son-of-a-bitch died today there would be no tears shed in this direction.

In a crazy way I was envious of Jacqueline despite the pain she was feeling. She had not one, but two men who adored her more than life itself. Two men had left Earth with the sense of duty towards Jacqueline no matter what, and I didn't have one who gave a damn about me. Thinking those thoughts made me feel worse than I cared to feel, so I suppressed them for both of our sakes.

I moved closer towards Jacqueline, her head rested on my chest as my right arm wrapped around her. I sipped beer and reminisced on our first trip to Helen when our romance was in its infancy. Two years later and there was a lot of change, but with change some things still remain the same. On one hand we were deeply in love and undoubtedly connected in a way unlike anything that I could ever have imagined. I was officially divorced from Marley, but Jacqueline remained at home with Duane. I was no longer bound by the confines of a marriage but she was. I could come and go as I pleased and see whomever I wanted to, but she could not. I was no more than a well-kept secret for Jacqueline. I was a matter of convenience and comfort when her world became cluttered and uncertain. I believed that she loved me in a way that she hasn't loved her husband but that was no longer enough for me. It wasn't enough to continue our existence in this manner. Here we were doing the same thing after two years expecting a different result. We were being insane. Something had to give, and it had to give soon.

"Jacqueline...I realize that you have been through a lot and you know that I would do anything to take away your pain." She nodded in agreement as she starred at me with those innocent brown eyes. "I'm not trying to pile on you, but I've been thinking. We need to decide what we are gonna do for the sake of us. I can't go on like this." Those words flew from my mouth like a bird leaving its cage. I felt a sense of release, but I could tell that she felt a sense of burden given her facial expression. This wasn't what she wanted to deal with; at least not in this moment. Suddenly I didn't really care about this nonexistent timetable that Jacqueline had us on. I was a bit more concerned with a thing called urgency. She seemed to be the only one comfortable in this situation. She had her life at home with her husband and their two children and she had me as a fall back plan whenever she needed it.

Maybe it was the whole finality of death that changed my perspective, but things crystallized for me since attending her father's funeral. I had begun to consider that since we all had an indeterminate amount of time on this planet that life came down to doing whatever it took to make that time count. No matter how many days a man saw in his lifetime, his life could be summarized in a matter of moments. A few brief periods of time would tell his story. It would tell if he were married, had children, his career exploits, and any affiliation he may have had. That would be it, no more, no less. A man's entire life could be summarized in a few paragraphs called an obituary. I had resolved to let death take care of its own business and decided to focus on life. I wanted to ensure that when I closed my eyes for the final time that I would leave this world with no regrets. I would leave knowing that I did everything that I could for Miles and that I did what made me happy.

Later on that night there would be more talking, more sharing, and even more lovemaking. The one constant that remained with us was how quickly time elapsed when we were together. Jacqueline and I slept snuggled in a lover's embrace as night became engulfed by the presence of dawn. Once again our moment had come and gone and it was time to head our separate ways. It was time to resume our respective version of normalcy. We had to leave the comfy confines of Fantasy Island and venture deep into the hustle and bustle of the real world. I would return to a world of pharmaceutical sales, an incomplete manuscript and a bachelor's pad while Jacqueline would return to her husband, rapid growth in the beauty industry and her two children. No matter how much we wanted to we could not take up permanent residency in Helen, Georgia.

We exchanged heartfelt goodbyes and tender embraces as we departed. Throughout our two-year romance she and I have parted ways many times but this one had a different feel to it. Although I couldn't figure it out at the time this goodbye would prove to be a defining moment in our relationship.

CHAPTER TWENTY-EIGHT

True to form as I drove away from Jacqueline she became an object that appeared smaller and smaller in my rearview mirror when I drove away until she wasn't even in sight. Miles between us would continue to grow as I headed towards Atlanta and she headed towards Charlotte. Just like that I was missing her already.

Her scent lingered on my flesh as I inhaled Jacqueline with every rise and fall of my chest. She was still with me. We were still together. I could feel her breathe against mine, her flesh against my flesh. I felt our tongues intertwined like musical chords in a well-played symphony. I replayed every single second of our time together and chased memories of time long gone, time that would be no more.

My trip home was consumed with thoughts of Jacqueline and all of the memories that we have made. Things were so much more different since Marley and I divorced. I had limitless options when it came to seeing other women, yet the one woman that I wanted more than anything belonged to another man. That man was her husband. Jacqueline was married no matter how I tried to slice that pie. She simply didn't belong to me. I only wanted her to and sometimes no matter how much you wanted something you simply had to accept what was.

The road trip allowed me to make sure that everything in my world was as it should be. Miles was on the up and up, Marley and me remained cordial, my mother was doing fine, and I was still ducking Marcus, while writer's block was kicking the crap out of me, I hated my job with every growing second, and I hated my father more than republicans hate Obama. I think that was it. That was my pathetic life in a nutshell.

After getting back to Atlanta I decided to make the most of my day. I needed to stay busy to distract my mind from thoughts of Jacqueline. I already knew that she was back home which meant she was back in her world as well. A world of increased responsibility and job growth with Genesis Beauty, a world of bath and story time with her sons and good night kisses, and unfortunately a world of wifely duties that provided the type of good night kisses for her husband. That thought made my stomach turn like bad dairy products. It made me want to vomit with disgust and envy. I absolutely despised the thought of her sharing her lips with him or making sounds like she made for me. I have survived in this crazy maze of love by convincing myself that Jacqueline only did those things for me. I was the only man who could make her yearn for me. Her G-spot was tucked away in a location that only I had the GPS coordinates to find. She was only home with Duane for the sake of the children, but there was nothing else. She was captive to a miserable marriage held together by Evan and Michael. Somehow leaving Duane would be too much devastation for them to handle. Jacqueline has said on numerous occasions that he was a wonderful father but a horrible husband. She wanted to stick it out for them. Taking a back seat to her boys was one thing, while taking a back seat to Duane was something entirely different. That wasn't going to happen.

I made several rounds to doctor's offices while I switched back into pay the bills mode. I reminded myself of how I actually earned a living and ate, no matter how much I grew to despise it. A man had to earn a living. My parents had taught me the importance of good work ethic so I was going to be a professional regardless. I flashed both my charming smile and my ever-growing knowledge of antidepressants and erectile dysfunction medication. I knew that one pill would make a man not want to have sex and the other could make him become a porn star. The government sanctioned both; meanwhile some politicians were trying to legislate birth control for women. Didn't make a whole lot of sense to have a bunch of hard penises running around and not have women on birth control, married or otherwise. It was hard to make sense of an anti-abortion, anti-birth control, pro-erectile dysfunction stance but that seems to be the overwhelming consensus of these right wing nuts in congress.

After my professional duties had concluded I headed home seeking refuge in my tiny condo. I unloaded my duffle bag from my trip to Helen, Georgia to see Jacqueline. My place was clean because I cleaned it before I left. Old habits die hard. My mother always made sure she cleaned up before leaving so she could return to a clean home. It was the way she did things and now it was the way that I did things. It made sense then and it makes sense now. I put on some laundry and thawed out some chicken for my dinner. Eating out was not only expensive but it was getting old. I would grill some chicken breasts and sauté some spinach.

Marcus had sent a dozen text messages after I had ignored just as many of his phone calls. I was avoiding him like swine flu because I knew that I wasn't mentally in the place where I needed to be in order to write. I was trying to buy time and time was very costly these days. It was out of my price range and offered no layaway plan or finance options.

I needed to clear my head of Jacqueline, Marcus, legalized drugs, my father and anything else that required sustained mental focus because I had none to offer. Mentally I was a poor man without a roof over his head that didn't know where his next meal was coming from, didn't have a pot to piss in not to mention throwing it out of a window. I was hanging on by a thread that was rapidly giving way.

A run was what I needed. It was the only thing that I didn't have to think about doing in order to do. I would just put one in front of the other and run until my exhaustion conquered any lingering thought that occupied my mind like citizens occupying Wall Street. I changed clothes, grabbed my Garmin Forerunner to map my course and calculate my mileage, as I set out on a quest to outrun my problems.

I picked up Peachtree in Midtown Atlanta opting for a little more scenery than Stone Mountain provided me. I was familiar with the terrain after running the Peachtree Road race a number of times since moving here. The timing couldn't have been more perfect given that it was after rush hour and the city wasn't nearly as busy as it was earlier, in spite of Atlanta's growing tourism. I had more than enough to distract me as I ran the main streets of the Peach State's capital city.

The more I thought of Jacqueline the more I ignored my body's subtle whispers to stop and take a breath. I kept on pushing through the physical pain and fatigue that my nearly 40-year-old legs had offered me. It was no match for the emotional pain and mental anguish that I was feeling.

As I approached the exact point in which I started running it signified the end of my run. I was sure that I had seen the finer points of Atlanta and all that Peachtree street had to offer but the entire 9.45 miles that I just ran according to my Garmin all seemed like one big blur. I didn't remember a thing and for a person trying to forget a lot this was good. I stopped my watch, gathered my breathing and began to stretch. The hour and twenty-three minutes it took to finish was time well spent and thus far put me in the mental space I needed to be. My head felt clear and for the first time in a very long time I was focused.

My mental clarity accompanied me back to my condo and decided that it would stay for dinner. It seemed to be in no rush to leave, which I decided to take full advantage of the opportunity. I contacted Marcus to get the specifics regarding the business end of writing and beyond. I was having my share of apprehension over being judged by so-called critics and doing publicity. That was new territory for me, but necessary to make this all happen.

Marcus explained that he used a few sample chapters to garner interest and explore options that I had never considered. The meeting with producers was to sell me on the idea of converting the novel into a screenplay and doing a movie. All of this sounded great and was a tremendous honor but there were just two minor complications. Number one the book wasn't finished, and number two I was having some serious writer's block. My creativity was as scarce as good ideas at a republican convention.

I ended that call with Marcus understanding that I needed to get focused to maximize this wonderful opportunity. Things usually didn't just happen by themselves without people making them happen. This was something that I needed to make happen.

Later on that night, consumed with what felt like dead legs I attached myself to my bed with plans of getting some much needed sleep. Before I knew it I was deep inside of REM sleep, which allowed me to dream. As I lay in the image of death my thoughts from my subconscious flashed by like a movie projector. Everything seemed so real and most of it was enjoyable until I got to my childhood. Images of a broken hearted child with my face were constant. Times when my father first left home; times when he promised to come and get me and never did; and times when I remembered becoming less and less significant to him. I relived that hurt as if it just happened. No matter how much you repressed certain moments in your life the stained memories never leave you. No matter how absent my father was in my life I clung to irrational hope that he would want to be a part of my life. The more hope I held, the more he disappointed me. He consistently disappointed me until I finally stopped holding out hope that he would ever be my father again. After crying myself to sleep one night I made myself a promise that I would never shed one more tear for him. I committed my father deep within my memory's museum and considered him a "use to be." My dreams had taken me to a place I didn't want to visit and made me feel things I didn't want to feel. Sleep was overrated I thought as I abruptly awoke from my slumber.

Looking around provided instant comfort that I was only dreaming and I immediately became oriented to time and place. Even though I was no longer sleeping, the feelings of hurt and vulnerability remained and clung tightly to my emotional state. It made me think of my role as a father and it made me grateful of the relationship I had with Miles. My son knows that I love him and I was looking forward to him moving with me next school year.

My mind shifted to Jacqueline, but this time I considered her sons in a way I never have before. Thankfully, I was no longer clouded by selfish aspirations of she and I being together regardless of everyone else. I thought of what that would do to them. I thought of the looks on their faces if they didn't see their dad each day or how divorce would drastically change their lives. I wondered how many nights they might cry themselves to sleep. Wondered how they might grow to hate Jacqueline for leaving their father and reject my very existence in their lives. I wondered how long it would take them to put Duane in any other place mentally than the one they already had for him. No child deserves that. No man deserves that either in spite of what I felt for Jacqueline.

I would have to do what I never thought that I could do when it came to her. I would have to be the one to make the decision regarding our fate and not leave it to Jacqueline. I wouldn't burden her with having to choose between her family and me. I didn't want that on my conscious. I didn't want to repeat the same sins of my father through selfish actions of my own.

During the early hours of what was the dawning of a new day, with only my mental clarity to accompany me I decided to fall upon my own sword and end our affair once and for all. I couldn't take it back, but I could make sure that it was no more. This is what was best for everyone. Sometimes what was best wasn't what was easiest, but it was what needed to be done.

I emailed Jacqueline in the most sincere and clearest words I've ever written and told her my decision. I asked her not to contact me and I would do the same. I apologized for the manner, the tone, the lack of closure, and for the lack of response that I would give from this point forward. I didn't apologize for meeting her, or even falling in love with her and maximizing that love in our limited existence. I told her that I didn't have any regrets that I could think of and that was accurate to this point. I wished her and Duane well and I begged her to insert herself fully into her marriage. I never wanted to be the reason why Jacqueline divorced her husband. That was a burden that I didn't want to carry with me. Hopefully her life without me would provide answers to the questions that she needed answers to. I told her that I was truly thankful for the memories and promised to never let them go.

Just like that I hit the send button as I swallowed a very tough swallow. Email wasn't the best way to tell a person you loved like I love Jacqueline goodbye but in our case it was for the best. There was no way that I could gaze upon her face and look into those beautiful brown eyes and let her go. This was by far the toughest thing I've ever had to do but I did it anyway.

Alone with mental clarity I continued the theme of forward thinking by opening up the document that was my incomplete manuscript and re-dedicated myself to finishing what I had already started. I sipped herbal tea and fell back in love with my ex-girlfriend, who I'd neglected for so long. I fell in love with my writing again and took full advantage of the opportunity this moment provided.

CHAPTER TWENTY-NINE

Watching Kennedy drive away was torture. I missed him already and his car was only a few feet away. I thought for a moment as he lingered in his car before pulling off about that scene in The Bridges of Madison County, where Clint Eastwood pulled in front of Meryl Streep and her husband at that traffic light and waited for her to come to him. She had her hand on the door handle but couldn't muster the strength to go through with it. I felt like getting in the car with Kennedy throwing caution to the wind, leaving this life behind and living in the moment with him for the rest of my days. Just like Meryl Streep, I did nothing in spite of what I felt.

`Being with him for the last day and a half had provided me with the only measure of true happiness in what seems to be my darkest hour since losing my father. I never realized how much I absolutely adored this man until our latest encounter. Just when I thought it was impossible to fall, I fell further. I could truly say that I loved Kennedy completely and without reservation. I loved him with my mind, body, and with my soul. It was as if God himself put Kennedy on this Earth with implicit instructions on how to love me. He was the only person who truly got me. I didn't have to pretend to be anyone other than Jacqueline.

I only wish that I had met Kennedy first and I never would have made the biggest mistake of my life by marrying Duane. The boys were the only good thing that has come from our marriage and nothing else. As harsh as that thought might have sounded it was the truth. I was regretting more and more every day being married to Duane. I was beginning to hate my husband simply because he wasn't Kennedy King.

Kennedy has been more adamant about making a decision but I don't think that he truly understood my situation. I'd leave my husband in a heartbeat but there was so much more to consider. He thought that everything was black and white but there were gray areas and maybe even hues of different colors when it came to leaving Duane. I didn't think that he was being totally fair but I could empathize with him. He was single now and I was still married. Kennedy could pursue any woman he wanted to, yet he was waiting on me. It was tough to think of another woman being in his arms; him holding her or kissing her or looking at her the way that he looks at me. Those images were too much to stomach so I dismissed them and shifted my thoughts to finding a solution to this mammoth sized problem.

I didn't want to put my boys through an ugly divorce and uproot them from a stable two-parent environment. I didn't want to have the burden of sifting through a messy divorce and have to face uncertainty. I finally admitted to myself that deep-rooted fear was a huge factor as well. I had never truly considered my own fears; fears of Kennedy and me not making it, being a single mother, and how people would look at me now especially my mother. No matter how I sized up this dilemma I was a coward plain and simple.

I trailed his car as we cascaded down the mountainside through the beauty that Helen, Georgia had to offer. This time of year autumn had commanded the leaves to show a multitude of colors that were simply breath taking. I took in the German style architecture in this tiny but unique town that boasted a population of no more than 420 people. Helen was probably best known for being home of the Cabbage Patch dolls I adored as a little girl, its version of Oktoberfest, and for hot air balloon races. For Kennedy and me Helen would be known as the place where we fell in love with one another. Helen would always be the place where we truly bonded in every way that two people could possibly bond. I would cherish those memories for the rest of my life.

I watched as my lover traveled in his direction, then I traveled down my own road. Parting was such sweet sorrow. It was always great seeing Kennedy, but agonizing when we had to leave. Time was very cruel sometimes and had its own agenda giving little to no consideration for others.

The closer I got to Charlotte the more I was reminded of why I needed to get away in the first place. There wasn't much about the life of Jacqueline Tate that made sense to me lately and as a result I wasn't very happy to say the least.

It was one thing to have your father die and it was two things to find out that your father died before you were born and you didn't find out until after you buried the man you always knew as your father. It was even confusing to think about. It totally changed things that I thought were solid in my life. I was questioning what else was false that my mother hadn't told me. I totally adored my father and I missed him dearly. What he did was totally admirable and I know that most men would not have done so regardless of how many times someone saved their life. That was a once in a lifetime occurrence and I was grateful for Stanley

Michael Evans. He would always hold a place in my life that no man could ever take and nothing could change that.

I wanted to know more about the man I never met. I wanted to know what type of man Lionel Jackson was. I wanted to know if I had any of his physical features or personality traits. I wanted to know the man whose blood was my blood, the man who matched my mother's 23 chromosomes with 23 of his own and provided the X to match her X, which made me a female. Were there traits that ran in his family that I need to be aware of for the sake of my boys and myself? What are my biological relatives like? Did they know about me? My mind was working overtime but clearly there were more questions than answers to this point.

Despite everyone sympathizing nobody truly understood because it wasn't them it was me. I was the only one who knew what I was going through and one was very lonely company. In fact it wasn't even company at all. Emotionally I felt like I was stranded on a deserted island with no resources whatsoever to sustain life and time was running out on my entire existence. I felt displaced in the life that up until now I understood, had accepted and it had accepted me. I rode those turbulent thoughts all the way back up I-85 north to Charlotte as I searched for a glimmer of optimism that things would work out in my favor. So far I hadn't found any. Instead I shifted my focus to seeing the look on Evan and Michael's faces when I got home. Those faces always had a way of making everything right that was wrong. I couldn't wait to catch up on everything in their respective worlds.

By the time I got home Duane and the boys were still at work and school which allowed me some time to prepare dinner, unpack, and tidy up a little bit. Duane was a complete slob and it seemed that he had done his best to convert our home into a disaster area. Clothes were all over the house, no laundry was done, the boys' beds weren't made, toothpaste was in the sinks, and carry out containers were gathered atop my kitchen counters. I wanted to scream but figured it wouldn't do any good. I was raised that cleanliness was next to Godliness so I focused my efforts on bringing order back to my home.

With some serious multitasking things were back to my standard in no time. All toilets were cleaned, tubs sparkling, mirrors clear, counters disinfected, floors swept and mopped, and the dishes were done. Now I could cook. It was one thing to clean up after children but an entirely different thing to clean up after a grown man disguised as a child. Inexcusable, I thought to myself.

I heard the garage door opening, which alerted me of my family's arrival. The boys barreled into the kitchen from the garage nearly colliding with one another in total disregard of my strict rules about indoor conduct. They were excited to see me and I was more excited to see them so I overlooked their rambunctious play for now. "Yay, mommy's home!" They both exclaimed in unison. Michael was hugging my right leg and Evan clung to my left leg. I knelt to hug them both. Even though it had only been four days since I last saw them it felt longer. It was as if they hit a mini growth spurt in my absence.

After several rounds of rapid fire I was adequately abreast of all the happenings in their lives. I knew everything from what they were learning in school, to the latest kindergarten gossip at recess.

We all ate together including Duane who seemed a bit distant and caught up in an entirely different world, which was fine with me, but different for him. The boys didn't put up much of a fight and ate their vegetables so dessert was in order. I was quickly falling back into my mommy routine of dinner, baths, and bedtime. The boys were in their pajamas and in bed. Michael insisted on his choice for story time, but I let them both choose one in the spirit of fairness. I seriously doubted if Duane had been reading to them the last several days anyway. I kissed them both as we said our good nights. "Mommy, where is grandpa?" asked Evan. "He's in Heaven" inserted Michael before I could respond. "Well, when is he coming home? We miss him." These were the conversations that no parent wanted to have with their child. Even as an adult I had more questions about death than I had answers for. The boys were getting smarter every day and I knew that they would naturally have more questions. I explained to them that their grandpa was with God in Heaven and that one day we would see him again. I did my best to fight back tears so they wouldn't get more upset. I told them that each time they prayed at night they could say a special prayer and ask God to give grandpa the message so that he would know they were thinking of him.

I knew that this would be an ongoing thing especially since they were so close to my father and he was the only grandfather they have ever known. When I left Evan and Michael I knew that a good cry and some alone time was what I desperately needed. I was grateful for the distraction that Duane's long day provided and I took full advantage of the moment by soaking my body in a warm bubble bath. Consumed with thoughts of what if, why me, and what next, the next half hour came and went in a blur.

I was out of the tub, had dried off, moisturized my body and dressed in pajamas that were all about comfort. I didn't want to communicate anything sexual to my husband whatsoever and made sure my body language reflected that. After making my rounds through the house the boys were sound asleep and Duane was in the basement. Cigar smoke permeated the basement and seeped out when I opened the door, along with musical notes from yesterday's legends. He was consuming his favorite cognac, lost in a daze. His cup was half empty in more ways than one where I was concerned. I left him in his world and decided to turn in for the night in preparation for a busy workday I checked my email account.

Checking email for me was a task that could take hours and tonight was no exception. There were some hard deadlines that Genesis was up against regarding upcoming shows, product distribution, and all things related to marketing. I was playing some serious catch up and with a new title came new responsibilities. Mr. and Mrs. Dillard didn't need to tell me that with extra pay came even higher responsibilities because I put that pressure on myself. No matter how compassionate people were during your bereavement period they would expect you to "get over it," at some point even if you weren't. I was fully prepared to put my best foot forward in spite of my emotional state. Several hours had elapsed after I responded to the emails and I was about to power my laptop down and catch up on some rest when I saw an email alert from Kennedy. This was a pleasant surprise since I never close my eyes without thinking of him. With great anticipation I clicked onto his email to see what my lover had to say.

CHAPTER THIRTY

To: jacqueline tate
<JacquelineTate@genesisbeauty.com
From: kennedy king<Kking@me.com
Sent: Thursday, October 18, 2012 1:46 AM

Subject: Us

Jacqueline you know that I love you. I knew from the moment that our eyes met that there was something about you that I could not resist. It's the reason why I couldn't go on and never see you again. It's the reason why I have overlooked your husband and the fact that you remain married even though I am not. When I met you I had my share of problems with Marley but feeling what I feel for you helped me to realize that I would never feel that way for her, so we divorced. I wanted her to be happy and I want to be happy so it made sense.

You have said that you love me like you have never loved another. Part of me believes that, but lately that part isn't getting the benefit of the doubt. You are going to have to deal with the part of you that has allowed this situation to last for two years. I'm afraid to say it, but if not there will be other Kennedys. Take that for what it's worth and simply know that I can't do this anymore. Please understand. I hate it had to come to this, but it has. I will not contact you and I am asking you to not contact me. This is not the way that I wanted us to end, but there never would have been a good time.

I realize that I love you in a way that I have never loved any woman, but you are someone else's woman and not mine. In a very irrational way I believed one day that you would come to me free and clear. That is no longer my expectation. I am going to have to move on. In a perfect world we would be together and we wouldn't have to hide our love from anyone. This is not a perfect world and we are not perfect people. I will continue praying that you get peace and understanding concerning your father's death.

I truly wish you well in your career endeavors and I hope that you insert yourself fully into your marriage for the better. I don't want to be what holds you back or be the reason your marriage ended. I don't want that burden Jacqueline. I wish that we could maintain some level of a friendship, but there is no use in kidding ourselves; we can never simply exist as friends. There would never be a day that I hear your voice or look into your eyes without wanting to be with you.

The last two years with you have been the best two years of my life and in a crazy way I don't have any regrets meeting you, or falling in love with you. I only regret not being the man that you chose to spend your life with. I regret not meeting you sooner but I understand why you stayed. I will cherish every single memory that we have made, while keeping my fingers crossed that maybe we'll meet again under different circumstances. Take care Jacqueline Tate and know that I enjoyed every moment.

Kennedy

Kennedy's email jumped off the screen of my 15-inch monitor and rang loud and clear. I was pleading with my brain that maybe my eyes weren't working, that somehow I hadn't read what I just read. This had to be a mistake. The lump in my throat made it difficult to breathe and my heart pounded with desperation and suffering. I pulled my bottom lip into my mouth and clenched it with my teeth as I finger combed my hair with my right hand. Clearly agitated and confused, I couldn't believe Kennedy's words after such a wonderful two days in Helen. I was in total shock unable to conjure up any rational reaction to his words. He didn't have the courtesy to say any of this to my face. It was as if he was planning to disconnect and I was the last to know.

He chose to send an email like a damn coward. How could he do me like that? How could he simply reduce our existence to a faceless correspondence over the Internet and ask me to not respond? I wanted to call him at that exact moment but cooler heads prevailed.

My emotions vacillated; one moment I was angry and the next moment I was on the verge of tears. I didn't know how much I could take lately. Kennedy had been the one constant in my life over the past two years. I have grown to count on him in ways that I have never counted on another human being in my entire life. I have trusted him with my most intimate feelings, and had shared things that made me embarrassed to even think out loud. Most importantly I had given myself to him in a way that I didn't even know was possible. I had done things with Kennedy sexually that I hadn't even done with my own husband. At the end of the day he sends an email to do his dirty work for him. Not a phone call, or a face-to-face encounter; a fucking email. I was pissed.

After pacing around my bedroom for what seemed like a mile back and forth I forced myself to swallow two Xanax pills to keep from hyperventilating. My doctor prescribed them to help me relax and cope with my father's death. I wasn't a fan of medication, but felt the need to throw caution to the wind and control this category 5 emotional hurricane that was on the horizon. I was feeling vulnerable and destructive and didn't like either of those emotions and I changed course moments after the medication began taking effect. My breathing returned to normal, which decreased my rapid heart rate. Despite the loopy feeling it did allow me to calm down enough to fall asleep. I was looking forward to taking an uninterrupted timeout from the chaos that consumed my world. We all slept in death's image, totally oblivious to that which resembled life.

That night I slept on the metaphoric hard bed that my mother always warned me that being hard headed and stubborn would cause. As much as I hated admitting that she was right, most of the time she was and this was no exception. This was a hard bed to sleep on, and the rest that it provided me wasn't a good one. All because I ignored what I knew in my mind wasn't right to begin with has put me in a place where my heart has steered me directly into this pitfall. How could I have allowed this to happen?

I sat up in my bed reflecting on this whole experience searching for perspective on everything. I thought back to every encounter with Kennedy. Thought of how easy our conversations flowed out of nowhere. We could talk about anything and oftentimes, we did. Our compatibility expanded all comprehension. It made what we were doing make perfect sense. It justified our actions in spite of all the reasons why they were wrong in the first place. Anytime a person felt just in their actions, they were capable of doing anything that came to mind from murder to adultery and everything in between.

The moment our eyes met that night over two years ago and I reciprocated the smile that he offered me, lingered in his presence, and exchanged phone numbers and met him for dinner was when I began justifying the actions of being in an affair. I had invested my emotions into a man that wasn't Duane and I did it for two years. I had created an entirely different life with Kennedy separate from the life that I was supposed to be living. Every night before I slept he was the last person I thought of and the first person I remembered when I opened my eyes the next morning. I have grown so accustomed to Kennedy that I knew getting over him was not going to be some shrug of the shoulders. It was going to take some time, especially under these circumstances. Everyday I'd wonder if he was slowing down enough to eat and hope that he wasn't overdoing it with work. I would always miss his subtle text messages just when I needed to smile, or his words of wisdom when I was feeling overwhelmed. I'd always miss having someone to share everything with and knowing that I wasn't being judged, but totally understood.

Later that morning, I did my best to conceal the pain and confusion that I was feeling since resting on Kennedy's words via email. Duane and the boys were out of the house and off to school. I knew that sulking in the house was not in my best interest so I decided to go into the office and distract myself with work.

CHAPTER THIRTY-ONE

A whole two weeks had passed since I emailed Jacqueline and we have not spoken since then. No emails, phone calls, text messages, FaceTime, Twitter, Facebook, LinkedIn, telegrams, Instagrams, or telepathic exchanges. There was no contact whatsoever. This was a first. We had never gone this long without some type of exchange, but it was for the best. It was painful and I wanted to cave in and reach out to her just to see how she was doing, but I didn't. I wanted to know that she was doing okay. I wanted to know that she was healing from her father's death, and getting answers to the questions that bothered her the most. I wanted to take away all that frustrated Jacqueline, but that was no longer my role. In fact it never was in the first place. I desperately wanted to hold another man's wife in my arms as if she were mine. Thinking those thoughts, as painful as they were helped me to put things in perspective.

My mental clarity remained a close companion which allowed my thinking to become crisp, rational, and void of fictitious happy ever after thoughts. It was bitter and difficult to stomach at times. It reminded me of frat parties of yesteryear when I consumed my share of liquid spirits that went down easier than Mitt Romney tells lies and made everything seem fun only to come back later and haunt me in the worse way. Jacqueline had been like a drug to me. To see her, touch her, smell her, taste her, and feel her made me fall deeper and deeper under her seductive enchantment. The more I had the more I wanted. She had penetrated the core of my emotional fortress like a Trojan horse and taken my heart as her prisoner. I was seeing her when she wasn't there and even smelling her upon my flesh when it had been weeks since we bonded last. I was having withdrawals kicking this sweet drug called Jacqueline Tate. My empathy for addicts was increasing daily and I was praying the Serenity Prayer while working my own 12-step program.

I knew that simply avoiding Jacqueline wasn't going to make me forget her so I had to find a way to channel that part of me into something productive. Every time I thought of her I wrote. When I wasn't thinking of her, which was rare; I wrote. I took full advantage of my clear mind and became a disciplined writer using Jacqueline Tate as my muse. Every conversation, every moment of contact, every embrace and every minute of our existence traveled the highways of my mind nonstop. The night I sent her that email I wrote for hours. I wrote until night gave way to light, only pausing to answer the call of nature. I ignored my cell phone and constant complaints from my overworked fingers in the form of cramps. When I finally stopped that morning my word count was 30,000 words in approximately 6 hours. I was in a writer's zone and my fingers seemed like they were magical. They were tap dancing atop the keys of my word processor like Sammy Davis, Jr. In one night I was able to double the output of what had taken over two years to produce. To that point I was only able to give Marcus three chapters, and made excuse after excuse for my literary shortcomings.

He pulled some strings to have my chapters reviewed at some pretty big publishing houses as well as some reviewers with clout that rarely if ever reviewed work from un-established writers such as myself. They were putting pressure on him, which meant that he was putting pressure on me to produce a finished work. Some would say that pressure bursts pipes and that was true in some instances. I would counter that pressure also makes diamonds, and in this case it helped me to produce a gem. I submitted my 86,354-word manuscript to Marcus ahead of my self-imposed deadline, although it was severely behind the one that I had long ignored.

The hard part was over and now I had to cross my fingers and pray that other people liked my work more than I did. Writing was such a subjective process I thought to myself, but it was what it was. I would have to be patient and allow the process to run its course. In the meantime I still had bills to pay and doctors needed samples for their patients so I continued to work the job that I hated to afford the lifestyle that I loved having; a very simple equation.

After a few days of a normal work routine I was meeting Marcus for lunch. It had only been 48 hours since I sent him my manuscript but it seemed closer to a decade. Waiting was torture and it seemed as though every second lingered like a bad memory.

I arrived before Marcus did, which gave me some time to grab a good table at the quaint coffee shop in Midtown Atlanta. It was lunchtime so the daily grind of hustling and bustling was on full display in the city that was now becoming the "Black Hollywood." Atlanta was once again changing up the entertainment industry pretty much the same way it did with Hip Hop music in the 90's. Now television and movies were being shot in Atlanta and not just the ones that Tyler Perry was doing. I sat down in nervous anticipation, with only the company of a medium roast cup of coffee drizzled with Splenda and a drop of half and half to lighten it up. It tasted perfect I thought as I sipped my coffee and waited on Marcus.

People came and people went as I waited for Marcus to arrive. The anxiety manifested itself through my left knee as it bounced up and down while I manipulated several applications on my smart phone. Halfway into my cup I was greeted by a pair of $1000 dollar grey suede loafers that gave way to a complementary blue pin striped suit, crisp white shirt, and grey tie. It was Marcus and he was in full business mode, talking on his iPhone while he was texting on his other iPhone. The life of an agent was a bit much for me I thought as I stood and waited my turn to shake his hand. He ended his call and put his phones where they rested best, one on his right hip inside of a black case and the other atop the table in reach of his left hand.

"What's up man?" I blurted out. "How do you do it all? The clients and the women." I joked.

"Sorry I'm late, but you know how it is. He countered. "It's a hard job, but somebody gotta do it." He returned a joke of his own and we both laughed. His arrogance was ever present. Marcus declined on my offer to buy him coffee and instead he began to inform me of where things were. The anxiety that dissipated while we joked had returned tenfold. My heart felt like it was beating out of my chest cavity. With a business tone and a poker face Marcus sensed my anxiety and urged me to relax.

"Take it easy K2, I haven't seen you this nervous since we were pledging back in college. I had your back then and I have your back now." Marcus taking me back down memory lane didn't make me laugh, but it helped to ease my anxiety and put things into perspective. I sipped my coffee and did a better job of listening and breathing at the same time. He explained news that was difficult to accept but I had no choice because I knew that he was serious.

Marcus told me that he submitted my manuscript to three publishers and they each wanted to purchase the rights. They couldn't believe that I was a first timer and felt like the book would resonate with readers both male and female. Two of them even felt like there was a chance of movie potential. It was a good thing I was sitting down. I couldn't believe what he was telling me. He continued detailing the next steps of choosing the best deal, which would no doubt offer, the best advance, royalties and priority ranking. There was editing, formatting, cover designing, author photo, dedication, acknowledgements and about a hundred second glances to ensure it was market ready. It all sounded so intimidating but I shrugged it off and figured it was all a part of the process.

Marcus continued in agent mode and remained a zillion steps ahead of where my mind was. He talked about photo shoots, radio and television appearances, and book tours. I was a private person and never once thought of myself as the celebrity type. Maybe this was why I had kept my writing to myself and procrastinated for so long. "Don't worry Kennedy, I will take care of everything. All you gotta do is be where I tell you to be. Got it?" He smiled an arrogant person's smile and I nodded a reluctant person's nod.

"My friend, your life as you know it is about to change," Marcus proclaimed!

My mood became cautiously optimistic as I did my best to embrace this moment. I searched for all the good and focused less on my insecurities. Instead of what if, I asked why not? Marcus's phones began ringing in harmony, which alerted him that our meeting was over and he had to focus his attention on his other clients. He mouthed his exodus and focused intently to his other business while walking towards the exit. I sipped my remaining coffee as I swallowed his words.

Not wanting to count chickens before they hatched, I didn't see anything wrong with sharing the good news with the people who matter the most in my life. I called my mother, and I called Miles to fill them in on everything I figured they needed to be filled in on. My mother was excited pretty much in the same way that she was excited about everything I've done since pooping on my own. I could always count on her support. Miles was excited and supportive; telling him meant telling Marley as well. There was something missing even in my moment of triumph. I couldn't tell the person that I loved and had grown accustom to sharing so much with. I couldn't tell Jacqueline about having my book published and see in her eyes that she was equally if not more excited for me. I fought the urge to call Jacqueline with everything inside of me as I headed towards my vehicle leaving the scene of a productive business meeting with my best friend who doubled as my agent while roasted coffee permeated my olfactory and ushered me outside in the same manner in which it had welcomed me moments earlier. I decided to embrace all the possibilities of what was going to happen next in my life and focus less on what had already happened.

CHAPTER THIRTY-TWO

With what seemed like the weight of the world on my shoulders I began to feel my knees buckling and my grip of life as I knew it was slipping away. I was no Atlas and the internal social worker in me knew that I couldn't last at this current pace without having a nervous breakdown or worse. I was missing Kennedy like an orphan missed their parents. There was nothing that I could do to keep me busy enough to make him go out of my mind. This man was undoubtedly etched onto my soul and my soul yearned for him every passing minute.

Gabby obviously sensed that I wasn't close to being myself earlier when I saw her for my hair appointment and insisted that we meet for drinks. Normally I wouldn't think that alcohol consumption in the middle of the week made sense given the fact that I wasn't much of a drinker and with my hectic work schedule, but today it made perfect sense.

The world I knew and loved was rejecting me like the rich rejected the poor. My marriage was a joke in poor taste, I was grieving the loss of two fathers one of which I knew and one I never knew, most importantly Kennedy was no longer a part of my life. It was too much at one time; too much for two lifetimes.

Despite our sometimes rocky friendship and awkward moments Gabby was once again proving to be a dependable person during my time of need. She listened intently as I shared my inner most feelings about Kennedy, Duane, my mother and fathers. The more the liquid spirits went down the more my inner feelings came up. Martini after martini she fed me my therapy. It felt good to be honest about my situation in a way that I hadn't been before not even with myself. The truth could sometimes be a bitter pill to swallow and very ugly when it was revealed. Even in the midst of my ugly truth I felt a sense of relief in sharing it with Gabby. She didn't judge me or tell me what she thought I needed to do; she simply listened to a friend whose life was in shambles.

All of my masks were removed and I was totally uncovered in plain view, vulnerable to Gabby's scrutiny. I waited on it to rain on me like a monsoon. She wasn't one to hold her tongue for anyone and possessed no filter when it came to others. Gabby was a lot of things but most importantly she was honest. I braced for her harsh judgment; even wanted it but it never came. Instead she simply held my hand, looked into my eyes and remained a supportive listener. It just felt good to be heard, felt good to be understood. Lately it seemed like I was existing in a foreign land and Gabby was the first person who spoke my language.

Our one sided conversation helped me to put some things in perspective. I was able to reflect on Kennedy's words in his infamous email about not making the same mistake and inserting myself back into my marriage. I could go on for days about Duane and his shortcomings and I would be accurate in my assessment, but I had never considered my own contributions to our marriage. I had long since disengaged emotionally from my marriage before I ever laid eyes on Kennedy King. There was no way that I could have become that involved with another man if I hadn't. Duane wasn't perfect by a long shot but even he didn't deserve what I had done to him. I had to make sure that I exhausted every measure possible to salvage our marriage. I had to make sure that if things ended that I would truly have no regrets.

I was going to have to bury my feelings for Kennedy and move on with my life. The weight of our existence was worse than the fact that we were no longer involved in each other's lives. At least this way I wouldn't have to operate in secrecy or feel forced to choose between my husband and my soul mate.

My ugly truth had been birthed during my conversation with Gabby and it was now a living and breathing entity. It rode shotgun in my SUV as I departed Gabby and a place called MEZ located in the Epic Center in down town Charlotte.

I decided to re-insert myself into my marriage and assume the position that I vowed to over seven years ago. I'd overlook the multiple disappointments that Duane has dished out, his dismissive ways, his filthy ways, his caveman DNA, his cigar smoking, his poor physique, his lack of affection, his poor attention to detail, the fact that he doesn't even know I prefer wild flowers over roses, his lack of consideration for my career, and most importantly the fact that he was not born Kennedy King. I would learn to look past those epic fails that in no way compared to my indiscretion for the last two years. That truth I knew would remain with Gabby and it would remain with me until my dying day. He didn't need to know that.

My life was like America's economy. There were more than enough problems to go around but no quick fixes.

It was going to take not only a good plan of action, but also patience to turn things around.

Duane and I have talked about taking the boys to Disney World but hadn't gotten around to doing so. I figured now was as good a time as any and they were old enough to remember the experience. Putting good use to our timeshare I booked our resort for the Christmas holiday when both Duane and the boys would be out of school. I would invite my mother as well. Not only did we need to mend our relationship as mother and daughter, but she needed to get away and do something other than cry herself to sleep. This would be the first Christmas since my father's death and I knew it would be difficult. Holidays were more depressing after the loss of a loved one. I recalled my professional experience doing grief-counseling groups during my social work days so mentally I was bracing for that challenge. Only now it was personal for me. I was the one grieving the loss of someone I loved dearly. I figured what better time to begin a new tradition. It was bad enough that my father wasn't coming back, but it was worse that I couldn't take away the pain that my mother was left with.

I couldn't wait to see the look on the faces of Evan and Michael when I told them that we were going to Disney World for Christmas. I couldn't imagine them being more excited than I was. I remembered my parents taking me to Disney World as a child, just the three of us. Sitting atop my father's broad shoulders as we entered the gates to Magic Kingdom is a memory that I will always treasure. He always told me that I was his princess, always told me that I was beautiful. I embraced the emotions afforded by those thoughts and became even more appreciative of his role in my life.

After a good cry I began to smile as if my father was wiping away the tears that streamed down my face in the same manner that he had always done when I was a child. I had that same feeling of comfort when he demanded that I look him in his eyes when he assured me that everything would be okay. No matter how bad things were in my mind he made them better with his words. Even after the expiration of his physical existence his words that resided in my heart were still making things better. I wished that I could just have one more conversation with my father to tell him how much I appreciate everything that he did, but I knew my wishes would go unanswered. Instead I began to write him a letter. Even though I knew that his earthly eyes would never see it, I hoped his spiritual eyes would. It was another intervention that I had done with my clients to help them process their unresolved grief issues. I pulled out a legal pad from my workbag, a black ink pen and began writing my deceased father a letter that he would never get.

Since you've been gone, things have changed considerably. Okay, things have been a living hell for me. My heart is broken and it has been since you died. Seeing you at the hospital and knowing that we would never hold hands, talk, laugh, or embrace again in this life was the hardest thing to accept. I am doing my best to look after mother the way that I know you would want me to. She tries to appear as if things are fine but I can see that she is really struggling and there is nothing I can do. This has all felt like a nightmare that I can't awake from no matter how hard I try. I wish I knew that you were doing well. I tell myself that you're in Heaven but I don't really know what happens to people when they die. Knowing the type of man that you were and the life that you led I would like to think that God has you in His plans. By the way tell God that I'm not as mad with him as I was, but clearly not happy at all. The boys miss you and ask about you all the time. They pray for you every night. It seems like sometimes they understand the finality of death and other times they don't. I hate they had to experience death so early in life. It feels bad as a parent when you can't shield your children from the horrors of this world. Guess I gotta come clean about some things. I know that you aren't my biological father and I must admit that it angered me initially. It was too much at one time. I have had time to think and your actions made me even more proud to call you father than I ever have been. You are the man that has always been there for me and nothing will ever diminish our relationship. I carry you around with me every day and I am even passing you onto Evan and Michael. I am so proud of the sacrifice that you made for not only me but also for my mother when you didn't have to. Thank you for proving that a person's word is truly their bond. You kept your word to Lionel Jackson and you never wavered. You knew that my mother didn't love you, but you married her anyway so that I would have the father in my life that Lionel Jackson wanted me to have. I will never forget that and I intend to do everything in my power to make you never regret the choice you made. I am however curious about the man who was my biological father for a number of reasons. There had to be something about him to make you feel personally indebted to him. I wonder how he looked and I wonder if there is any surviving family that knew about me. I understand now why I never truly felt bonded to your side of the family and why they never seemed to embrace my mother. It makes perfect sense now after all these years. I hope that you don't for one moment feel slighted by my position. There is not a man alive or otherwise that could ever take your place in my life. I will always be your little princess. I know that you said over and over that I could never disappoint you but I am afraid that I have. In spite of the way that you and mother raised me, I managed to veer off course morally. I cheated on Duane by having an affair for the last two years. Quick math should tell you that it was going on way prior to your death. I have fallen in love with a wonderful man named Kennedy. Even though I knew it was wrong and had opportunity after opportunity to end it I did not. Kennedy finally ended things because I couldn't. Honestly speaking father I have no remorse whatsoever and I know that sounds bad. I have never loved anyone like that, never felt more alive, never desired anyone like that, and I don't know if I will again. It taught me that true love is not a myth and in spite of the obvious wrongs, it was a beautiful experience. You would have loved him too if you ever met him. I know that you were not always Duane's biggest fan but you believe in the institution of marriage and what it means to take vows seriously. I'm sorry for letting you down and I understand if you see me differently. I have decided to put that behind me and really focus on Duane and trying to do my part to fix our marriage. I am gonna try my best to uphold my vows and not contact Kennedy even though I want to badly. Christmas is in a few months and Duane, Mother, and me are taking the boys to Disney World. I know how much you loved the holidays and how different this sounds, but we are all adjusting to a different world without you. I know I rambled on a bit, but we haven't spoken in a long time and so much has happened. Try to send me a sign letting me know that you are well, and I will take care of things that mattered to you the most on this side. Just make sure you don't do anything that spooks me out. You know I'm a bit of a chicken. I love you so much and miss you in ways that you cannot imagine. I'm going to go to bed now. Talk to you later, your princess always Jacqueline Evans Tate.

My left hand rested atop the legal pad, the ink pen seemingly empty after all of the scribbled words to my father were done. I put my pad back into my workbag and secured my belongings in my home office when my eyes took notice of the figure that took residence in the center of my desk. It was an hourglass figurine that Kennedy had given me. He said that time was cruel whenever we were together. It never lasted quite long enough, but took forever until we saw each other again. He said that the hourglass would represent each and every moment that we had shared and that anytime I looked at it, I'd be reminded of all the good times between us never to forget them. His words never made more sense until now.

I sat at my desk and reached for the figurine until I held it in my hands. All of the sand rested in the bottom as if time was no more. In many ways it represented the end of our great love. As tears rose in my eyes and began to free-fall down my face I turned the hourglass over to begin again. With every bit of sand that sifted its way from the top to the bottom I was reminded of good times with Kennedy. I was taken back to the first time our eyes met, our hands touched, our lips kissed, our genitals mingled, and our souls blended. I remembered falling in love all over again in Helen, 20 orgasms in Tampa, and making love for the first time in Atlanta after the Bronner Brothers show. I remembered countess conversations about any and everything that lasted for hours and hours, yet they never quite lasted long enough. I had shared my fears and ambitions in life with Kennedy. He knew a side of me that not even my own husband knew.

Although the circumstances couldn't have been more wrong, I knew with everything inside of me that we were supposed to be together. For every excuse that I'd offered about the timing not being right, or not wanting to break up my unhappy home, the bottom line was that I simply made a choice. Every choice in life had consequences and my choice to remain with Duane would present its consequences to me very soon. I just hoped and prayed that they were consequences that I could live with.

CHAPTER THIRTY-THREE

D ear father, as promised I am doing my best to keep you in the loop with the comings and goings of your beloved family. It's nearly Christmas again, which means that we are taking the boys to Disney World. They enjoyed the experience so much the first two years when we took them that we just kept on doing it. They have gotten so much bigger since the last time you saw them which was over two years ago. They are seven now and I can't wait until their front teeth grow back. It is getting increasingly difficult to understand a word they say. I am making sure that they never forget their wonderful grandfather and how much he loved them. They send up prayers to Heaven every night on your behalf. I hope that you are getting those.

Also as promised I am making sure that mother is taken care of. She and I have both gone to grief counseling and although she misses you she is doing much better. I have even begun teaching groups at the hospital on grief. It is helping me to deal with my loss by helping other people deal with theirs. Even though she tried to live on her own, we decided to move Mother in with us to keep an eye on her. My job is requiring a bit more travel and it is comforting to know that she can care for the boys and not have the responsibilities of maintaining a house on her own. We sold the house, which was so hard to do considering all of the wonderful memories there but it was for the best. Maybe it will provide cherished memories for another family.

It should be noted that I have never contacted Kennedy King and he has never contacted me again. I still think of him and I will always have a place in my heart for him as long as it continues to beat. I believe those feelings were real, so I'd be lying to you if I said that I didn't regret my decision to not leave Duane for him especially after all that happened. I dove back into my marriage and did my best to set aside our differences to really see if it was salvageable. Things did get better for a moment and then the bottom fell out. Two years ago we took the boys down to Orlando after the first time I wrote you and things could not have been better. I had never seen them so happy, at least not in a long time. Mother was happy and it did all of us some good to leave our grief and awkwardness in Charlotte to escape to Florida for nice weather and a needed distraction.

Duane and I started actually talking to one another and it seemed as though our communication was headed in the right direction. Anyway midway through the trip I was up checking my work email while everyone was asleep and the truth leapt off the screen and bit me. Duane was the last to log onto my laptop and didn't log out which meant that his email was still open. I know that I probably should have simply closed it out in the spirit of trust considering my own lack of untrustworthiness but I looked anyway. It wasn't really hidden. There were hundreds of exchanges from him and a woman that he has been seeing for some time now. She knew all of his whereabouts, she knew that he obviously wasn't happy with me, and she talked graphically about their sex life. They both talked about their amazing sex.

My initial reaction was to douse him with a pot of boiling water as he slept carefree but cooler heads prevailed. I forwarded the messages to my email just in case he tried to deny it. I swallowed that truth like liquid fire. It did not go down easy. I did it for the sake of my boys and my mother and not for Duane. They didn't deserve a tense vacation in the wake of all that was going on. I smiled and played the role of loving wife, mother, and daughter so that everyone else could have a great Christmas. I learned to smile through my teeth shielding a lie to anyone who thought that I was happy.

That year ended as the worse year in my entire life. I made a promise to myself that I would make sure to do everything in my power to make things better. I started attending the grief counseling and my therapist helped me to put some things in perspective. I had some things going on within myself that I was in denial about. It helped me to deal with Duane and our situation in a more appropriate manner. I was hurt that he was cheating and rather carelessly at that, but so had I. Even though I was sure there had been more women throughout our marriage none of that mattered. When I finally confronted him the straw that broke the camel's back was his lack of denial. It was as if he wanted to get caught. It was in a man's DNA to lie; yet he didn't. I was even willing to overlook this considering my own indiscretion but the look in his eyes let me know all that I needed to know and that was, that no love resided among us anymore.

We had been two people in a marriage where we fought more than we made love and both of us had arrived at a place where there was no fight left. Honestly I was at the same place before I ever laid eyes on Kennedy and didn't want to admit it. He wasn't the first man that I had seen and thought that he was attractive before, but considering where I was in my marriage and seeing him when I did was a perfect storm. I have never felt the depths of love for any man like I did for Kennedy and while it was beautiful it was also scary at the same time. I feared it because of the circumstances and I am prayerful that I will experience it again only without limits.

I never brought up Kennedy to Duane, but I did let him know that I knew about his affair and that I thought that if we cared enough about not only our boys but also ourselves that we should divorce and move on. I understood Kennedy's words better about not wanting to be what tore Duane and me apart. He was right in so many ways because our affair was actually helping to keep me married. It was how I coped with being unhappy for so long and if I would have stayed married to Duane I probably would have found someone else like Kennedy. I didn't want to be a serial adulterer. One time was enough.

So, on that note we divorced each other a little over a year ago. In the end it ended up being a simple process that neither of us contested. It wasn't messy and we have shared custody of Michael and Evan. Duane continues to take them to school each day, and I pick them up. Having Mother has helped the process tremendously and Duane and me do our best to shield them from the ugly side of divorce. We go to all of their school functions together and we even decided that vacations together for now would make the most sense.

I know that one day as he moves on and I move on things will get complicated, but so far it hasn't happened.

It's been about a year and yes I have dated a guy or two, but I'm in no rush. I even thought of reaching out to what was familiar by calling Kennedy, but haven't found the strength to. I'm sure that he has closed our chapter and moved on with his life. I don't think I could stomach being rejected by him. Life has already shown me that timing is everything when it comes to love, and time waits for no man or woman. Who knows, maybe I'm hoping to stumble upon Kennedy or a man just like him someday. Crazier things have happened and a girl can still dream right?

Anyway, with the help of my counselor she helped me to also realize that my unanswered questions about my biological father Lionel Jackson required answers. I didn't like the prospect of going the rest of my life not knowing. I had to know, so I took a trip to the Deep South in the heart of the Confederacy. My journey led me to Selma, Alabama. Between Google and the Veterans Administration I was able to locate his place of burial with no problem. I kept on telling myself that I was doing this for all the right reasons each time a sliver of doubt crept into my mind. It's what kept me going every time that I wanted to drive away from a world that never knew me only to head towards one that I didn't want to know anymore. Talk about being between your rocks and hard places. Something in my spirit made me press on, provided me with comfort, and told me that it would all be worth it.

I didn't tell Mother that I was going because I didn't think that she would understand. I thought that she would feel somehow as if I were disrespecting you. I certainly hope that you don't feel that way. I sincerely hope with everything in me that you understand my need to know more about what has been kept a secret for my entire life. Finding that out has made me empathize with people who find out they were adopted later on in life. Even though you're grateful to the people who chose you, you will always wonder about the side of you that you know nothing about.

I had the greatest father a girl could ever ask for, yet I still want to know about the father who never got to see me take my first breath, first steps, smile, invite him to tea parties, or wipe away tears and tell me it would be okay, tell me I was beautiful even when I didn't feel like it, or walk me down the aisle to be married. I am blessed that you did those things for me, I truly am but I'm sad that he wanted to but could not. Hope that's no too confusing to you. Hope that you understand the thoughts that clung to my mind and reminded me every chance they could that they were here to stay. They ate at me the way flesh-eating bacteria devours flesh. I took flowers to his gravesite pretty much the same way that I do for you. His tombstone was smaller and obviously more worn down considering the amount of time that it has been there. When I got there it felt awkward, as if I didn't belong or had made a mistake. It was like introducing myself to a stranger but I pressed on fighting my anxieties to make the most of the opportunity. I introduced myself as I sat beside his grave. I thanked him for being the type of man that could touch another man's soul to the degree in which he touched yours to make you do what you did. I let him know that even though we have never met a day on this Earth that I was proud of him all the same. I told him how wonderful you were as a father and how he should be proud of you as well. I bought photo albums of me in my childhood from birth to recitals, graduations, proms, college, sorority, wedding, and pregnancy pictures which made me embarrassed at how much weight I had put on. I thought that he would want to know about his twin grandsons that he never met either. I lost track of time as I rambled on and on all the while vacillating from laughter to tears at a moment's notice. In a strange way I felt a connection to that part of me that had caused so much conflict since discovering my truth. In my moment of revelation what happened next was startling. I was jarred back into reality by the polite tap on my right shoulder that nearly made me wet my pants. You don't sneak up on people at cemeteries I thought to myself as I frantically turned to confront whoever it was. As much as I wanted to say my words to Lionel Jackson certainly didn't want any super natural experience.

"Sorry sweet heart, didn't mean to startle you," she said. I stood to greet the silver haired senior citizen who was alone and indeed a fleshly being like I was. She was no ghost even though gauging from her wrinkled face, hands which clutched her cane, slumping posture, the thickness of her eyeglasses and her aged voice she had no doubt lived longer than most of the people who were already lying in rest. I was wiping the seat of my pants as I stood face to face with the senior citizen who had interrupted my time with Lionel Jackson. I couldn't help but feel defensive being in a strange place on a personal quest for answers; meanwhile granny had spooked me out. I exercised good manners the way that you and mother always taught me to.

"I'm okay ma'am, it's no big deal," I countered. The old woman's expression froze as she studied me. She was back to making me feel weird and uncomfortable. Then she removed her thick eyeglasses and looked into my eyes as if she were peeping into my soul. The old woman began crying as she reached for my hand. Her frail, wrinkled, and arthritic hand clutched mine as she searched for words to justify her actions. She spoke in a very southern accent that told me she hadn't had much of a formal education and had lived through some dark times during Jim Crow days and never thought Obama was possible in her lifetime.

"What took you so long baby? To come home...I knew you would return." Clearly she was having a demented moment I thought to myself totally dismissive of her words until she told me that she was the mother of Lionel Jackson. It all made sense. I was holding hands with the paternal grandmother that I never met. The woman who had the same eyes as me once the eyeglasses was removed. She told me that they were also Lionel Jackson's eyes and she knew it when she first saw me. Now we both were in tears. She told me that she knew about me and never forgot me. She also encouraged my mother to marry you after Lionel Jackson died. She knew it was best for me and it was what Lionel Jackson would have wanted.

To make a long story short meeting her made the whole trip worthwhile because she helped me to answer so many questions. I now know how Lionel Jackson looks, how he was as a child and I know about his character as a man. I understand how he touched your life and moved you the way he did which ultimately has touched my life.

Even though that meeting was a year ago I continue to keep in touch with her.

Anyway father, I know that I have said a lot but a lot has happened the last two years. As promised we are about to head to Orlando for yet another Christmas away from home with the boys; mother, me and Duane. I will be bunking with mother and Duane will bunk with the boys. So far everything is falling into place and working itself out day by day. You continue to rest or whatever people do in Heaven and know that I am taking care of things down here. I love you, and tell Lionel Jackson I love him too. Thanks for making me feel like the most beautiful girl in the whole world even in your death.

Until next time, your loving daughter Jacqueline Evans.

CHAPTER THIRTY-FOUR

When Marcus told me that my life was going to change that day we met in Midtown, he didn't quite prepare me for what to expect. My debut novel, "No Regrets" was a highly anticipated release following the buzz that had been created by the reviews and overall positive feedback by top reviewers and bloggers. These people had the type of influence that could either make or break a writer in this industry. If their opinion said that it was good, everyone wanted to know why. I was fortunate and humble that they found favor in my literary exploits.

In life timing was everything and I was intent on not letting this moment escape my grasp. The title in many ways seemed appropriate for not only my novel but also for my life moving forward. I had my share of regrets in life and my relationship with Jacqueline was probably my biggest regret. Initially I regretted the way that we ended, and that I didn't meet her before Duane did. I regretted not fighting for her and second-guessed my decision to simply bow out gracefully.   I regretted being so emotionally vulnerable given the limitation, but lately I have gotten to the point where I simply regret ever laying eyes on her. It took me almost two years after we ended to get to the point where I wished that I never even met her in some regards.   That truly would've been the only way to avoid the pain and humiliation that our affair eventually cost me.

I had examined and cross-examined every angle of our existence with the precision of a top crime scene investigator. I combed over and through everything and I even weighed the pros and cons. On one hand meeting her, knowing her, and loving her was a blessing of sorts. I had never met someone more compatible with me, or someone who was easier to get along with. I could just be me and she even understood my inner groans. She knew when I was happy, anxious, satisfied, or frustrated without me having to say a word. Jacqueline even delighted in making sure what was wrong became right. She would send me text messages to make sure that I had eaten because she knew I would get too busy to eat at times. My concerns were her concerns; my joys became her joys, and my sorrows she took on as well.

I was no amateur when it came to sex and thus I've had a beastly lion's share. Although I had been with more experienced lovers never had I been with a woman sexually quite like Jacqueline. It was as if she was the yin to my yang, the Mars to my Venus, the Quincy Jones to my Michael Jackson; we were good together. The loving was better every time, which made us both crave more and more. What she lacked in experience she made up for with her presence. She was always totally present in mind, body, and spirit. When I made love to her, I made love to her in all three phases all at the same time. Until that point I had only had sex with a woman's body only to mind fuck her later.

In spite of our limited existence we were able to create a lifetime of experiences that a part of me will treasure for as long as I can remember. She helped me to reach a level of intimacy that I didn't know was even possible. I anticipated hearing even the most insignificant details of her life. I still think of inside jokes that only she and I would know and find myself randomly bursting out loud in laughter.

Then there are the cons I'm left to deal with. As great as we were and in spite of the fact that we met under less than ideal circumstances it was difficult to really believe that she felt the same for me as I felt for her. When I began to fall in love with Jacqueline it helped me realize that I was only holding Marley back. I knew that I really loved Marley at one point and I would always have love for her but not the kind of love necessary to endure the rigors of a promise that ends when death dials you up. It made sense to me for us to part ways for everyone's sake including Miles. While Jacqueline didn't cause my marriage to fail, she certainly provided confirmation that I had long since emotionally checked out. My emotional portfolio was empty and there was nothing further to invest in stock that consistently underperformed. I thought that eventually she would do the same after declaring her feelings for me. Her countless I love you like no other rants became less and less convincing without any actions whatsoever to support them. It became too difficult to overlook the fact that she went home every night to lay beside a man as his wife regardless of how she felt about me. At the end of the day the titles were what mattered most. A wife had certain duties to perform whether she wanted to or not. 14 years of marriage have taught me that. I can't count the times that I couldn't stand to be in the same room with Marley, yet we managed to get through sex just fine. It simply became too difficult to block out the image of her doing the same things to Duane that she had done with me; her making the same sounds, calling his name instead of mine, or declaring that he was the owner of what rested between her legs like she had done for me. Those images rose in my mind and beat the crap out of me on a daily basis. They beat me into submission and made me resent Jacqueline to a degree.

I resented her for making me so damn vulnerable to that type of hurt and rejection. I resented her for sleeping with her own husband; for not leaving the man she said she never loved and coming to the one she said she believed she was meant to be with. I resented all of her Libra and Gemini head games that made me lose my way; made me forget who the hell I was. I realized that my being with Jacqueline wouldn't make her leave Duane. It actually made being with him easier because she had the best of both worlds. I was her escape from all the bad in her marriage and in spite of her feelings for me they weren't enough. I was enabling her to tolerate the intolerable. My being in her life wasn't helping her to draw strength; it was actually making her weaker.

If you aren't helping someone then you in fact are hurting them. She was hurting me by keeping me on hold, which kept me from moving forward. I was hurting her by not allowing her to see if her marriage could be salvaged, and her children stood to be hurt the most by parents exposing them to a cold and loveless marriage.

I knew about that firsthand with my parent's messy marriage and even messier divorce. In the end the cons disproportionately outweighed the pros and continuing to do things the same way made even less sense. My mother had taught me as a child that when you truly loved something and let it go, that if returned to you it was meant to be and if it didn't return it was never yours. As a child her words confused me because all I wanted was for my lost puppy to be found, but as a man I found myself clinging to those words like an optimist clings to hope. I let her go knowing that I was doing the right thing, meanwhile hoping that maybe one day she would return to me. Hoping all of her talk of true love and soul mates would prove true. Hoping the stars and planets would perfectly align themselves again for us so that our paths would cross, then maybe the timing would be better.

That was two years ago and although I still think of Jacqueline that hope has diminished and I have moved on with my life, as I'm sure she has as well. Marcus and his team did an awesome job in branding me to make me more marketable and credible. The book advance and royalties have been enough to step away from my life as an FDA approved drug dealer. My days in pharmaceutical sales are behind me and there are truly no regrets in that regard. I am no longer consumed with drugs coming on or going off line, quotas, meetings for the sake of meeting, being asked to cover larger territories for the same salary and the mounting pressure of potential layoffs. I do miss the doctors like Felicia who honestly still have patient care as their number one focus and not personal perks in the name of corporate greed. It was good to know that there were still good guys out there among the creeps.

Team Kennedy took advantage of my boyish good looks, my speaking skills, and most importantly my literary prowess to book engagements on television and radio that dealt with relationships and healthy living. It made me thankful for every experience that I've had personally and professionally. To include, everything from my track days, 14 years of marriage and subsequent divorce, being a single parent, and even my experience as a pharmaceutical salesman. Each of those experiences gave me a unique perspective when it came to lending credibility to a particular topic. It also gave me an opportunity to plug the book, which produced even more sales.

It's not every day that a fiction novel from an unknown author makes it to the New York Times Bestseller List. Never in my wildest dreams could I have fathomed that happening. It was like a dream, only this time it was one that I didn't want to wake up from. I had interviews on radio with everyone from Tom Joyner to Michael Baisden, and Rickey Smiley. I had done television appearances on GMA, Today Show, Ellen, Wendy Williams, and Atlanta Live, even Dr. Oz. I gave feedback on marriage, divorce, raising children after divorce, dating, running, and even sex.

It was a wonderful opportunity to travel places, sign

autographs, and speak with people I never knew. It also afforded me to spend more time with Miles because not only is he 16 now but he has been living with me in Atlanta for almost two years now. I am more proud of my son than I am about anything that I have accomplished.

Marley and I have remained friends as good as friends could be considering our past. She has moved on and I am truly glad for her. There are no regrets where she is concerned because she gave birth to my son and she is a great mother. I have dated off and on over the past two years but nothing even remotely serious. Part of it has been the busyness of my schedule with interviews and tour dates and making sure that Miles is adjusting, but the other part was because I wasn't ready to be in a relationship. I didn't have my heart to give to a woman and I made that abundantly clear in the beginning. I was tired of the need for everyone to fix me with what they felt like was the perfect woman for me. What were the odds of this perfect woman being perfectly single? It was as if being single meant that you were either gay, or had some form of modern day leprosy. I just didn't want to lead someone on or have to pretend to listen to someone and pretend they were interesting when they weren't. What was attractive to me 20 years ago wasn't as attractive to me today. I met women who were physically gifted yet not as much intellectually or vice versa. The two often ever matched.

Under the constant badgering of Kevin Wade and his gorgeous girlfriend Lisa I decided to go on a blind date with their friend. I figured that Kevin obviously had taste and as fine as Lisa was even if her friend was a few notches lower she'd still be prettier than most. I wasn't wrong; however in the spirit of irony I had already met this perfect woman. We burst into laughter when they introduced us to one another over dinner several months ago. It was Lisa's best friend Elise better known to me as my divorce attorney. We both found the irony of the situation amusing.

Elise and I have dated since then when our schedules have permitted us to do so. She was attractive, and obviously very intelligent. I understood her when she said it was complicated regarding her status as a single woman. She had a demanding career as an attorney who was named partner a year ago. Her heart wasn't hers to lend after losing out on a guy some years ago before law school. I knew all too well what she was going through and certainly didn't press the issue. The heart wants what the heart wants. She knew about my divorce, which meant that I didn't have to discuss it. We remained at a safe place in spite of our chemistry and potential. The easy out was there for the taking with no penalty whatsoever.

Elise had flown in from D.C. to be my escort for the premiere of "No Regrets" on the big screen. The success of the book made it a no brainer for the movie to follow just like Marcus said it would.

You get to the point in life that you realize mistakes are inevitable and I had made my share of them, but given the outcome I'm not sure if I'd change one thing. I believe that life is a series of opportunities to accomplish tasks both big and small. We will have hits and misses. Those who are successful will focus on the hits and overlook the misses. I embraced my moments of solitude before I became engulfed by the hundreds who would attend the screening and after party to follow. I realized that I was the sum total of my life experiences both good and bad and that it was impossible for me to embark on this moment without the bad. My father's insecurities, my mother's pain, their divorce, my divorce, and even my bitter ending to my affair with Jacqueline were all necessary ingredients for my recipe to success. As I took one last long look into the mirror after dressing for my big night, I could truly say that I don't have a single regret.

Acknowledgments

The book that you have just finished reading is a work of fiction and it isn't real and certainly not based on my life or anyone else I know. I'm sure that I will have to repeat this a few times the more people read the book. Anyway moving on… I truly thank God for blessing me with a number of things, but most importantly as it pertains to writing I thank him for a creative mind that is forever thinking and asking "What if?" I thank him for courage and boldness to implement my talents and to see a project through until the end.

Many thanks to my entrusted readers who will read unedited chapters at a moment notice and provide feedback that is genuine. You know who you are. I appreciate it. It helps more than you know.

I would like to thank my fans that go all the way back to 2009 and have read Closure, and Getting Closure. The fans that will read this book and any other book that I will write in the future. Thanks to the fans who appreciate creative writing and enjoy an escape every once and a while. You are the reason why I write and you are the audience that I write for.

As usual I would like to thank my family as a whole, especially my wife Tamala, my children AJ, and Arrington, my brother, sister, and mother. Kenny Boyd thanks for your talents my man, I love the cover. Ashford family, Broome family, Murrill/Phillips family, C.A. Johnson family, South Carolina State University family, Omega family; especially Epsilon Omega spring 1999, and ASY family I love you guys.

I went in the last time naming names and got myself in a little trouble so I'm not doing that, besides I named names that didn't even purchase or read the first book. Keeping it real. I love you anyway. If you truly love me then you won't be expecting a shout out in a book as proof of our bond.

Back to the book itself, this book is actually number two and I am excited about the project itself. As a writer I embrace building on previous works and challenging myself to do something creatively different.

In this book the challenge was to go inside the mind of a female and bring forth the emotions that Jacqueline was feeling from a first person account. Any writer would agree that first person is a bit more difficult versus third person because you are speaking from a more expert vantage point. Third person simply tells others what you saw the situation to be, while it isn't wrong it certainly isn't that person telling you what their inner most thoughts and feeling are. Not saying that one is better than the other, just explaining the challenge I faced as a man in telling a woman's story.

Being a therapist I am burdened with the task of understanding the way someone thinks in order to understand their behaviors, so my writing has benefited in that regard. Both Jacqueline and Kennedy are regular people with dilemmas and agendas and I think very realistic although fictional individuals. Anyway I wanted to do a love story, but not just for the sake of doing a love story. This entire novel started with a thought. The thought stemmed from the notion of love at first sight, soul mates, and chance meetings. It all started with "what if?" There is one person on the planet that was meant for you to be with. What if you met that person and the moment you laid eyes on them you knew it? The therapist in me would convince my clients that while such a notion was possible it was extremely improbable, and that they didn't need to wait on this magical encounter. It's a good thing I lock that part of my thinking away to explore the possibility with Kennedy and Jacqueline. It was an interesting run for the both of them and who knows what would have happened had they never met. The hopeless romantic that resides within me resisted the urge to somehow have a happy ending. It is fiction, but I think good fiction resembles reality. In the real world situations like that rarely work out. In life things happen and it's up to us to interpret whether they are good or whether they are bad. I left things rather unfinished in many regards because sometimes we don't get answers when we want them. Maybe Jacqueline showed up to the premiere and surprised Kennedy and they are together right now. Maybe she showed up and she's married to someone else, or maybe they saw each other and simply didn't feel what they thought they would. Any of those scenarios are possible and I wrestled with each of them and decided not to. Maybe these guys show up in another story down the line and you will get the answers you are looking for. At the least it should make for very clever and interesting book club banter. Feel free to invite me either in person or via Skype or FaceTime. They responded to the casting call and blew away the director to earn the parts.

Those of you that go back to Closure will recognize Kevin, Lisa, and Elise and see where life has taken them since 2009. As far as what's next, let's just say that there is no shortage of ideas floating around in my mind. There are some characters popping into my head with some pretty dark secrets and even darker backgrounds. Everything from swingers, to bank robbers, to serial killers so stay tuned because things are going to get interesting.

I hope that *In the Moment* has provided you with literary entertainment and that you are looking forward to what's next. I am officially signing off on October 23, 2012 at 12:38 p.m. inside of Starbucks at the corner of Trenholm and Forest Dr. Dressed in a striped sweater, Levis jeans, and vintage Polo boots from 1995. Laura Izibor is playing in my ear. I'm two cups of coffee in and done with people watching for today.

Take care,

Aaron L. Ashford – iWrite

www.ingramcontent.com/pod-product-compliance
Lightning Source LLC
Chambersburg PA
CBHW020903200626

46814CB00001BA/151